ACCLAIM FOR *Cereus Blooms at Night*

"*Cereus Blooms at Night* is a gem, a wonderful flower of a first novel; Shani Mootoo can be counted as one of our most gifted new writers."
– *Vancouver Sun*

"Sifts intrigue, mystery, and a heady sense of the natural world into a harrowing family saga. . . . Highly recommended."
– *Library Journal* (starred review)

"The fecund and fertile cycles of Caribbean life pervade this powerful first novel from Mootoo, who invokes all the senses. . . . "
– *Publishers Weekly* (starred review)

"Her language and characters seduce us away to a mythic place that is, by turns, as sweet as the first knowing of love and as hard as a callous blow. Inside the grand sweep of the story are the finely tuned details which mark a brilliant storyteller."
– Jewelle Gomez

"Working with magic, grounded by psychological insight, Mootoo weaves a deft design of vivid and sensuous scenes."
– *Quill & Quire*

"This ethereal first novel employs myth and magic reminiscent of Isabel Allende."
– *Out Magazine* (U.S.)

"A swirling cauldron of cross-generational history filled with violence, romance, aching beauty, and heart-breaking mystery."
– *Sojourner* (U.S.)

"This is a new writer with a generous spirit and a gift for storytelling. We should watch where she travels next."
– *Globe and Mail*

"Like the titular cereus that blooms once a year at night, Mootoo at the climax releases a dense burst of aroma into this exquisitely exact novel."
– *Georgia Straight*

BOOKS BY SHANI MOOTOO

FICTION

Out on Main Street & Other Stories (1993)

Cereus Blooms at Night (1996)

He Drown She in the Sea (2005)

POETRY

The Predicament of Or (2001)

Cereus Blooms at Night

Shani Mootoo

EMBLEM EDITIONS
Published by McClelland & Stewart Ltd.

First published by Press Gang Publishers 1996
First McClelland & Stewart trade paperback edition published 1998

Library and Archives Canada Cataloguing in Publication

Mootoo, Shani, 1957–
Cereus blooms at night / Shani Mootoo.

978-0-7710-6400-5

I. Title.

PS8576.O622C47 2002 C813'.54 C2002-901226-0
PR9199.3.M6353C47 2002

We acknowledge the financial support of the Government of Canada through the Book Publishing Industry Development Program and that of the Government of Ontario through the Ontario Media Development Corporation's Ontario Book Initiative. We further acknowledge the support of the Canada Council for the Arts and the Ontario Arts Council for our publishing program.

The author gratefully acknowledges receipt of a writing grant from the Canada Council for the Arts during the course of working on this book.

SERIES EDITOR: ELLEN SELIGMAN

Cover design: Brian Bean
Cover photograph: © Photonica/Katrin Thomas
Cover inset image manipulation: Brian Bean
Text design: Val Speidel
Series logo design: Brian Bean

Typeset in Minion by M&S, Toronto
Printed and bound in Canada

EMBLEM EDITIONS
McClelland & Stewart
a division of Random House of Canada Limited,
a Penguin Random House Company

www.randomhouse.ca

8 9 10 11 17 16 15 14

For my parents, Indra and Romesh

I

By setting this story down, I, Tyler — that is how I am known, simply as Tyler, or if you wanted to be formal, Nurse Tyler — am placing trust in the power of the printed word to reach many people. It is my ardent hope that Asha Ramchandin, at one time a resident in the town of Paradise, Lantanacamara, will chance upon this book, wherever she may be today, and recognize herself and her family. If you are not Asha Ramchandin — who could, for all anyone knows, have changed her name — but know her or someone you suspect might be her or even related to her, please present this and ask that she read it. Might I add that my own intention, as the relater of this story, is not to bring notice to myself or my own plight. However, I cannot escape myself, and being a narrator who also existed on the periphery of the events, I am bound to be present. I have my own laments and much to tell about myself. It is my intent, however, to refrain from inserting myself too forcefully. Forgive the lapses, for there are some, and read them with the understanding that to have erased them would have been to do the same to myself.

THE CEREUS IN the yard will bloom soon. We planted a slip from the original cutting at least a year ago. That is how long it has been since I left my village on the other side of the island and moved to Paradise. I had to cajole Mr. Hector, the gardener here, who thought the plant nothing but an unruly network of limp, green leaves. Too gangly, he said, to be kept in a garden under his charge. When, recently, deep alizarin buds pushed through, his curiosity was piqued and he now visits the cactus daily and pats the cow manure around its trunk.

Judging from the way things turned out, I am sure you will agree it was no coincidence that I and the eye of the scandal happened upon Paradise, Lantanacamara on the same day.

The town seemed empty and quiet when I arrived. That was because everyone had left what they were doing and taken off to the house on Hill Side to see for themselves what was happening. Even though Paradise is spreading out, inch by inch, and taking over the sugar cane fields that surround it, it remains one of the smaller towns in Lantanacamara, so small that merely the news of one stranger passing through can be enough to ignite a wild fire of curiosity and jabber among its citizenry. But my arrival was eclipsed by the scandal on Hill Side, the discussion of which quickly became Paradise's most favoured pastime. Even the days following brought me little notice; Paradise was clutched by a menacing cloud that hung low over the town for several days and would not budge. The only sources of light in the town were the electric street and house lamps that remained lit all day. In a situation like that I could not have expected to be noteworthy.

Being an outsider at that time — and I suppose I still am and may well always be — I thought it best to exercise propriety. I was well aware what was unfolding but refrained from taking part in the daily dissections of new gossip and from helping its spore-like dispersal. By the time interest in the scandal had abated I was past being a novelty. Hardly any fuss was made of me when, in fact, I might well have been celebrated! I was, after all, the only Lantanacamaran man ever to have trained in the profession of nursing. I had taken courses abroad, in the Shivering Northern Wetlands where, to my astonishment, there were a number of men, albeit a small number, in attendance. But I was and still am the only man in the profession here. Not just in Paradise but in all of Lantanacamara.

Nevertheless, despite all my formal training abroad, and considering that nurses in Lantanacamara generally receive their sole training on the job, the matron of the Paradise Alms House, when assigning me my first chore, pointed toward a bucket, a square of cobalt-blue soap and a scrub brush, and sent me off in the darkness of the day to scrub the residents' shower stalls. So was the tone set for my duties. Later I was called by this one or that one to run errands and do menial chores. Regardless, every morning I presented myself wearing a freshly washed, starched and pressed white shirt and meticulously pleated trousers, both of which I had made from the same cotton as were the nurses' uniforms, all in the hope that I would be sent to tend a resident. What I really wanted was to make at least one old person smile or feel that she or he was of some value.

It is an interesting quirk of fate, I think, that for all the prattling by almost everyone at that time, sowing and tilling and reaping idle rumours about the Ramchandin family, and for all the scant attention paid my presence, I am the one who ended up knowing the truth, the whole truth, every significant *and* insignificant bit of it. And I am the one who is putting it all to good use by recording it here in the hope that any existing relatives of Mala Ramchandin, be it her younger and, to this day, most treasured sister, Asha, or anyone else, might come forward and pay the old lady a visit.

Three weeks after I arrived — the suffocating cloud had mysteriously lifted by then — I was out in the yard at Sister's request, sweeping the path. The home's regular yardboy, Toby, stood watching from afar, sucking his teeth and shaking his head and spitting low curses in my direction, when a black automobile pulled up. The arrival of any motorized vehicle was still cause for a gathering in this place, where people had not easily let go of donkey carts for labourers and broughams for gentler folk, but an austere, black police vehicle brought an added element of excitement. The gathering of nurses and residents — those alert enough to notice — watched anxiously as two slender men alighted, walked to the back and opened the rear doors. Even the gossipmongers among the nurses were silent when the stretcher slid out. On it lay the home's newest resident.

Mala Ramchandin was never tried in court. Judge Walter Bissey had dismissed the case in minutes. Several times he asked the prosecution, "I'm sorry. I can't seem to follow your logic. Tell me again, what is the evidence? What is the charge?" He shook his head in disbelief that his time was being taken up in such a manner. He thought for a minute how to avoid insulting the police and the prosecutors, and finally said, "But you say you cannot present a victim. No victim! You say that there are no witnesses. No witnesses! And there is no evidence that a crime was ever committed. Regardless of what the police reportedly saw? And you want to put a crazy lady on trial. You don't have a case. Am I missing something here? Hmmm?" Had there been any evidence as alleged by the police, he explained, it would, in any case, certainly have been inadmissible due to contamination by the ravages of time. He was not about to have an old woman, a crazy old woman, tried in his court based on a lot of words and no hard-and-fast proof of anything. No victim, no evidence, no witnesses — no crime. A waste of the court's time and taxpayers' money.

However, out of compassion for her health and welfare, he ruled that Mala Ramchandin be taken into the alms house in Paradise to receive proper care and attention until the end of her days. It is said, incidentally, that on the day of Judge Bissey's ruling, the life-robbing cloud began to break up and shift south over the ocean, letting light shine in Paradise once again. Even now a handful of people remain disgruntled about the dismissal and the ruling. They felt cheated of the rare opportunity to have a woman criminal in their midst. Some citizens believe that a crime was committed and that she was its perpetrator. Come to think of it — they scratch their heads, think a moment and pronounce — they remember this and that and the other. And for the constable in charge, the mystery of an unsolved death, evidence of which he himself saw, is like an infestation of ripe mites swarming under his skin, and the judge's ruling a cruel disallowal of his craving to scratch.

Sister, too. On hearing that hers was the chosen home for Miss Ramchandin, Sister went to Judge Bissey in protest. She was forced to accept his decision.

Now Sister's hefty heels clopped down the path toward the police vehicle. The two officers carried the stretcher, which appeared to be empty except for a white sheet strewn across it.

"Yes, we knew she was coming, but not *when,*" I heard Sister say. "I should have been given fair notice. I was not notified. There is no room ready. You can't just come and drop people off like that. This is not a train station, you know. She is an extra mouth to feed. We have to plan for these kinds of things."

"Ah! No, no, no," an officer responded. "That would be the least of your problems, in truth. Look at her. She does hardly eat. They leave a plate of fowl for her one day and when they came back, they find the plate and all the food scatter all over the floor. Then another day they give her salt fish and she didn't even go near it. She don't eat, in truth. Even a biscuit and some hot tea would be plenty enough for her."

The two men carrying the stretcher approached me. They could not have been much younger or older than I, and they looked heroic in their uniforms. Observing the narrowness of their waists where their close-fitting khaki shirts slipped neatly into slim-belted khaki pants, a fiery heat rose on my cheeks. I felt diminished by these two officers of the peace but rather pleasantly so. As they passed I averted my eyes and looked at the woman on the stretcher. Only her head was exposed. Except for a fan of yellowed silver hair, I was unable to see more because she faced away from me.

Sister kept pace with the two men, ranting that there was no room ready and no security in place. "This is an alms house. This is for poor people. This is not the place for psychiatrics. There is no room . . ." When she reached me she grabbed my arm and pulled me along. At the entrance to the main office, the officer said, "Well, Sister, we have to leave her here with you. Those are the orders. Later, I advise you, go and talk with the judge if you want. But right now we have orders. If you have a bed, we will carry her to it and save you the trouble. In any case she is not heavy, a child could lift her with one finger, she so light." He spread his legs slightly and let go of one of the rods to show that, even with one hand, he was capable of hoisting the stretcher. He gave the impression of having Herculean size and strength, and a rustle of not-so-discreet ooohs and ahhhs came from the gathered nurses. I was in full agreement with their admiration but I, more prudently, merely smiled good-naturedly.

Still perturbed, Sister watched the men gently rest the motionless body on the floor of her office. She reluctantly penned her signature on the court receipt.

On his way out, a policemen turned to Sister and said slyly, "Don't 'fraid she. It have nothing to be afraid of. Unless, of course, you used to go and pelt her house and tief she mango!" Sister's head spun around so fast and her face paled so instantly that I guessed his arrow had hit its target.

The crowd of nurses, babbling low at the office door, parted to let the officers through. I was happy to see them leave. One can engage in the act of admiring for only so long before the frustrations of desire, envy and self-criticism begin to cast shadows across one's vision — or turn one's knees to jelly.

Sister dispersed the nurses, except for two whom she took to arrange Miss Ramchandin's accommodations. I was told to stay in the office to "guard" the strapped-down figure. I had rested my broom against the wall but before Sister left, she grabbed and placed the broom in my hands. "Keep this handy!" she told me gravely. I took the broom, proud that it was not assumed that I, the only man among the nurses, ought to be strong and fearless and without need of protection.

It was the first time I had been given such an important assignment, the first time I was asked to care for one of the residents. I had spent most of the past three weeks on my hands and knees scrubbing the concrete paths around the residents' bungalows. I had prodded and poked at spiders' webs in the high corners of all the rooms on the property. Out in back yard I hosed down the garbage pails. I was assigned — only once, thankfully — to assist Toby with fixing a leak on the roof. (I will refrain from dwelling on the verbal rocks he tossed in my direction and say only that he made no effort to hide his disdain for my ways. At the end of the ordeal he told me plainly that he was going to leave the job if he was ever put to work with this pansy again.) Another time I helped Mr. Hector move heavy furniture from one bungalow to another. I saw him watch curiously as I struggled with the weight of some items and the awkwardness of others. He kept a distance but at least he was more helpful than most. When I tried to fix a broken stool, he showed me how to hold the hammer's handle lower to get more leverage, and he watched to make sure I was not about to hurt myself or ruin the stool. But I was anxious to begin nursing again.

For such a tiny spectre of a being, the new resident breathed deeply and loudly in her drugged sleep. I squatted at the side of the canvas stretcher, peering at her. I expected her facial skin to be grey but it was ochre, like richly fired clay. Her skeletal structure was clearly visible, her thin skin draped over protruding bones and sagged into crevices that musculature had once filled. Even so, it did not take much imagination to realize that she must have once had a modest dignity. She slept on soundly. If she had slept through the trip over Paradise's dreadfully pockmarked roads, my peering was unlikely to awaken her.

The urge to touch overcame me. I rested my palm gently on her silver hair. I expected it to be coarse and wiry, qualities that would have fit the rumours. But her hair, though oily from lack of care, was soft and silken. This one touch turned her from the incarnation of fearful tales into a living human being, an elderly person such as those I had dedicated my life to serving. I needed to know the woman who lay hidden by the white sheet. Still clutching the broom, I inched the sheet off her shoulder. "Flesh and bones," I thought, but it was the predominance of bone that truly caught my attention. I wrapped my hand around the ball of her upper arm where it met her shoulder. It was like a large marble, and cold like a marble. She did not have the sweet yet sour smell I had come to expect whenever close to an old person. Instead, an aroma resembling rich vegetable compost escaped from under the sheet. I felt the skin on her neck. It was an old person's skin, in truth, nothing remarkable about its thinness or looseness, but damp and cold. I could feel the fear trapped in this woman's body, even as she slept under sedation. I was gripped by fury as I remembered the officer's words—"a biscuit and some hot tea"—and I wondered if, after she rejected fowl and fish, tea and biscuits were all that she was fed or all that she would eat. Either way, I felt as though I were witnessing a case of neglect.

I drew back the cloth further. A pile of fine bones, starling bones, on my dinner plate at the end of a Sunday meal flashed through my mind. I dropped the broom and unstrapped the thick leather bands that pinned her to the stretcher. I am not a very strong man, physically; I never have been. And neither am I known to anger easily or to express anger directly. But that day, I slipped one arm under her shoulders and one under her knees and lifted Miss Ramchandin off the stretcher. Having judged only by her frail looks, I was surprised at her weight, forgetting for a moment the density of bone. Nevertheless, outrage gave me the strength and courage to descend the office steps with her in my arms. Making my way along the path, I again became aware of her odour. She had a curiously natural smell. The words of the officer came to me again, that the plate of fowl had been scattered and the fish untouched. I realized she had likely not eaten animal flesh in a very long time.

Needless to say, when I arrived with Miss Ramchandin in my arms at the door of the room being prepared for her, Sister and the two nurses shrieked. None of them would approach me and my human bundle. Sister demanded that Miss Ramchandin be taken back to the office. I suddenly felt her weight and began to buckle under it. When it looked as if my bundle would fall, Sister again shrieked and ordered me to deposit Miss Ramchandin on the bed, which had not yet been made, and to strap her down again. I hardly had opened my mouth to explain that Miss Ramchandin was too frail to inflict even a bad thought when Sister screamed at me for being insolent and blatantly disregarding her authority. I placed Miss Ramchandin on the bed yet still hesitated to get the straps. Sister scuttled out into the yard and came back shortly with a length of rope from Mr. Hector. I raced back to the office, yanked the straps off the stretcher and returned in time to contain Miss Ramchandin myself. I made a production of pulling at the straps but in truth only loosely buckled them. Faced with the threat of losing my job, I agreed not to unbind her again. Sister did not want me anywhere near Miss Ramchandin's room, but no other nurse would tread there and neither would she. Miss Ramchandin's care was therefore left in my hands, and I was finally able to employ my nursing skills.

The sedative wore off slowly. As the weight of induced sleep lifted, sobs escaped my new patient. By evening she tried to turn but was too weak to fight the restraints. She had opened her eyes and seemed now to be almost afraid to close them again. Tears rolled from her face. I began to talk to her, to tell her where she was and who I was, but on hearing my voice she began a deep, fearful moaning. It did not take me long to realize that my movements, no matter how slight, terrified her. I sat still on a chair by her bed, and for an hour she watched as I tried to remain still, even as the room filled with attacking mosquitoes. The light outside faded and through the window I could see electric light bulbs shining in the valley. Still I did not move. Eventually I became dizzy from hunger and started to get up. She began to moan and pulled back into the bed, as though afraid that I might hurt her. I had no choice; she had to eat and it was clear that no one was going to bring her food. I inched out of the room. Her eyes followed me to the door and her breathing became heavy. I could not tell if she wanted me to stay or leave.

The other residents had already been fed and the nurses were finishing their meals in the dining room of the house we share. Sister regarded me coldly as I went toward the kitchen.

"It's past the residents' meal hour. And past the staff's meal hour also. Exactly what are you up to?"

"I was in Miss Ramchandin's room, Sister. She woke up and I detected what I think are symptoms of trauma so I did not want to leave her alone."

"Mr. Tyler, I know that you had formal training and it was abroad and all of that kind of thing, but that does not give you the authority to make up rules for yourself. You will always find troublesome residents but in the end, at their age, they are all like children. And when children misbehave, you have to discipline them. Not so? don't get too thoughtful over that Mala Ramchandin. She committed —"

"Sister, I beg your pardon, but there was no trial and no concrete evidence that she ever did anything. She has not eaten for several hours. If she does not eat something now, she will surely slip away."

I heard a sigh of exasperation from one of the nurses at the table. Sister remained silent for a moment to confirm her agreement with the sigh, and then she continued.

"She is old and may well slip away whether she eat or not. That is the nature of working in a home for old people, Mr. Tyler. It have dasheen soup and egg sandwiches for the residents. See if she will eat that. If she doesn't, there is nothing else you can do. She will eat if and when she is good and ready. But if you go and make too much fuss of her, she will be no end of trouble for all of us. Is best not to start them off with bad habits. You understand me, Mr. Tyler?"

"Yes, Sister."

"You are assigned to her room tonight. Do not take the straps off until I take a look at her tomorrow morning. You understand me? I will judge when she is not a danger to herself or to any of us."

Before going back to Miss Ramchandin's bungalow, I went to my room to regain my composure. I could hear the nurses' scandalous laughter and their chatter through the floorboards. I combed my hair back and tied a 'kerchief around my neck to ward off a chill from the night air. On my way out, I had to pass the nurses again in the dining room. Sister had already retired for the evening. The chatter fell silent and all eyes turned on me. One of the women spoke up.

"But, eh-heh, Mr. Tyler! Where you going dress up so?"

"You are referring to the addition of my neckerchief?"

"Eh-heh!" And she turned to the others and said, "But it nice, eh? You really know how to look good. What material it is?"

"It is nothing fancy, just a light cotton 'kerchief against the cold."

"But it suit you well. Is a nice colour! I will have to consult you sometime, yes!" They nodded among themselves, making additional comments, all in the same condescending tone. It was the kind of notice one might shower on a child. But I am not a child and I knew there to be malice in their words. Behind the flattery, the edge of mockery was plain to anyone who must, as a matter of survival, learn to detect it. I could detail for you the number of times I have come across that same tone. I am aware of the subtleties and incremental degrees in a hostility — from the tight smile to the seemingly accidental shove — and I have known the gamut. But what would be the value of laying it all out before you? The temptation is strong, I will admit, to be the romantic victim. There is in me a performer dying for the part, but I must be strict with myself and stay with my intention to relate Mala Ramchandin's story.

I will add this and nothing more: I employed then the one strategy of survival that has saved me time and time again, here and in the Shivering Wetlands. Since I couldn't hide and knew better than to flaunt, I was quietly proud and did not enter into a façade of denial. I smiled at the nurse and said, "Yes, I would be happy to give you a pointer or two. I would quite enjoy that. Sorry I have to run now, though. Enjoy your evening." I picked up the food before another word could be spoken, and considered the encounter a relative success.

From outside Miss Ramchandin's bungalow I could hear nothing but squealing crickets and frogs. I knocked on her door, not expecting an invitation to enter, but to announce that I was back. When I entered, her eyes were already alert and on me.

I began a quiet chatter. "It's soup. It smells good. I brought a cup for me, too. I thought we could eat together." I did not watch her but could feel she had not taken her eyes off me. She made no sounds, even her breathing seemed consciously regulated.

"It's cool outside. The frogs and the crickets like it when it is like this. Can you hear them? They sound like they are making music together. May I rest the tray here?" I set the tray with two cups of soup and some slices of bread (no eggs) on her bed and pulled up a chair. I noticed her eyes, wide open and expressionless, glued to my movements. I was afraid to look directly at her for fear that the spell might be broken. Without meeting her stare I looked at her hair.

"I'll just smooth back your hair a little." I stroked her forehead twice. There was no hair on her forehead to smooth back but I wanted her to feel in my touch that I would not harm her. Happily, she was no longer damp, though she was still rather cool.

"Miss Ramchandin, are you cold?"

No response.

"Well, I'll just throw this sheet over your feet. If you get too hot, you can push it off. You know, just give it a little kick." I felt awkward, not meaning to bring attention to the restraints. There was still no recognition that she heard me. I became acutely conscious of my movements and the subtleties of my tone, which may have been all that communicated with her.

"Mmmm, this smells so good. It's dasheen soup. Only fresh dasheen leaves, water and salt. Nothing else. Just try a little." I put a half-filled spoon to her lips, then realized her head needed to be propped up to avoid a mess. She did not make a move or even look at the spoon. She just continued to stare at me. Then I detected a slight change in her face, the slightest frown, perhaps perplexity or wonder. I put the bowl on the tray, found her towel and made it into a little roll that I placed under her head.

"How does that feel? If it's uncomfortable, let me know and I will fix it for you." When I brought the spoon to her mouth again, she turned her head away slightly and muscles around her mouth twitched. Still her eyes were locked on mine. Even though her actions suggested she did not want the food, I was overjoyed to have been given an indication of her will.

"All right. If you don't want the soup, that's all right. But it's too bad to let it waste. It tastes good and clean. Just eat a little piece of bread. You must eat something. Look, I'll just make it nice and soft for you." I broke off a piece, the size one would give a baby who had just gotten its first tooth. I dipped it in the soup and mashed it against my finger. Balancing the morsel on the tip of my finger, I put it to her closed lips. She did not protest. The bread lay in her motionless mouth. I held my breath and busied myself preparing another piece, giving the impression that I trusted she would swallow and be ready for another. I made no notice when her mouth moved, but I took the opportunity to make the next piece a little bigger. She parted her lips this time, only barely. I prepared a piece similarly for myself. As we both chewed I looked up at the ceiling, aware that she was still watching me. Then I looked out the window, at the food on the plate, at my nails, and tried to come up with something to say that might elicit a response or at least help the trust building between us. Suddenly, however, the only things that came to mind were the very things I knew better than to bring up. Her father. The prison. The rumours. The thickness and quality of the leather straps that still held her firmly. Fowl. Salted cod.

My actions spoke more eloquently than any words. She ate a full slice of soup-soaked bread and took some sips of water. Then her eyes, still fixed on me, fluttered until they closed and she slept. Filled with a sense of success, I pulled the sheet up around her neck and quietly left.

I lay wide awake for more than an hour. My eyes ached with a gritty tiredness but my brain was giddy, joyous with constant recitations of the events with Miss Ramchandin. While they played in my head, I imagined further successes, immeasurable feats that I might accomplish with my great understanding and magnanimity. Finally, nausea at my own ballooning sense of self wore me down and I slept.

It seemed I had been sleeping for hours when I awakened to find Sister over me, a flashlight in her hand, shaking my shoulder.

"Something the matter with Miss Ramchandin. Listen! Come quick, quick."

I heard a mournful wailing. How could I have slept through such an eerie and agonizing din? I threw on my dressing gown, even though I was well aware it would be commented on later. I hurried, fearful that Miss Ramchandin had become ill, and disappointed that this might be a major setback to the evening's progress.

When I reached the bungalow, I found several night-shift nurses milling around outside. Residents had pushed their windows ajar and were peeping out. It was a frightful sound Miss Ramchandin made. Without knocking, I entered the bungalow. Sister, attired also in her dressing gown (plainer than mine), stayed at the door. I switched on a lamp. The wailing halted abruptly, only to be replaced with breathless gasps of fright. Miss Ramchandin's hair was damp, pasted to her face and neck. Strands were in her mouth. I wiped away the wetness. Her head resisted my touch. She stared ahead, past me.

"Miss Ramchandin, what's happened? What's happened?" I whispered. The sweet smell of an old person's urine was strong.

Now that she was certain the straps had not come undone, Sister tentatively approached. "What is all that noise about? You all right? What happen to you?" The loudness of her voice, as if Miss Ramchandin were hard of hearing, did not mask Sister's nervousness. "You keeping everybody awake. You not feeling well or what? You want to see a doctor?"

Miss Ramchandin shifted her stare even farther away. I wanted to offer her an antidote to Sister's harshness but I knew better than to oppose Sister. To convey my concern, I felt Miss Ramchandin's neck and cheek, as though checking her temperature. Then I drew back the sheet. I gave her damp shoulder a quick and gentle rub. There was nothing to be alarmed about but I noticed her clenched fists and recognized in them a fighting spirit.

Under her breath, Sister muttered, "Hmm! This is not a place for crazy people. Hmm! I don't know why they send her here, na!"

I jumped in quickly. "Sister, I think the straps might be uncomfortable. You know, lying for so many hours in one —" Sister glared at me and then I saw an idea crawl across her face. She spoke loudly and clearly to Miss Ramchandin.

"Miss Ramchandin, you can hear me? Listen to me. I will remove the straps tomorrow if you behave yourself tonight. You hear? You go to sleep now and don't make no more noise. And tomorrow morning I will make sure they take them off, and that Doctor come to see you. But if you make any more noise they will stay on for another day. You hear me? Then Doctor will have to give you something to make you sleep. There are other people here trying to sleep, you know. Now you go to sleep and behave yourself nicely."

Miss Ramchandin's breathing deepened to a low growl.

One thing still troubled me. "Sister, one of the nurses must come and clean her up." Not to offend, I made sure my tone was one of concern only. Sister inhaled deeply and let out a sigh. She stared at the wood floor as if waiting for me to solve this problem. I had no qualms about doing the job, but out of respect for the woman on the bed, and not wanting to bend house rules, I remained quiet.

Sister sucked her teeth. "I will never get any nurse to come in here."

Still I offered nothing. Sister stormed out. I watched her speak at length with two nurses outside, awaiting, no doubt, further morsels of gossip. Although I could not hear their words, the nurses' gestures were loud enough. They recoiled several paces. Sister returned.

"Please. If you don't mind, I know you are not on night shift, and I realize that you are a man . . . but since you . . . well, what I mean is . . . the other nurses —" She paused, clearly hoping I would simply offer my services. It worried me that Miss Ramchandin could hear such a conversation. In the struggle of wills between Sister and me, my self-preserving prudence prevailed. I nodded my head in agreement to the unstated question. Relieved, Sister exited hastily.

Miss Ramchandin did not help me turn her body. I understood and did the job quietly, trying to be as invisible as is possible when working on her private parts. She was beginning to perturb me, not because I feared her but rather because I felt an empathy for her clenched fists, defiant stare, pursed lips and deep, slow, calculated breathing — an empathy that words alone cannot describe.

She was unlike the other residents, whom, in all fairness, I had been given the opportunity to know only from a distance. Since her arrival Miss Ramchandin had been lying strapped, except for the brief moments when I carried her, yet I detected a glint of stubborn independence quite different from the easy reliance and uncontested compliance the other residents seemed to thrive on. My training in the Wetlands dealt with general nursing and palliative care of the elderly, not medical or psychiatric nursing, so I have no authority in these matters. But my intuition was that the woman on the bed was going to prove herself to be neither crazy nor failing in health, and that she would fare better given more freedom. On the other hand, perhaps my intuition was nothing more than recalcitrant yearning, for I did fancy that she and I shared a common reception from the rest of the world.

I paced Miss Ramchandin's room. I desperately wanted to unstrap her but when, for a moment, I came close to defying orders and removing them, I found myself afraid. What if I removed them and then in anger — not pure craziness, but reasonable anger — she were to hurt herself or someone else?

I brought my face inches away from hers and whispered, "If I were strapped like that, I would hate it, too." And then I felt foolish, for what was the point of empathizing without taking more positive action? I wanted to touch her again but I left and returned to my room feeling impoverished and weak.

I had not even taken off my dressing gown when the wailing started again, this time low and less frenzied. I jumped up and was heading out my door when Sister stopped me and told me flatly to let Miss Ramchandin cry until she fell asleep. She promised to call the doctor to get sedatives for the following night and to discuss getting Miss Ramchandin committed to the crazy house. Sister went back into her room and closed the door firmly, leaving me standing in the corridor.

The wailing continued. I waited long minutes until the light under Sister's door went out, and then I slipped away and headed for Miss Ramchandin's room. This time when I entered she did not stop crying. Tears streamed down her face and her body was contorted.

Fuelled by outrage I undid the straps around her feet. Then I unfastened the ones around her thighs and across her chest. She continued to cry as if unaware of my presence, and her body slowly tightened even more into the contortion the straps had temporarily curtailed. I sat by her head, slipped my arm under her back and pulled her into my arms. I held her against my chest, rocking her until the first streaks of morning light broke through the pitch-black sky. She had by this time fallen asleep, her head leaning on my chest. I continued to rock her and stroke her hands quietly. As much as I wanted to doze, I stayed alert. When I heard the sounds of the nurses awakening, I slid from behind Miss Ramchandin and lowered her on the bed. I shook her shoulders. She opened her eyes with fear. I held her face in both my hands.

"Shhh, shhhh, shhh, it's all right, it's all right," I whispered inches from her face. "Everything is all right. I have to go now. But I will come back a little later and I will stay with you all day. I have to put the straps back on, but I promise you, I promise you, it won't be for long. Please forgive me for doing this, but trust me. You must, you *must* trust me! Try to go back to sleep and when you awaken I will be here." She looked at me blankly, more fatigued than frightened, and she remained still as I tied the three straps around her again.

She stayed quiet and watched my eyes, the fire of life beginning to burn in hers again, until the door closed between us.

As I walked back to the house quickly, nervous that Sister would catch me, I tried to decipher the words in her eyes. I did not see fear in them but a pleading. I took that pleading to mean she hoped I would be true to my word.

Miss Ramchandin had hardly been in the home a full twenty-four hours before she had visitors. Three gentlemen in one day. The home's doctor was the only one Sister permitted. The other two neither Miss Ramchandin nor I had the opportunity to see. Sister received them and their gift of a plant clipping. She then turned them away, explaining that the new resident was incapable of having visitors so soon. She brought the plant to me and said "Do something with it."

I recognized it immediately. I had seen one in bloom in the Exotic Items Collection of the SNW National Botanical Gardens: the rare night-blooming cereus. Without blossoms the plant appears to be little more than an uninteresting tangle of leafage, hence Sister's dismissal. However, in bloom it is stunningly gorgeous. I put the ample greenery in a milk can filled with water to let it catch. When I entered her room, Miss Ramchandin watched me closely but paid no attention to the clipping. (Without blossoms the plant soon became as much a part of the room as her bedpan and even I forgot all about it — and about them, the visitors. I had decided, illogically, that they must be solicitors or the like.)

That the doctor's presence made me blush is not important to this story, but to ignore how alive and frisky I felt in his presence would be to deny the part of me that hopes for freedom. What he thought of me as I tried to accommodate his needs during that visit I do not know. What I do know is that he talked and joked with me in the same manner he would have with any of the other staff. I know my propensities are not invisible yet he did not recoil. For the first time in weeks I was not a curiosity. I was so accustomed to being seen as one that when treated like a regular fellow, I fumbled and blushed. And became aware of how desperately I want to be — and be treated as — nothing more than ordinary.

The good-natured and good-looking doctor laughed rather nervously when he saw the straps still on. He teased Sister about being afraid of an old, frail woman, and reiterated that no one knew if she really committed the crime. I refrained from interjecting that no one knew for certain that a crime had even been committed. He made a show of regarding Miss Ramchandin pensively, walking (elegantly) around her bed and taking her in from different angles. He then pronounced that, based on his experience, she did not have the personality of a criminal and removing the straps would bring about no incident.

"Unless, of course," he said jovially, "you were one of the people who used to harass the poor lady!" The comment seems to have been the joke about town.

The doctor himself unbuckled each strap. As he chatted with Sister about a mutual acquaintance, he coiled the straps around his brawny right hand and slapped the three blunt ends against the palm of his left. He left Miss Ramchandin's bungalow taking the straps with him, wishing her and me, with no special nuances, I should add, a good day. Miss Ramchandin made her biggest gesture since arriving at the home. She followed his body not only with her eyes but with a turn of her head.

That night I fell asleep holding her, just in case. When I awoke in the middle of the night she was sleeping, her face serene.

The next day I put her in a wheelchair and rolled her along the path. The other residents were not as wary as the staff. They passed close by, a couple of them trying to introduce themselves and make conversation, happy and curious that there was someone new to get to know, to show around or show off to. They quickly lost interest in this new resident though; she was uncommunicative and seemed to live in a world that did not include them.

Miss Ramchandin made no sounds besides crying, moaning, wailing and sighing. I talked often to her though I truly thought she was unable to speak, and I watched her eyes, which I had come to believe were what she used for communicating. Then one evening, perched on the edge of the grounds, we were taking in the yellow sunset and the purpling of the distant valley — well, I was taking it in; I did not know what she was up to in her mind — when a pair of parrots flapped across the sky, squawking leisurely. She made no movement but I distinctly heard a perfect imitation of the parrots' calls. I dropped to my knees at her side.

"Miss Ramchandin! Was that you? That was perfect! That was so beautiful! Can you do it again? Please?" She did not respond but I detected a brightening of her eyes, whether at the sight of the parrots or my surprise I could not be sure. Then, as I rolled her back to her bungalow after the sun had fallen behind the hills, I heard a high-pitched, pulsing tremolo and saw the vibration in her throat, as though a cricket had begun its evening ritual. I looked into her face, my jaw dropped in admiration and disbelief. She looked directly and proudly back, for the first time a hint of a smile lighting her face, and continued the humming long into the evening, not missing a fraction of a beat.

Days passed with her calling out, only loud enough for me to hear, perfect imitations of all the species of birds that congregated in the garden and dotted the tropical Lantanacamaran sky. I would catch her watching me through the side of her eyes, as she did bird, cricket and frog calls as though she meant to entertain me.

The rumours about Miss Ramchandin continued. The staff quickly sensed that I was becoming protective of her and would hush their tales in my presence, but I could tell they were still talking. Sometimes, I have to admit, I thought of the stories I had heard. I would edge myself out of Miss Ramchandin's sight whenever I tried to imagine her in the roles they had cast her in, for it did occur to me that this unusual woman might know what was going on in my head.

I remember the first time I heard the name Chandin Ramchandin. It was long before arriving in Paradise to work in the alms house. Indeed, the recent rumours were elaborations of what I had heard many years ago when I was too young to pay attention.

I was ten or so. I was in the back of our house passing time with Cigarette Smoking Nana (to differentiate her from Bible Quoting Nana, whom I couldn't bring myself to get too close to, nor she to me since I was not turning out to be boyly enough for her church-going satisfaction). We were sitting on the back steps, and I was working up a froth pondering the specifics of family relationships. Could a nephew be the father of his uncle? I wondered, or could a mother ever be any other relationship to her child? Could she be the father? (I implore you, please keep an open mind and hold your judgement. I was, I remind you, a child, and children were innocent, if not ignorant, in those days.) Could your sister be your brother too? Could your brother be your father? I decided finally to ask Cigarette Smoking Nana.

"Nana, I have something on my mind."

"Uhuh. Tell me. What is on your mind, child?"

"Nana, can your Pappy be your Pappy and your Granpappy at the same time?" Nana cocked her head toward the sky and wrinkled her nose.

"Huh? Come again?" Exasperated by her slowness to catch a question that seemed plain enough to me, I merely repeated myself, but slowly, stressing and drawing each word out. She stared at me grimly for a long time. Her eyes were open wider than usual. I thought the look on her face was because it was, after all, such a good question and it made her think extra hard. She took a long, pensive drag on her cigarette and she thought and she thought and she thought and made several attempts to answer, but she kept hesitating.

Then finally she said, "Yes, child, it could happen. The father could be the grandfather too. But it doesn't happen often and it's not, well, it's not good, it's not nice, you know, son."

"Yes?" I said, and waited. I had no idea what she was trying to say.

"Tyler, boy, why you so inquisitive? Why you thinking about these things?"

Still I waited. Suddenly she seemed to perk up as if she'd seen a vision of the perfect explanation. "Look here, son, you see, there was a fellow . . . not from near here, he was from Paradise, a fellow name Chandin, Chandin Ramchandin. You know, he only had a handful of years over me but when I was your age or so, they used to tell us that we must study hard so that we could have the luck of that Ramchandin fellow. Hmmm, I wonder what become of him? Nowadays you don't even hear his name. It's like he disappeared off the face of the earth."

Nana took another pull on the stub of cigarette, and as she exhaled long and slow she stared up into the sky.

OLD MAN RAMCHANDIN, who was only ever known as Ramchandin, was an indentured field labourer from India. He was relaxing as he did every evening after work, rocking himself in the burlap hammock that hung from a cashew tree at the back of the estate barracks. His eyes were closed but as usual he was not asleep. The old man kept himself awake by worrying about the future of his only child. He had been turning mathematical estimations this way and that, inside out and upside down in his head. He had, as usual, whipped himself up a headache with his obsessive predictions of what the state of his finances could be if he and his wife, Janaki, were to work one hour more, or even two hours more per day, so that enough funds might be accrued to send Chandin to a college in the capital, or even abroad to study a profession. With the rhythmic flicking of his thighs, he rocked in the hammock and calculated how many years it would be before Chandin were eligible for enrollment in a college, how many extra hours there were in that many years — times two if his wife were also to work the extra time, factoring in a possible raise in their salaries — and he even went so far as to do a little division and addition to account for the inevitable rise in the cost of living.

Old man Ramchandin thought about life in the barracks and life in India before his recruitment to Lantanacamara. There was no difference. But by making the long journey across two oceans, he hoped to leave behind, as promised by the recruiter, his inherited karmic destiny as a servant labourer — if not for himself, at least for his son who had been born just before they left India. In Lantanacamara it was easier to slip out of caste. He planned to work hard, save money and educate Chandin out of the fields.

In the midst of all this mental confusion he heard the crunch of gravel and the ruckus of a horse and buggy manoeuvering the dusty path. Ramchandin pulled himself out of the hammock. His daydreaming evaporated like dewdrops in morning heat. Before him lay the harsh reality of his two-room ajoupa quarters in the barracks. His two thin cows were yet to be tied up for the approaching night. He was exhausted. He could have told Chandin to tie up the cows but he considered the task too menial for the gold bead of his life. Ramchandin straightened and smoothed his white kurta and dhoti, which hung loosely on his stiff frame, and made his way to the front yard with as much dignity as age and fatigue would allow. His son stood by the front porch and scratched the dry clay soil with his bare foot. The rumble of the buggy coming down the path so late in the day had not surprised the boy as much as his parents. He was, in fact, awaiting the arrival of Reverend Thoroughly. His mother, smelling of coals and charred eggplant and a sweat that embarrassed him with its pungency of heated mustard seed, had left the clay oven at the back of their quarters. She quickly pulled her orhanie over her head and nose and mouth, and hurried around to the front.

The graceful Reverend pretended not to notice the large cloud of dust his horse and buggy had whipped up, or that he was covered in it. He declined a cup of well water and stated his case without formalities.

Before the Reverend had returned to his own home, his visit and the name of Chandin, son of Ramchandin, were known to immigrant workers throughout barracks across the width and breadth of Lantanacamara. Even at the farthest end of the island, in Nana's humble and unremarkable village, the Reverend's visit and Chandin's bright and prosperous future were discussed and debated.

"Is a Reverend who come from the Shivering Northern Wetlands. A white man who set up school and church for Indians. Is he who make the trip inside of the cane field area up to the barracks."

"So he gone all that distance in all that dust!"

"He travel dirt road to bring them such a news. And I hear he face and he hair and he clothes and he shoes was covered, like white sheet, in dust by the time he get to the house."

"Eh-heh!"

"So he taking the boy to go and live in he own house?"

"Yes."

"In he own house. Hmmm!"

"To raise like he own child?"

"Eh-heh."

"He is the oldest student in the school, so that mean that he will be the first one, the oldest one, to make the first graduation, with ceremony and thing, na! And the Reverend want to send the first graduate from his school to college to study. So he taking him to make sure he study good good."

"But that child lucky! What is the family name again?"

"Ramchandin. The child name Chandin. Chandin Ramchandin."

"Well, the father and wife lucky!"

"You think so? I hear they did have to convert. That was the condition if they wanted the child to go to school. I can't do that. No. I just don't want to do that."

"What you talking? What you mean you don't want to do that! If it is the only way for your child to get education and not have to work like a horse sweating and breaking back in the hot sun for hardly nothing, you wouldn't convert? I will say my piece now. Listen. Since the Africans let go from slavery, all eyes on how the government treating them. It have commissions from this place and from that place making sure that the government don't just neglect them. They have schools, they have regular and free medical inspection. Now, you see any schools set up for our children, besides the Reverend's school? When we get sick and we have pains, who looking after us? We looking after our own self, because nobody have time for us. Except the Reverend and his mission from the Shivering Northern Wetlands. All he want from us is that we convert to his religion. If I had children, I would convert! Besides, nobody but you really know which god you praying to. Convert, man! Take the children yourself to the mission school.

And when you praying you pray with you eyes and you mouth shut. Simple so. That is all."

"Is true. Yes. I suppose is true. It make sense."

"Mm-hmmm."

"Chandin Ramchandin will be the first one of all of we to get profession. The first Indian child in Lantanacamara to get a title. Remember that name. I tell you if I had children is what I would want for them too. I don't see nothing wrong to want the best for your child."

And so the news of Chandin's fortune spread, and even before he entered the Reverend's seminary he was unwittingly helping to convert Indians to Christianity.

Nana rolled herself another cigarette. I liked the smell of sulfur when she outed her match and was fascinated by the way she cupped the cigarette in both hands and sucked erratically before she got a good enough light.

"He was bright, Nana? He went to study abroad?"

"He was bright, yes. But I don't think he went to study abroad." Seeing my face fall, because she knew it was my dream to go abroad and study, she slowed down.

"He didn't have to go abroad. I'll tell you more. You see, the Reverend set up a seminary right here in Lantanacamara, right there, in Paradise and it is there he went . . ."

Once the Ramchandin boy left the barracks he was not inclined to return. He hardly saw his father but his mother went to church services at least once a week, especially to see him sitting up there in the front, looking very foreign in spite of his dark skin, all dressed up in his jacket and tie, right next to the Reverend's wife. The few times he went back to the barracks to visit it was evident his mother had not really converted to Christianity. When he inquired after the foot-long brass crucifix the Reverend had given her to put above the doorway, she shyly said that she had wrapped it carefully in a clean white cloth and put it away, for safe-keeping, in a trunk. However, he noticed that the number of statues of Hindu gods and goddesses lining the walls had increased since his move to the Reverend's house. Sometimes sacred camphor and incense used in Hindu prayers coloured the air, and always a faint cloud of pooja smoke permeated his parents' hair and clothes, replacing the odour of coals and spices that used to emanate from his mother's body. He was embarrassed by his parents' reluctance to embrace the smarter-looking, smarter-acting Reverend's religion, and there soon came a time when, to his parents' dismay, he no longer visited.

A name change for Chandin was briefly discussed by the Reverend and his wife. Mrs. Thoroughly thought that a Christian, if not Wetlandish name was more suitable for a son of theirs. Chandin was eager to have his Indian name replaced. Mrs. Thoroughly suggested Matthew, Mark, Luke or John. Even Ovid, Errol, Oscar and Atticus were considered. She half-joked that it was her first and probably her last opportunity to name a boy child. The thoughtful Reverend, however, suggested that Chandin Ramchandin would one day be a Christian teacher, theologian and missionary whose success in the field would be due, certainly to the blessings of God, but also to the novel idea that people were most likely to be swayed by one of their own kind. Chandin and Mrs. Thoroughly gave in to the Reverend's idea that Chandin's own name would win his people's trust.

Chandin went everywhere with his new family. When they travelled to other towns and held church meetings under tents, he sat on the stage among the other Wetlander missionaries and was often the centre of attention. He was introduced as the Reverend's son, and his story, already well known to every labourer, was expounded as a tangible benefit of conversion.

Being the adopted son of the Reverend and Mrs. Ernest Thoroughly, Christian missionaries from the Shivering Northern Wetlands, did have its benefits, the greatest of which, in Chandin's mind, came to be the daily presence of Lavinia Thoroughly, his newly acquired sister.

Chandin's favourite time of day was after the evening meal when the family gathered in the living room for an hour of relaxation. At other times he was unsure of his place in this new household. He often felt conspicuously lost. But evenings, sitting quietly in the living room with his new family, he had a very definite place. The Reverend had a chair that he alone sat in, as did Mrs. Thoroughly, and Lavinia invariably lay on her back or stomach on the very same portion of rug, or sat on a footstool near her mother. Chandin found that a straight-back upholstered chair had come to be marked as his. Although it was only a physical place, the chair became an antidote to the chaos of his uprootedness.

He was mesmerized by the chandelier that hung low in the middle of the room. While he should have been studying he would spend long moments staring at the leaf-shaped glass pendants that kicked off flickers of blue, red and violet light. He wondered how many of the people in the cane field barracks had ever seen such a fine thing. He wished he could show them not only that item, but also the fine cabinets, carved chairs and side tables and lamps with fancy shades. At first he wanted the labourers to see it all because everything was new and exciting. Then he desperately wanted them to see the inside of the Reverend's house so they could embrace not just the Reverend's faith but his taste. In his innocence he felt that his people's lack of these things was a result of apathy and a poverty of ambition. He thought of his parents' mud house and the things there, the peerahs they used for sitting on, the rough planks of wood used as shelves, the cattiyas instead of mattresses on high wood frames, the enamel wares, the paltry pitch-oil lamps, and most saddening of all, the latrine with that particular odour that etches itself on one's brain. He felt immense distaste for his background and the people in it. Gazing awestruck at the chandelier, he would daily renew his promise to be the first brown-skinned person in Lantanacamara to own one just like it.

The living room had two large windows through which scented breezes from undulating fields of sugar cane sailed in from the valleys below. While the Reverend and his wife cooled themselves in the benevolent breeze, chatting one minute, silent the next, absorbed in reading or in writing in their journals, Chandin observed his new family and listened to their conversations, the kind that families have only among themselves. At those times, he felt most thoroughly assured of a place, more significant even than a chair, in this new family.

When he first went to live in the Reverend's house, Lavinia was a quiet, unremarkable child, a little younger than he, who begged not to be noticed. As far as Chandin's classmates were concerned, her only noteworthiness was in her fair skin, her white hair and the fact she was the principal's daughter. Those attributes, however, were more than enough to win her admirers. The boys would perform antics and heroics in her presence in the hope that she would glance their way, but she appeared self-absorbed and blind, which only made them try harder.

There was only one other girl in the school but the boys were not as concerned with her. She came from the same barracks as Chandin. Her parents had made a more convincing conversion than his, taking name changes for every person in the family. She had been given the name Sarah by Mrs. Thoroughly. Sarah was the only person in the school whom Lavinia was close to. The only thing that pleased Chandin about the friendship was that it indicated Lavinia was not prejudiced against people like himself. A friendship with Sarah, to Chandin's mind, would encourage her to become comfortable with the Indians, and so with him. Chandin would regard Sarah jealously and wonder what attributes she had that he lacked. He wished Lavinia would talk and laugh with him the way she did with the small, dark girl from the barracks. On days that Chandin and Lavinia were encouraged to invite one friend each from the school to spend the day, Lavinia uniformly invited Sarah, while Chandin, ashamed of the boys' barracks ways, invited no one.

Over the course of a couple of years, Lavinia, confounding even her parents, sprang into an unusually tall and handsome young woman. Her sullenness turned into an attractive independence. At the mission school, interest in Lavinia, which for a while had waned, was renewed. The boys became even more absorbed by her presence. They competed against her remarkable strengths on the playing field and her brilliance in the classroom, both of which, coming from a girl, stunned them and made them more attracted than before.

Chandin watched the other boys' brash, competitive ways. A rash of jealousy darkened his days and made his nights sweaty and fitful. Dizziness would drench him whenever he saw her. He spoke with her less and less as his words seemed to jumble in her presence, and he would momentarily lose his ability to make such a simple decision as whether or not he was thirsty. For a while he stopped looking at her, fearing that the flame he could feel burning brightly in his cheeks and the odd and unspeakable sensation filling his trousers and the pleading in his eyes were all too visible. His feelings were all the more unbearable because he knew that he dare not express them.

When Lavinia failed to notice him, his passion did not wane but was transformed. Embers of adoration and desire smoldered but what sprang up were flames of anger and self-loathing. He began to hate his looks, the colour of his skin, the texture of his hair, his accent, the barracks, his real parents and at times even the Reverend and his god. It began to matter to him that he and Lavinia were not in fact siblings.

At school the flames of self-loathing were fanned. Lavinia remained uninterested in any of the boys despite their willingness to perform miracles for her, so the boys decided that a girl like her would fall in love only with a boy like herself. They would then jokingly mimic the Reverend's gait and gestures. In the privacy of his bedroom Chandin watched himself in the long mirror on the door of the armoire, and saw what he most feared: a short and darkly brown Indian-Lantanacamaran boy with blue-black hair. Without question, he resembled the other boys in his class and from the barracks in the fields.

He would change, he decided once and for all, what he had the power to change. Chandin took note of the Reverend's rigid, austere posture, so unlike his own father's propensity to bend or twist or fold his body whichever way the dictates of comfort tipped him. He practised sitting upright, with his back unswayed and his legs planted firmly on the ground or crossed severely at the knees. Other times he diligently studied and imitated the Reverend's pensive stroking of his chin or tapping of his fingers against a book. When he walked, even though he had, by the age of fourteen, reached his full height and was quite short, he made strides as wide as the towering Reverend's, and he clasped his hands, similarly, in a little entwined knot behind his back. His usual thoughtfulness turned weighty. He now brooded with an air of romantic sullenness. He stroked his chin habitually and revelled in the tragic knowledge that his love-sickness could bleed so freely within him and yet be invisible, or so he thought, to the family with whom he lived and to his schoolmates.

It came, then, as a surprise when Reverend Thoroughly burst into Chandin's room one evening to invite him to the rectory, an invitation that seemed more like an order. The rectory was hardly a five-minute walk away. The Reverend placed the palm of his hand on the back of Chandin's fleshy neck and held it gently but firmly, as if ushering Chandin along. His hand was hot and its weight reassuring, intensifying an intimacy between them that Chandin welcomed. In the bond of that moment he considered confiding in Reverend Thoroughly his feelings toward Lavinia. He would, he decided, take more time to consider his words, to avoid any ineloquence, and then within the week he would seek the Reverend's counsel.

Inside the rectory Reverend Thoroughly sat at his desk and began leafing through a ledger. Chandin stood about idly, as he imagined a son might stand and wait for his father. He went to the bookshelf and fingered the spines of a few volumes, feeling the little gullies the letters made. His mind strayed back to the living room. He walked over to the window and pressed his face against the glass, cupping his hands to block out the light's reflection. He stared in the direction of fields that had long ago been sucked up into the dark night. He thought only of Lavinia and wished he was back in the living room with her and her mother. She had been lying on the woven straw rug reading. He wished he was brave enough to move onto the rug with her and ask what held her attention. After all, he reasoned, even though they were not really siblings, they were supposed to treat each other as such, and a sibling should be allowed to do that. At the same time he knew that once on the rug next to her he would shake like a mango leaf in a hurricane. As he pulled his face away from the window, he could see in its reflection that Reverend Thoroughly had swung his chair around to face him.

"Chandin! I am talking to you!" Reverend Thoroughly had never called him so sharply before.

"Oh, sorry sir. I was . . . I was just . . ."

The Reverend softened. Lowering his voice he asked, "What were you thinking about?"

"Nothing really. Everything. Nothing." Chandin half-smiled, again considering taking the Reverend into his confidence.

The Reverend remained serious. "I will speak as plainly as I might, Chandin. If I sound harsh, please forgive me. I have found from experience that to deal with delicate matters too delicately serves only to prolong and unnecessarily muddle discussion."

Chandin's dark brown ears immediately flushed scarlet. He had never heard the Reverend speak so formally or firmly, except at the pulpit when in prayer. Chandin felt his chest shrink and his breathing become shallow. He crossed his legs against an urgent need to run off and find relief in one of Mrs. Thoroughly's flower beds. He wondered if he were about to get a lecture about his school studies. Had he disappointed the Reverend and his wife? For a long moment Chandin had the uncomfortable feeling he was about to be informed that he was to be sent back, a failure, to the cane fields, to live forever in the midst of his parents' shame and disappointment.

"Sir?" The word he intended to say with dignity came out in a gravelly whisper. He stared with discomfort at the concrete floor.

"Your brooding has not been unnoticed. Besides being as unpleasant as those sour cherries of which you boys seem so fond, or as a thunderstorm at a garden party, brooding will never charm a young lady."

Chandin's eyes flicked up to look at the Reverend. His face burned. So his interests had not been invisible. Believing he heard an ounce of advice in the Reverend's comments, he broke into a nervous grin. The Reverend stood up and walked to the bookshelf. With his back to Chandin, he continued.

"Chandin, how long have you been sharing our home with us, with my wife and I?" Instinctively Chandin felt that what was about to come was not a smiling matter, but the muscles in his face twitched and his grin, a grin of embarrassment, grew wider.

The Reverend spun around on the heel of his shining shoes and looked directly at him.

"You are having a good time, are you? Answer me! How long, Chandin? Three years. Hasn't it been three years, son?"

Chandin tried in vain to wipe the painful grin from his face. He looked at the floor and nodded.

"Do we not feel like a family to you?" There was disappointment in the Reverend's voice.

Tears collected in Chandin's eyes. His smile had become rigid and aching.

"I have, in good faith, taken on the role of your father. Mrs. Thoroughly has done a good job of being a mother to you, hasn't she?"

Chandin nodded, unable to give sound to his answers.

"If I have performed as your father and my wife as your mother, what is the relationship of my daughter to you?"

Chandin's heart leapt up in fear. The room seemed to spin. He prayed that no tear would fall and embarrass him. Finally the smile dissipated.

"I think you understand me well. Your attentions have not been unnoticed by my wife and me."

He paused as though waiting for a response. When none came he shook his head in exasperation and continued.

"Look here. You are to be a brother to Lavinia and nothing more. A brother. She is your sister and you her brother. A brother protects and helps and supports and comforts his sister. There is no harm in loving your sister. Or your mother or your father. But that love must remain pure, as pure as God's love is for his children."

The Reverend walked to his desk and slammed the polished mahogany top with his fist. "You cannot, you must not have desire for your sister Lavinia. That is surely against God's will. Do you understand? Do you understand me, Chandin! Otherwise, otherwise . . ." The Reverend, seemingly spent, sat down in his chair. His tone softened as though he were enormously tired. "It is past your bedtime. I will stay here and pray to our Father in heaven. I suggest you go to your room and do the same. Go on, now. Please tell Mrs. Thoroughly not to worry, that I will stay here for a while longer."

Chandin did not immediately return to the house. He stayed outside holding his stomach, which had turned into a hard knot. It cramped unbearably and he was unable to stop an onslaught of hot tears. His world seemed suddenly to have shrunk. He looked up at the stars and mumbled to himself. "Imbecile! Why do I have to grin and smile whenever I am embarrassed. Imbecile! Grinning like an imbecile. She is not my sister. Why couldn't I say that instead of grinning? She is not my sister. It's not really wrong, is it? It can't be."

It was some time before he noticed the fireflies flickering in the pitch-black night. One would glow for a few seconds, then shut out and disappear. Soon somewhere nearby a tiny light would burn again. His eyes still stinging from crying, he began to try to trace an insect's flight by its flickering light. Absorbed in this manner an idea dawned on him, which he took as a response to his question. His love for Lavinia would never die. He would hide it away so well that no one would be able to trace it. Only he, in the privacy of his room after he had turned out the light, would know his love still glowed. And when the time was right he would take it out and it would burn as brightly as the cane fields afire, by which time Lavinia would be older and would declare her interest in him.

So, in the years that followed, even past the time that he graduated from high school and moved into quarters at the seminary some miles away, the Reverend and his wife remained pleased that Chandin had responded to that night's talk with remarkable maturity and earnestness.

Chandin Ramchandin was the only person of Indian descent at the seminary. He was, in fact, the only non-white person there. He and seventeen other men lived together in the institution's dormitories. The others had all come from the Shivering Northern Wetlands to study theology and get first-hand experience in a tropical climate among non-Christians. Most of the young men planned to remain in Lantanacamara, while some had intentions of joining the church's other missions in India and Africa.

Chandin seemed to be well liked by the taller, fair, heavily accented men, but he wondered constantly whether it was because he was the Reverend's adopted son and Lavinia's brother, or because he was of the race that it was their mission to Christianize. He scrutinized every aspect of these men. Most were his age yet seemed so much more worldly. He copied their manners and dressed like them in the white shirts and trousers the Wetlanders considered the height of tropical fashion. He would turn their accented phrases over and over in his mind until he was brave enough to air them: "I'd be very much obliged, Chandin, my good fellow . . ." ". . . upon your honour!" ". . . how infinitely superior . . ."

Often they all congregated in the Thoroughlys' garden for tea or croquet, and Chandin watched them flutter around Lavinia. She flirted back good-naturedly but if she paid special attention to anyone, it was to him. He might have been honoured yet he knew all too well that it was their supposed sibling relationship that brought her to him with giggles and little whispered confidences about this or that seminarian. Pray as he might, nothing indicated that she might ever be drawn to him or expect one day to share his life. He feared that without some firm action on his part, someone else with more aplomb would step in and steal her away. He had proven himself in school and in the seminary. They were now both adults. And furthermore, they were not siblings, he shouted in the silent space of his own head. He decided he would speak with Lavinia at the first opportunity.

The opportunity came quite unexpectedly. A cricket match for the seminarians had been arranged by the Thoroughlys and two missionary families from other parts of the island. It was to be a fun-filled day to celebrate the end of the dry season, which coincided with the coming holidays. Lavinia, who had just graduated from high school, was there, as was Sarah. Sarah was the only other non-Wetlander besides Chandin. Each man, dressed in brilliant cricket whites, seemed to be batting, bowling and fielding for the two young women.

Chandin batted long and hard. After each stroke he would adjust his V-neck sweater and glance proudly toward Lavinia. At the start of his batting she cheered him on, calling out, "Bravo! Bravo!" Her public acknowledgement all but dizzied him. When the game broke for lunch, Chandin was still not out. Reverend Thoroughly, holding a plate of cheese sandwiches, called him aside.

"Chandin, what splendid batsmanship, my boy! Inspired, simply inspired!"

Chandin, sweating in the heat yet still wearing his cricket sweater, blushed and mumbled thank-you. He was aware of being spoken to by the Reverend as though he were a third person standing off to the side observing the two of them.

"I must tell you of our great fortune. I ought to have informed you a while ago but with all the business of graduations it simply slipped my mind. Lavinia has been accepted into the seminary."

Chandin thought, You are the seminary, in other words, you

have accepted her. But he succeeded in sounding pleased when he answered, "Good news! Well done! She must be very happy."

"Indeed, she is. We all are. And this is the thing. Before the term starts up again, I have decided to take the family to spend the next few months back home in the Wetlands. You know we have not been back in a long while."

Chandin's heart leapt, thinking he was to be included in the family journey.

"Mrs. Thoroughly, Lavinia and I will leave in a matter of days," said the Reverend.

"But, sir, there are no sailings for at least four more months, until the end of the storm season," Chandin interrupted indignantly.

"Ah, but an unscheduled sailing takes place in three days, precisely to beat the storms. Fortunately our affairs are such that we can leave on short notice."

The Reverend continued to talk as Chandin became filled with fear. In her homeland Lavinia was bound to meet some Wetlander with whom she would fall in desperate love and marry. He heard the Reverend saying something about how much they would miss him. Chandin's only concern was to declare his love to Lavinia right there, that very day.

She and Sarah were strolling along the edge of the field, heading away from the crowd. Chandin took off in a little run, shouting Lavinia's name. She seemed not to hear. When he caught up, he did not excuse himself but grasped Lavinia firmly by the elbow.

"Lavinia, I must talk with you."

"What! What on earth could be the matter? You have not even excused yourself, and why this?" she said looking down at his hand still clutching her.

"Please excuse me. Sarah, would you please excuse us. I have a matter of some urgency to discuss with Miss Thoroughly."

"Chandin, Sarah calls me by my first name. You know that. Why so formal? What can be so urgent?" When Sarah walked off with a hint of a glare, Chandin apologized and softened his manner.

"I have been meaning to talk with you for a while now, but I haven't had the opportunity before today's match ..."

"By the way, you batted marvellously! I had no idea that you were such an asset!"

He stepped in front of her and took both her hands, bringing them up to his chest. "Every one of those was for you, Lavinia. I have been meaning —"

Understanding his intent all too clearly she pulled her hands out of his and said in disbelief, with a hint of a laugh, "I think you better stop right now!"

"Lavinia, listen to me please. I think only of you. I have only ever thought of you. I must tell you that I love no one quite as much as I have always loved you. Your father has just informed me that you are to leave in a matter of days. I will wait here for you, and when you return I will ask your father —"

She slapped her thigh.

"You will do no such thing. You are nothing more than my brother."

"Lavinia, stop this please. We are not siblings. I love —"

"No! No! No! This is ridiculous. Let's just stop this conversation right now. I think you must have batter's sunstroke."

Chandin fell silent. He stared blankly at her.

"Don't speak a word of this to anyone, Chandin. Please. I disapprove and do not consent —"

"Lavinia —"

"Shhh, shhh, do not speak to me of it either." She turned and saw her mother carrying two pitchers of mango juice. Without another word she ran off to relieve her.

Chandin was caught out with the first ball of the first inning after lunch. From the corner of his eye he could see that Lavinia had not even noticed. Her back was to the field and she was chatting with Sarah, who was laughing, clearly unaware of the state of the game.

The holidays passed miserably. Chandin, with little or no appetite, dwindled in size. One letter came from Mrs. Thoroughly, who wrote only that they were thrilled to see their relatives and happy to meet old friends again. She added, "We miss you and talk of you often," but said nothing about Lavinia. On the day of their return Chandin took special care in his grooming, changing his clothing no less than three times, trying to find the look that might catch Lavinia's eye without being too obvious. He arrived at the harbour in time to watch the steamer coast its last half-mile to port. Among the hundreds of pairs of hands waving wildly he picked out the Reverend and Mrs. Thoroughly, who had long ago spotted him, one of the few brown-skinned people on shore not employed in bringing the ship in. He was unable to see Lavinia.

The Thoroughlys warmly greeted him. The strained smile on his face, his nervous laughter and his scanning of the crowd were not unnoticed. Mrs. Thoroughly held both his hands, squeezing them in hers.

"Lavinia has stayed on in the Wetlands, Chandin. But not for long. Not for too long. My, my, it is indeed rather hot, isn't it? We have hardly been away for very long and I have already forgotten just how hot this place could be! I am delighted to be back, though. How are you, Chandin?" Her Wetlandish accent was thicker than Chandin had remembered. She let go of his hands and fanned herself with a scented handkerchief.

Reverend Thoroughly was quiet. He had his eyes on porters unloading trunks of luggage. As fast as he wiped perspiration from his forehead and neck with a large handkerchief, beads sprang up again. Seeing their luggage he excused himself. Mrs. Thoroughly faced Chandin squarely and began to talk quickly, as though trying to answer the questions she read in his eyes.

"Our family has very strong ties in the Wetlands, Chandin. All my family and Ernest's, I mean, Reverend Thoroughly's, live there. And they all know everything about you. You were the subject of many wonderful conversations, and people who have never met you have sent their greetings and blessings! It is good that Lavinia will stay on. But she will not be absent long — only until the very next sailing. As you know, Chandin, it had been many years since Lavinia and her grandparents had seen each other. She met cousins, several of whom were either babies or not yet born when we left to come here —"

Pain engulfed Chandin. He had an urgent need to say something, if only to assure himself that he was still breathing. "What about her plans," he interjected feebly "to attend the seminary? Does she not want to attend?"

"Of course she will attend! Her father has promised to hold her seat for her — she will, after all, be the first woman to attend! She will return, Chandin, on the next sailing. She is just so fascinated with the Wetlands. So much family there, you know, so many relatives. And it's so damp, so cool, so richly damp . . ."

The Thoroughlys regularly invited Chandin for supper, but it was impossible for him to enter their house and not obsess over information about Lavinia, about her pending return or her interest in him as her life's companion. Citing the need to study for this examination and that test, he more often than not declined. He spent much time by himself, sequestered in the library or his room in the dormitory. Despite what Lavinia's parents said, he had lost hope that she would return. His lack of appetite continued. His nights were sleepless, and he grew thin and morose. Even his gait changed; his muscles sagged and his bones seemed to bow under the weight of despair. The will to imitate the Reverend's posture of confidence and power had completely withered.

A month had not passed since the Thoroughlys' return when the Reverend arrived unannounced one afternoon at Chandin's room in the dormitory. The instant Chandin opened the door he felt a tired resignation in the pit of his stomach.

"Come walk with me, Chandin. The kanganilla are in bloom. Have you seen them today?"

Out on the lawns in brilliant sunshine Chandin remained quiet, thinking, Well, come on, I am waiting. I am ready. I know very well that you have not brought me here to see the kanganilla. Tell me whatever it is you must.

But he was not ready for the news. Reverend Thoroughly reached into the breast pocket of his jacket and pulled out a thin, twice-folded paper. He held it up as if to verify its existence yet did not unfold the sheet. A telegram from Lavinia, he said, and touched the page briefly to his lips. Chandin's heart leapt with fear and excitement. He wanted, at the very least, to brush the piece of paper with his hand, but Reverend Thoroughly had already slipped it back into his pocket.

"It is wonderful news, Chandin, simply wonderful news for a parent. Lavinia is in love—" Chandin, breathless, came to an abrupt halt. Even as he knew it to be in vain, an ember of hope spat at his heart. "—and requests permission to marry, Chandin. Our little girl, your sister, is to marry!"

A rush of blood to his head made him dizzy. Tears sprang into Chandin's eyes. He turned away to look toward the distant valley.

"Ah." The feeble response fell from his mouth.

"Fenton Thoroughly. A lovely chap, lovely! We . . ."

Chandin was startled. "Thoroughly?"

"Yes. He is my nephew."

Chandin turned to face the Reverend, uncaring, suddenly, that his disappointment would be visible. "Her cousin! She is in love with her cousin? I don't understand. And what about her schooling? I don't understand. Her cousin, sir?"

Reverend Thoroughly looked up at the sky, over to the kanganilla, at the seminary building, and continued on, trying to sound as if he were doing nothing more than confiding in a trusted family friend.

"Yes, Chandin. I was sure that you would mention it. He is not truly her cousin. You see, my brother married a woman who had been married once before and brought with her a child — Fenton. My brother was good enough, wouldn't you say, to bring him up as his own child, give him his name and all of that sort of thing . . . but as you can see he is not a true relation. He is a marvellous gentleman by every standard, and on maturing he is slated to inherit a rather large estate from his blood father. He is a medical student."

"And he is in love with her?"

"Well, of course! We have given our blessings to them both. There will be a marriage as soon as —"

It might as well have been night time. On cue from the word *marriage,* Chandin's world spun and blackened as if the sun had suddenly been switched off. He broke out in a sweat and began to shiver. The words spilling from his own mouth surprised even himself.

"I have been meaning to talk with you. I wanted to talk with you and Mrs. Thoroughly. I too . . . I want to . . ."

"What is it, Chandin?"

"I too have been thinking about marriage. I wanted to ask your permission also."

"You?"

"I, I, it's time for me also. I have been thinking of Sarah. Sarah, you know, Sarah." Chandin wanted nothing more than to collapse in the security of a woman, a woman from his background, and Sarah was the most likely possibility.

"Sarah! Well, what a surprise! I had not realized . . . Sarah, eh? Look here, son, shall I write her parents, or go and see them on your behalf? I am . . . speechless. So surprised. Her parents will be delighted. Thrilled. But not half as delighted as I am. We must inform Mrs. Thoroughly right away. Come on, come on."

Six weeks later Chandin and Sarah were married.

REFLECTING NOW ON the story that Cigarette Smoking Nana had begun to relate to answer my boyish query, I realize I had known of Miss Ramchandin for many, many years. I often want to call out to Nana up in the heavens — where I am sure she is and quite sure that Bible Quoting Nana is not — and say, "You were right, you were right. There was indeed a Chandin Ramchandin. But there is much more to that story!" It was as though Nana had introduced me to Miss Ramchandin, and Miss Ramchandin had confirmed Nana for me.

After a few days in the wheelchair, Miss Ramchandin was strong enough to walk. I held her by the elbow as we wandered across the grounds. Being outside was what she most loved. She came alive and made her bird and insect calls. That day as we strolled across the grounds a young stray cat scuttled by, unsure but curious about us. Miss Ramchandin made her most decisive gesture yet. She dropped to her knees, put out her hand and meowed like a kitten. The cat responded immediately, running to her hand. She picked it up, stood and pressed the creature to her chest. I was perplexed, wondering if this cat might have belonged to her and found its way back. Miss Ramchandin rested her cheek against the cat's head and whispered her first words since her arrival.

"Pohpoh, Pohpoh," she cooed into its ear lovingly, seeming to call the cat by name.

When I asked if it was her cat, she closed her eyes. "Pohpoh, Pohpoh," she said again. It was a common nickname affectionately given to children and I supposed not an unnatural name for a kitten as well.

The cat came back to the bungalow in Miss Ramchandin's arms. That night I hesitantly asked Sister if it were possible to keep the animal. She shrugged and said, "It have mice in the kitchen. It might be a good thing."

That Miss Ramchandin got to keep the cat was both fortunate and a mistake. Fortunate because it gave her something to exercise concern about; a mistake because in time I learned that when she had pressed her cheek against the cat's body and called the name Pohpoh, it was not a cat that she was calling.

By the time Nana got around to addressing my specific question, she was, in the end, unable to tell me everything.

"So Chandin Ramchandin married this Sarah and she made two children, two girl children," she said. "And well, you know, Tyler child, one thing lead to the other and, well, to make long story short, Chandin pick up with the older daughter. Now she never had any children with him but it could have happened. That is the thing. It could have happened, yes! Now if the daughter had made a child for him, that child would be his —"

Right then we heard the front door open. Nana stopped, outed the cigarette and tried to mash it into the earth, swiping frantically at the smoke with her arms. She got up quickly, making herself look busy. You see, Ma had just returned from her day's work in town. Nana's talk came to such a screeching halt that I sensed from her stony silence that the story had ended right there and then because these were things my Ma, her daughter, would have disapproved of her telling a little boy like myself. Even in its pre-empted state, what she was telling was alarming. The insinuation at the tail end of her story stayed with me. Over the years I pondered the gender and sex roles that seemed available to people, and the rules that went with them. After much reflection I have come to discern that my desire to leave the shores of Lantanacamara had much to do with wanting to study abroad, but far more with wanting to be somewhere where my "perversion," which I tried diligently as I could to shake, might be either invisible or of no consequence to people to whom my foreignness was what would be strange. I was preoccupied with trying to understand what was natural and what perverse, and who said so and why. Chandin Ramchandin played a part in confusing me about these roles, for it was a long time before I could differentiate between his perversion and what others called mine. Some instinctual fear stopped me from bringing it up with Nana again, and I noticed that she avoided it, too.

Two decades and more have passed since then, and so too has Nana. She made a long story short yet I wonder how much she really knew. If she were still here, would she and I be able to go through and finish that conversation we started on the back steps, and now that I have grown up and found my own nature, would this particular nature be coarse sandpaper drawing blood against her? I wonder if she and I as adults could today have that same talk without grudges surfacing. I fancy the affiliation blossoming between Miss Ramchandin and me to be a clue to these musings. The relationship between Nana, my Cigarette Smoking Nana, and me, her Peculiar Grandson, was special, for we both had secrets from my mother, her daughter. Miss Ramchandin and I, too, had a camaraderie: we had found our own ways and fortified ourselves against the rest of the world.

I wonder what Nana would think if she knew the positions I was in that enabled me to gain the full story. For there were two: one, a shared queerness with Miss Ramchandin, which gave rise to the other, my proximity to the very Ramchandin Nana herself had known of.

SARAH GAVE BIRTH to her first child ten months after the marriage, and a couple of years later she was pregnant again. Chandin thought often of Lavinia but his love for her had soured and mostly he felt betrayal. He was a dispassionate husband to Sarah though he enjoyed observing his two daughters, albeit from a distance. He was composed and diligent performing his duties as Reverend Thoroughly's interpreter and field assistant. Yet he often felt chained to both the church and the Thoroughlys, and impotent to reverse the path his life had taken since the day the Reverend made that trip to his parents' quarters.

Even when news came from the Wetlands that Lavinia had broken off her engagement, Chandin could only think with curdling cynicism, I knew this would result! I could have told her that it would not have lasted! As long as she stayed in the Wetlands he would be able to keep at bay his unquenchable desire for her and his ferocious hatred, not of her but of the effect she wielded. But a crisis would arise, he knew, if he were to come face to face with her again — if, that is, she were to one day return to the island of Lantanacamara.

Before Lavinia returned to live in Lantanacamara, Pohpoh's parents seldom spoke to one another unless it was absolutely necessary. Sarah, whose reserved nature did not suit an occupation in the church, occupied herself grinding spices downstairs in the yard, which was cooler than the kitchen, or weeding the front yard once the sun had gone behind the house, or washing clothing.

Chandin's relationship with Reverend and Mrs. Thoroughly slowly changed. His body began to accede to its inherited nature. A faint echo of his father's curvature developed, all the more evident as he shed Wetlandish fashion and fell into dressing like an overseer. He gradually extricated himself from the Thoroughly family, a move the Thoroughlys did not comment on but seemed to respect and perhaps even welcome. In public, though, they displayed more warmth for Chandin, his wife and two children, Pohpoh and Asha, than they did for the other Indian converts, all of whom they treated as their children.

When Chandin was not at the rectory studying or translating a sermon, or at Reverend Thoroughly's house discussing church business, he could be found in his own home, which he bought with a loan from the seminary. Years before he had dreamed of a stone and mortar house with special rooms for this and that — a library, a pantry, a guest room — like the Thoroughlys', but Chandin bought land cheaply in an underdeveloped section of Paradise called Hill Side, and hired two men to clear all but one tree from its stand of mudras. Using the hardy wood, he contracted them to build a two-storey house typical of modest dwellings in the area. The house stood atop mudra stilts. On the top floor was a drawing room, an ample kitchen and two bedrooms, the smaller shared by the two children and the larger by the adults. Porches ran on the front and back sides of the upper storey, each with a stairway leading to the ground. Between the bedrooms was a doorway leading down an enclosed stairway, the only access to a storage space that occupied a quarter of the downstairs, commonly known as the sewing room, whether or not it was used as such. The other three-quarters was open air. At home Chandin, who took no interest in the house itself, was invariably to be found lying on his side in the hammock, rocking on the back porch, reading until the sun went down and blackness fell.

The families of other, younger clergymen, who were rapidly spreading across the country, took regular excursions — day-long retreats, they called them — to the seaside or parks in the city for communion with God's nature. Chandin's family seldom made such trips. Their main outing was to the church on Sunday mornings. Chandin had lost any verve he had in the days when the chance of seeing Lavinia was his sole motivation for living.

Then one day without warning, even to her parents, she returned. Everything changed overnight. Chandin had not seen her, merely heard of her arrival, yet he clearly brightened. His children were surprised and pleased when he pointed out butterflies and flowering weeds, and purple and mandarin in the sunset sky. His colleagues noticed that he was now quick to enjoy others' wit and humour.

Still, he was shy to visit the Thoroughlys' house. Sarah returned home one afternoon to say that she had gone to pay her respects to Lavinia and that Lavinia was to visit them within the week. Chandin was like an excited child. He returned home the next day with a modest chandelier, and paid a man to install it in the drawing room. He paid another to put two coats of whitewash on his weathered mudra house. He bought a small imported rug for the living room. Out came his white shirts and trousers. He had Sarah bleach, starch and press them. He bought himself an expensive straw hat with a narrow velvet band, imported from the Shivering Northern Wetlands and purported by the retailer to be the season's top Wetlandish fashion statement. He began to dress impeccably, to speak with the accent and strut with the airs of the Wetlanders he once again seemed to so admire.

Chandin woke unusually early the day Lavinia was expected. He complained a little to Sarah about feeling unfit and lethargic, and decided to take a walk up Hill Side. He returned after the children had awakened, just as Sarah finished preparing breakfast. He was in great spirits. He complimented his wife on the meal and, after eating, he cleared off the table and, to Sarah's surprise, passed the broom across the drawing room and kitchen floors. He then swept the front and back porches and stairs. Inside he arranged and straightened and rearranged the furniture. He went out on the front porch and re-entered the house, imagining what a visitor would see on first entering. He stood on the porch again, and looked in and admired his chandelier.

Lunch time passed and Lavinia had not arrived. Trying not to show his nervousness that she might not come, Chandin lay in the hammock on the back porch and rocked. He thought about his wife and felt strangely distant from her, unrelated to her, as if a thick veil had dropped between them. His children's skin seemed suddenly too dark and their manner of talking crude. He wanted to remove himself from his wife and his children but knew it was impossible.

Lavinia arrived around tea time. She seemed genuinely happy to see Chandin. She showed him the presents she had brought for his children, and though he appreciated the gesture, it unsettled him: she seemed too willing to acknowledge his married state. He took two kitchen chairs out on the front porch and invited her to sit with him, while he had Sarah make a pot of tea. When Lavinia motioned to help, he quickly said, "She has learned to make a good pot. Let her do it and you come sit with me. Tell me everything that has happened since we last saw each other." He put his arm on her shoulder to guide her to the porch. He patted her shoulder in large, visible gestures, hoping to come across as brotherly.

When Pohpoh and Asha, playing out in the backyard, realized that the much anticipated Aunt Lavinia had arrived, they pelted up the back stairs. Hearing their excited entrance, Lavinia rushed toward them and, in the midst of the commotion, tea ended up being served in the kitchen, much to Chandin's disappointment. When Lavinia gave them the presents — books of Wetlandish nursery rhymes and folk tales — they asked her to read aloud right there and then, and a bond instantly formed.

Lavinia was so taken with the children that Chandin, unable to chat quietly alone with her, felt she had once again dismissed him. He watched peevishly from the back verandah as she was willingly led on a tour of the yard by the eager children. Sarah ambled alongside, grinning at their excitement. By the time the visit ended, Chandin could already feel the familiar sting of Lavinia's unattainability.

Much to his relief, Lavinia and Sarah rekindled their friendship, and Lavinia visited often. The hours between visits tended to be filled with tension in the Ramchandin household. Asha or Pohpoh, unable to stand the waiting, would sometimes ask for Lavinia to come along on excursions to the beach or river. Pohpoh noticed on these occasions that both her parents would relax. Soon Chandin became bolder, initiating outings he knew well would be of interest to the adventurous Lavinia. She never turned an offer down. When Sarah began to extend her own invitations, Chandin became sullen.

"She and I knew each other long before I married you. I wanted to marry her before I really knew you. I am not in the least comfortable that she and you are so close," Pohpoh heard her father shout one night.

"But you and she grow up like sister and brother. You couldn't marry she."

"This is utterly ridiculous. You know very well that she is not my sister. And another thing, is this how you speak with Lavinia?"

"What you mean?"

"Why don't you speak as you were taught in school? It is appalling that the educated wife of a man like myself refuses to exercise her knowledge. It just doesn't look good. What on earth would Lavinia herself think?"

"If you still so concerned with she, why didn't you wait until she returned from abroad to marry? You and I married now, boy. Ask her if she still interested in you. Ask her. Besides she never correcting how I speak. Is only you who always correcting me."

On Saturdays, when Chandin spent the day with Reverend Thoroughly going over school and church business, Lavinia would head over in her buggy to the Ramchandin house. Sometimes she arrived with her long golden hair in knots and tangles whipped up in the windy ride, her basket filled with candies and sweet-smelling potpourris from her grandmothers in the Shivering Northern Wetlands. Other times she came with her hair piled in an untidy clump on top of her head, strands dangling in her smiling face, carrying the gramophone she had brought from the Wetlands. She would play the little disks all day, and the children would dance and prance and laugh until they were sputtering with glee in the drawing room.

Lavinia loved the freedom and wildness in Sarah's garden, so unlike her mother's well-ordered, colour-coordinated beds. She brought clippings and whole plants ripped from Mrs. Thoroughly's garden, the fresh, rich dirt still under her fingernails. She brought flame ixoras for Sarah, and one memorable day she arrived with cactus plants, one each for Pohpoh and Asha. Cereus, she called them, pronounced like the bright, fuzzy star, a climbing succulent whose leaves and trunk were ragged and unsightly until they bloomed.

"Only once a year," she said. "The flowers will offer their exquisite elegance for one short, precious night." She took them out into the yard and made a production of choosing the best planting spot. In the roots of one of the cacti was entwined a large, bulbous periwinkle snail in a gold and buff shell. Pohpoh insisted she must have the shell for an ornament. Aunt Lavinia held her back from prying the live snail from its shell, urging her to wait until it died and shed its housing naturally.

"Killing snails amounts to courting bad luck, sweetheart," she said, narrowing her eyes and shaking her head. "But let me tell you a little secret. Protect a living snail and when it dies, it doesn't forget. Snails, like most things in nature, have long memories. A snail's soul, which is invisible, mind you, will come back after it has died, looking for its old home. It will have grown bigger and stronger, and will hover around its old stomping grounds, guarding and protecting you in return — as long as you protected it first! Just wait until you find some naturally emptied shells, honey. And this is what you do: display them nicely so they can be spotted by the floating souls of the snails that once occupied them. You press them into the earth — around a bed of plants or just make pretty patterns — and you, my sweet Pohpoh, and your Mama and Asha, and everyone whom you love will be ensured the fullest protection of the benevolent forces in the universe."

Aunt Lavinia winked at her. Pohpoh giggled at the whole idea and at Lavinia's telling. Sarah smiled and shook her head, for she too enjoyed the many tales that Lavinia seemed able to spin in an instant.

"Just you wait," Aunt Lavinia, enjoying the encouragement, continued, "just be patient. You will have your collection. But I'll tell you another thing: recently emptied snail shells can have the most unpleasant, most nauseating smell — especially a bunch of them. You must make sure to boil all empty shells before you can keep them as ornaments. Boil them in plenty of water, for a long time, until the water has almost evaporated from the pot. And another thing: salt, lots of salt in the water is a must . . ."

During the week Sarah and Lavinia would make trips in the buggy to other towns or the market. Pohpoh and Asha enjoyed these outings. They stopped to play on the swings in El Dorado Park and for things to eat, and Aunt Lavinia was sure to shower them with pendants and charms for their hair. Lavinia commanded the buggy herself. Unknown to Chandin, she taught Sarah to handle it too, but Sarah knew better than to be seen taking the reins until she was past their village and deep into the cane fields, out of sight of the other villagers. Chandin admired things in Lavinia that he would have been ashamed to have his wife do. In the fields between towns Sarah would drive until Aunt Lavinia shouted out to stop. Aunt Lavinia would stand on the seat of the buggy or hop off onto the unpaved country trails, uncaring that the ground underfoot might be muddy or treacherous, and she would pull out her Eastman Brownie camera and click away. Before they reached the town again, Lavinia would once again take the reins.

Aunt Lavinia continued to visit but the Saturday trips to town and market gradually came to an end. It seemed to the children that their Mama and Aunt Lavinia were wanting to conduct all their visits indoors, or only as far outdoors as the backyard. There used to be a photograph of Mama leaning back against the kitchen sink, facing the camera. Perhaps it was only the photograph that caused Pohpoh to later imagine that Aunt Lavinia had also stood there with Mama, because she had an indelible impression of them both leaning on the narrow sink basin, their sides pressed tightly together. The image stayed in Pohpoh's mind, fortified with a memory of Mama trying to send her and Asha out to play, and of

Pohpoh feeling something was being concealed. She had a vague memory of leaving the kitchen, noisily descending the back stairs, and then surprising them by returning quietly for candy. She crept upstairs and stood outside the kitchen listening. It frustrated her that Mama and Aunt Lavinia seldom spoke any more except in soft, abbreviated sentences. They seemed to communicate more with their eyes, and with long looks.

Pohpoh's heart leapt when she saw the tips of Aunt Lavinia's fingers grasping Mama's waist. She understood something in that instant but save for a flash of an image of her father's face in her mind, she had no words to describe what she suddenly realized was their secret. She looked again. She tried not to let her eyes rest too long on Aunt Lavinia's fingers. Aunt Lavinia removed her hand and walked over to Pohpoh. Pohpoh stood frozen, sensing she had been caught and fearing the consequences. Aunt Lavinia squatted in front of her and took Pohpoh's face in her hands. Pohpoh inhaled lavender and remembered the little packages of potpourri.

Lavinia spoke gently to her. "Pohpoh, your mama is my very best friend. You have a very special mama. And you and Asha are very, very special. You're the best little children I have ever known. I wish you were my own children. I love the three of you very much." Pohpoh was unable to respond. But from that day on, she spent Aunt Lavinia's visits listening anxiously for her father. Whenever Mama and Aunt Lavinia did not seem to hear him return she would bound noisily up the stairs or barge in on them. At first Aunt Lavinia did not leave until Chandin returned home and she had spent some token minutes with him. But when Chandin started complaining to Sarah that Lavinia was losing interest in him even as her brother, she began leaving before he was due.

Chandin passed the school holidays travelling throughout the island with Reverend Thoroughly, dressed in white shirt, trousers and hat — like the minister — and spreading the Gospel and converting field labourers to Christianity. Aunt Lavinia and Sarah spent most of those days in the sewing room downstairs. They no longer tried to conceal their closeness from Pohpoh and Asha. The girls now woke early, anxious to see Aunt Lavinia, who still played games with them, chased them around the yard, and braided flowers, seeds and feathers into their hair. She made them garlands that tinkled with the shells of dead snails that she boiled first to dull the fetidness. After a night's rain, when the clay soil was well watered, Aunt Lavinia would gather a mound of the slippery earth, carry it to a bench next to the sewing room and teach them to mould baskets the size of her palm, and fill the baskets with clay eggs.

Even with her back to them, Pohpoh was aware of Aunt Lavinia and Mama down by the mudra tree whispering and giggling to each other, or Aunt Lavinia and Mama down in the sewing room, Aunt Lavinia and Mama sitting on the sofa bed down there, Mama leaning into Aunt Lavinia's arms, or Aunt Lavinia braiding Mama's hair or standing behind Mama with her hands wrapped protectively around Mama's waist. Pohpoh turned her head away when she saw them facing each other once, and she felt them come together and hug. She imagined them kissing. She imagined Papa finding them kissing.

One day during the holidays Papa hired a hansom and driver to take the family and Aunt Lavinia to the beach. Aunt Lavinia and Mama sat on one side of the carriage and Papa, Pohpoh and Asha sat on the opposite side. Pohpoh detected an unusual hardness in Papa's face and she lurched across, placing herself between Mama and Lavinia. She leaned against Aunt Lavinia, took her hands into her own and occupied them in one game after another. Asha slept sprawled on the vacated seat. Mama looked in silence at the fields and houses scattered in the countryside. As the moments ticked by Pohpoh was conscious of her father staring at her mother as if he were seeing her for the first time.

Mama and Aunt Lavinia did not go into the water. They walked the beach while Papa sat in the surf with Pohpoh clinging to his back, trying unsuccessfully to distract him. Asha sat on his outstretched knees. His body washed from side to side with the push and pull of each wave, yet he seemed always to keep Mama and Aunt Lavinia in sight. His children jabbered incessantly, but he seemed to hardly hear what they were saying.

After the children's swim, Aunt Lavinia took out her camera. She took a picture of Mama and Papa and then several of Pohpoh with Mama, Asha with Mama, Mama alone, Mama with both children. Pohpoh asked to be allowed to take one of Mama, Papa and Aunt Lavinia together by the water's edge. Papa got an idea from Pohpoh, grabbed the camera with playful force from Lavinia and told Pohpoh and Asha to stand aside. He watched through the lens. In the midst of their laughter and frivolity, he did not fail to see Lavinia place herself behind Mama, and he saw Mama press herself against Lavinia. Through the lens he watched carefully and saw Lavinia's hands rest tenderly on Mama's waist. He saw it all only because, that day, he intended to. And Pohpoh watched him as he did.

On the ride home, no one spoke. Even though the salt water, slapping waves, tangy sea breeze and play had made Pohpoh sleepy, she forced herself to stay awake for the entire trip. Had it not been for the wheels of the buggy crunching the stone and dried earth beneath, and the horses' hooves clopping along steadily, the speechlessness would have been unbearably loud.

That night, after the lights were put out, Pohpoh lay in her bed staring at the pomerac tree outside her open window. She listened hard but all that came from her parents' room were quiet, indistinguishable exchanges. Abruptly, there was silence.

Next morning she awakened with a start, angry at herself for having fallen asleep. She was terrified that she might have missed the outcome of her father's discovery, but he had already headed out to the school house. The only sign that something might have transpired was that Mama blinked her eyes rapidly until Aunt Lavinia arrived. She sent the children out of the house, and they too spoke in clipped, hushed voices. Pohpoh feigned sullenness so that Asha would prefer not to play with her, then she sat on the back stairs, pretending to scratch at the wood with a fingernail while straining her ears. Aunt Lavinia as usual spoke far more audibly than Mama. Pohpoh was unable to catch the full conversation but the snippets that floated down were enough for her to understand.

"We have no choice but to make a decision." There was a pause and then Aunt Lavinia said, "Don't worry. Please don't worry about that. I have known that at some time in my life I would have to face it. It looks like the time has come." Pohpoh could tell that her mother responded but was unable to hear anything distinct.

"I will leave them a note, partially explaining, and then I will write them in detail once we're there. But they will never accept any of this, and if they learn of it beforehand, they will separate us at once . . . Look, Sarah, either we do it now or we will never be able to. There would be no point for me in living if I was unable to see you every single day of my life."

Another pause. Pohpoh heard little of what Mama said.

"They are every bit a part of our lives. I too want them with us, no less than you. We will *never* be parted from the children. I promise you that."

Again Mama's words were inaudible.

"It is, dear. But I have access now to my inheritance. What better use to put it to than taking you *and* the children some place where we can be a family, where we will never be separated. Ah, my sweet, don't be afraid. Sarah dearest, tell me, is this what you want or shall we stop all of this at once?"

This time Pohpoh heard her mother. "Yes! Yes, of course. As long as the children can be with us, I want to go far, far away with you, some place where we can be together."

"Then I will get the passages. I will get them. I will arrange it all. We will be able to be together within the next few days. We can sleep at night and hold each other and . . ."

Mama did not go to the gate to see Aunt Lavinia off as she had in the past. Pohpoh suddenly felt very grown up. She also felt weak and dizzy, knowing that she and her sister and her mother were going to go away — where she could not imagine — without her father. While she had no desire to tell him, she knew she was holding a terrifying secret.

For the next few days Pohpoh shivered even in the sunshine, while Asha sweated in her ignorance. She withdrew from Asha and began to collect things in a little bag. She gathered seeds and shells from the garden. She carefully snapped a leaf off the cereus plant, which was thriving but had not yet blossomed. She was determined one day to see the spectacular blossoms that Aunt Lavinia had described so rapturously. When the white sap stopped flowing like blood from the snapped-off end, she wrapped the leaf in a handkerchief, also a present from Aunt Lavinia, and placed it in her bag.

During the next days, Aunt Lavinia did not visit. Mama and Papa avoided each other's eyes but it was noticeable even to Papa how busy Mama kept herself, and how much attention she was paying to getting meals on time, to cleaning up and straightening the house.

Then the day arrived. It was a cool morning. Rain had fallen all night and only recently let up. Insects were clamouring. Pohpoh saw the signs early that Aunt Lavinia would be coming. Once Papa was out of the house, Mama dressed in clothes she might have chosen for a special church event. She insisted on dressing Pohpoh and Asha, even though both were capable of readying themselves.

When Mama slid the new dresses off their hangers, Pohpoh knew they had been chosen a while ago, for the garments had been pressed and placed in the cupboard for easy access. She made them wear their fancy shoes and new socks. There was such urgency in Mama's actions that neither child protested or asked questions. Pohpoh wondered if Asha also understood what was happening, for she noticed how unusually agreeable and attentive she was to Mama's every wish.

Aunt Lavinia arrived before they had finished their breakfast. The children were startled but Mama didn't seem at all surprised, even though Aunt Lavinia had entered through the back gate, one that was used so seldom it had all but grown over with brambles. Neither did Mama seem interested that she had brought the buggy and horse all the way into the backyard instead of parking in front as usual. Pohpoh noticed that even though bright sunshine had followed the night's long rain, the buggy was fully covered. She observed too that Mama and Aunt Lavinia regarded each other with a strained formality.

Then Aunt Lavinia spoke quietly and urgently to Mama. "He has already gone off with my father. But I don't know how long they will be gone. We'd better hurry." Mama didn't move but held her hands up as if uncertain. Aunt Lavinia moved closer. Mama instantly backed away.

"You manage all the passages? The ship sailing today self? Look how it rain last night. It won't postpone, Lavinia, eh? It don't have another sailing for months, right?"

Aunt Lavinia stood still. She bit her lower lip. Then she very calmly but firmly said, "This is the last sailing before the rains. We *must* hurry, my sweetest."

Mama became unfrozen and began clearing off the table.

"Are the things in the sewing room?" Aunt Lavinia asked. Mama nodded and Aunt Lavinia bolted downstairs and started hauling boxes and trunks up into the drawing room, then down the back stairs and out to the buggy. Her shoes squeaked sharply with each step in the wet earth. Insects carried on their ruckus.

Pohpoh watched from a distance. There were already two trunks atop the buggy, strapped down with thick leather belts. She wondered where Aunt Lavinia got such strength. Asha followed Aunt Lavinia down the narrow stairs to the sewing room. Pohpoh could hear her asking Aunt Lavinia questions — what this was for and what that was for — and for the first time Aunt Lavinia was too preoccupied to answer carefully. Her tone was unindulgent and oddly sharp, and so the questions, obtuse and pointless, kept coming, as though answers were not what Asha really needed. Pohpoh stood in the doorway between the verandah and the kitchen and watched Mama busily closing windows and gathering photographs off the walls. Then Aunt Lavinia came up the back stairs and said it was time, and they must leave at once if they intended to make the sailing.

It was only then that Mama, holding the children's velvet hats in her hand, pulled Asha and Pohpoh close, stooped down to face them and whispered, as though there were someone else in the room who should not hear.

"We going on a long trip, far away. We going with Aunt Lavinia on a boat. For a long time. Papa doesn't know. Is a surprise. I pack up all your things. Everything pack up." She placed a hat on each child's head. She bit her lip and blinked her eyes rapidly as she pulled firmly on the ribbons and tied a bow, first under Asha's chin and then Pohpoh's.

"Now I want you to go like nice girls quiet-quiet inside the buggy. You have to sit down and stay quiet-quiet until we get far away, you hear me? Okay now go, quickly. Aunt Lavinia will take you downstairs."

Aunt Lavinia placed her hands protectively on their shoulders and ushered them down the back stairs. At the bottom they waited for Mama. The sun had suddenly come out and the wet leaves on the trees and shrubs were glistening. Mama stood on the top stair, looked around at the yard and then, with a deep breath, ran down.

Just as they entered the buggy Pohpoh remembered her bag with all the seeds and the shells and the cereus cutting.

"My bag, my bag. I have to get my bag." She ran toward the steps shouting.

Mama and Aunt Lavinia tried to grab her but she was already ascending the back stairs. Aunt Lavinia headed after her and suddenly stopped. Pohpoh came to a halt, for she too heard footsteps.

"Come on. Pohpoh, come now! Come here!" Aunt Lavinia snapped an urgent whisper.

Pohpoh froze in terror. Her father had returned. Unsuspecting, he had strolled up the front stairs and across the verandah, had already unlocked the front door and was walking through the drawing room toward her.

Pohpoh stood still, unable to breathe, the whole world turning black around her. She saw her father hesitate, the cock of his head and the sudden twist of his body revealing he had noticed that pictures were missing from the walls, that the curtains were drawn, that the house was uncommonly tidy. She imagined what he was seeing — things cleared away or cleared out. She heard his unsure footsteps walk to the bedroom he shared with Mama.

Aunt Lavinia no longer whispered. "Pohpoh, Pohpoh," she called out sharply. She tried to grab Pohpoh's hand when she heard Chandin cry, "Sarah!" The nervousness in his voice made her pull back. When he called the second time his voice was unrecognizable.

Chandin swept through the kitchen and onto the back verandah. Aunt Lavinia backed down the stairs in haste. He saw Pohpoh and ran past her. She turned to watch him but the sun had caught on the jagged edge of the porch's iron roof and the spot dazzled like a blinding star. She heard her father descending the stairs, two, three at a time. She heard everyone shouting at once. She heard her father screaming, her mother screaming and Aunt Lavinia's voice, suddenly deep and raspy, shouting her name and Asha's. She heard Asha screaming.

It was Asha she heard most clearly, "No! No! No! Pohpoh! Pohpoh, Pohpoh. I want Pohpoh. No! I want Pohpoh." Then she heard the buggy rolling swiftly through the yard. She lay in a puddle on the floor of the verandah, her nose against the damp wood floor, shutting out the sounds. She covered her eyes with both hands.

It seemed as though hours passed before her father dragged Asha, heaving with incessant dry sobs, up the stairs. He stood on the verandah in his Wetlandish whites, and not until the sound of the horse and buggy had completely died out did he move. He kicked the banister again and again, first with his right foot, then with his left. He hobbled into the house. The two children huddled on the verandah floor, unsure and terrified. He seemed oblivious to their presence. They watched as he swiped at the kitchen counter, sending pots and pans and cutlery crashing to the floor, clanging and spinning. Asha began a soundless, fitful crying. Pohpoh held her breath and covered her mouth. Her eyes missed nothing. Plates and cups and glasses shattered all over the kitchen floor. Her father tore through the house smashing ornaments. Asha and Pohpoh turned to face whichever direction he took, keeping him locked in their sight. He thundered into his bedroom, kicking and banging the walls. They heard the drawers of the armoire being yanked out. Pohpoh knew he was seeing emptiness. He came out with a tin, thundered into the kitchen, banged the container on the table. He rifled through photographs, pitching some on the floor. Those of his wife or Lavinia Thoroughly he crumpled into a ball, then spat on, all the while crying and making growling sounds. His children cried even more seeing him cry.

His task so blinded him that he did not notice Pohpoh tiptoe to her room. She walked straight to her Bible, which sat on the table where she and Asha did their homework. She shook the Bible and out fell a photograph. Her heart beat rapidly. It was the one of Aunt Lavinia and Mama that her father had taken at the beach not long before. She shoved it in her pocket and, holding her breath, made her way toward the verandah.

Her father's skin and hair were drenched in sweat. He staggered as though drunk and threw the crumpled photographs into the kitchen sink. He struck a match on the window sill and dropped it. It did not take long for the little flames to become one large one. The flame leapt up from the sink, burning blue and orange. Black smoke tumbled upwards and flecks of blackened ash sputtered throughout the kitchen.

The story of Chandin Ramchandin's wife and Reverend and Mrs. Ernest Thoroughly's daughter spread across the island with the swiftness of a brush fire and the quietness of ripples in a sugar-factory pond. The affair was not discussed during the evenings when villagers congregated in the shade of their favourite trees to take in the breeze, talk out their problems and hear a little gossip. More than half the labourers on the island had converted to Reverend Thoroughly's church and no one wanted to be seen or heard partaking in idle chatter involving his name. But when one person met another, under their breath and with hands perched at their lips, people did indeed speak.

"You hear about — ?" The sentence would remain unfinished, a flick of the head in the direction of the church being enough.

"What about the children?"

"By him, na!"

"Hmmm, he take up the bottle, I hear."

And that was more than enough for the talkers to feel pangs of guilt, for they felt as though they were discussing, not the Ramchandins or Lavinia, but rather their Reverend, their church and their God.

Chandin Ramchandin never set foot in the school house or the church again. The Thoroughlys, mortified by the actions of their once-treasured daughter and by Sarah, let go of their ties to him. He fenced off his house crudely with chicken wire and stayed indoors, waiting in a spot equidistant from the back door and the front door, expecting one or both of the women to return to try and nab the children.

He did not let them out of his sight. He stood guard as they showered in the outdoor bathroom. He waited for them not far from the latrine. For the first few weeks after the shattering of his world, he slept in his bed with a child on either side.

One night he turned, his back to Asha, and in a fitful, nightmarish sleep, mistook Pohpoh for Sarah. He put his arm around her and slowly began to touch her. Pohpoh opened her eyes. Frightened and confused by this strange, insistent probing, she barely breathed, pretending to be fast asleep. She tried to shrink away from under his hand. Suddenly, awakening fully, he sat up. Then he brought his body heavily on top of hers and slammed his hand over her mouth. She opened her eyes and stared back at him in terror. A sweat covered his face and neck, and dripped on her. Glaring and breathing heavily like a mad dog, he pinned her hands to the bed and forced her legs apart.

That is how it started. The following night he sent the two children to sleep in their own room, but they both came to know that he would call for one or the other to pass at least part of the night in his bed.

Soft-edged shadows danced on the wall: a dog with drooping ears but no sound to accompany its opening and closing mouth, a rabbit with long ears, a butterfly gracefully beating the wall with its wings as it ascended and then transformed into a giraffe's head on a long neck.

Late into the night, long after their housework and school studies were done, sleep was impossible. The flame in a kerosene lamp sitting on the floor jumped in the breeze passing through the window. Too exhausted to sit at the study table, yet too frightened and tense to sleep, Pohpoh and Asha lay together in the narrow bed against the wall. In the yard crickets chirped. From the other side of their bedroom door came the low voice of their father in the drawing room, mumbling tuneless phrases from church songs. Occasionally he muttered long and animated conversations with himself, sometimes crying or pleading or angrily cursing.

Asha lay huddled in Pohpoh's chest between arms that were magical and elegant, making creatures dance and transform gracefully. She hugged herself, her hands clenched into little fists. In the protective comfort of Pohpoh's warmth, Asha's eyes brightened, her eyebrows arched and a smile twitched and widened at each new animal. Pohpoh's mouth wore the strained shape of a smile for her little sister's eyes, but her forehead and her own eyes were dark and solemn, waiting for the inevitable ripping apart of the night. She heard every creak of the chair outside in the living room as her hands worked to calm and distract Asha. She hoped he would drop off to sleep right there in the drawing room, unable to budge with so much alcohol in his brain.

The chair in the drawing room groaned. The singing and chatter stopped. The smile on Asha's face disappeared. She squeezed her eyes shut and turned her face into Pohpoh's chest. Her little hands grabbed Pohpoh's upper arms and she clenched her fists. The sting of pinched skin felt good to Pohpoh. She pulled Asha closer to her and squeezed her, trying to save her by obliterating her.

"Asha," he called out from the drawing room. "Asha." Asha's body trembled as if she were naked in an icy wind. Pohpoh clamped her hand over Asha's mouth.

"Stay!" Pohpoh snapped. "Don't move. I'll go. Shhh, he too drunk. He'll never know the difference. Go to sleep. You close your eyes and go to sleep, Asha baby. Nothing will happen to you, I promise."

Pohpoh unwrapped herself from Asha and went. As if it were nothing at all.

THE GARDENER'S NAME was John Hector. Sister called him John. The staff referred to him as Hector, some of the residents and I called him Mr. Hector, and to the others he was "son." Mr. Hector was still curious about me. When I passed him, stooped shirtless on his haunches weeding a bed (almost too lean for a man of his fatherly age), he would put down his tools. His eyes would tickle my flesh as they followed me, the sort of tickle that jabs rather than titillates. His curiosity, though, did not have the same sneering intent that I felt from the nurses and Toby, the yardboy. Before the incident I am about to relate, which has, contrary to first impressions, more to do with Miss Ramchandin than with him or me, he had not spoken more than a polite sentence or two to me.

"Tyler!" Before I turned to see who had called, he was getting right to the point. "The old lady interested in gardening? I know she had big yard before it burn down. I hear it was full of all kinds of bush, plenty for teas for bad feeling and pain and thing. She had pretty-pretty plants, I hear. They say the yard also had some plants that was ugly like snake-face and dangerous like snake-bite, but plenty-plenty bush. It look like she used to take care of it — useful, pretty, bad, whatever. How she doing?" He held a stem of a yellow gerbera picked from the bed he was tending.

"Thank you for asking, Mr. Hector. She is well, all things considered."

"You know, since I growing up I hearing 'bout she. When I was a young fellow my Pappy used to threaten that if I didn't behave myself he would take me and drop me in she yard and leave me there. And now look at this, na! Is she who get drop and left in my yard!"

I quickly marched over to him, leaving Miss Ramchandin to amble in her world, hoping more than ever that it occupied her well enough to block out his conversation. I planted myself between him and her view of him, intending to block her view of the broken plant.

"Serious though," he continued, "plenty people used to go and harass the lady, but, you know, is strange, I was never one, myself, to torment anybody. Children used to go and pelt she and pelt she mango and come back frighten-frighten but still excited that they break a window or sling-shot a bird. You know how children could be, na. It was the thing to do, and though I didn't take part in it I didn't question it either. Hmmm. I never question them. Somehow you don't question things until you come face to face with the person and suddenly — suddenly you realize that behind all them stories it have a flesh-and-blood, breathing, feeling person who capable of hurting, yes! Well, ask her, na. Ask her if she want to garden. I thinking about starting a plot for the old people to have something to do. Some people say that gardening good for old people. I am proof of that!" he laughed.

I hesitated, still blocking his approach. Seeing that my focus was his cut gerbera, Mr. Hector clutched it possessively.

"Is for she. I pick it to give to she. What? You want it?"

"No, no, Mr. Hector. It's just that, well, I don't really know how to explain, but Miss Ramchandin might not react well to it. I think it is a very generous thing, that you want to give it to her. It's very touching, actually. No one here has really been kind to her."

His eyes roamed my face. I felt as though he was looking for an angularity to my jaw line and cheekbone, inspecting my moustache and other facial hair to help confirm a notion. The muscles of my cheeks became devilishly ticklish. I was afraid my eyes would begin to flicker on their own, as they were given to doing whenever I became shy.

"You see," I said, "I am beginning to understand some things about her and I think that she does not like things in nature to be hurt. To her, the flower and the plant would be both suffering because they were separated from each other. You know what I mean? It would be as if its arm had been cut off or something. I think it would upset her greatly and set her back."

He thought a while. "That make some sense, if you look at it in a particular way. Well, you want it? Take it, na. It pick already. No sense it go to waste."

It was an awkward moment, for no sooner had he offered it than he became uncomfortable. His eyes, whose aqueous tranquillity I was noticing for the first time, now glanced across the yard.

"I don't mean nothing by that, you know! I mean, don't take it the wrong way. I married and thing. I not funny, you know. Is just that the thing picked already—" He was so nervous that the flower fell out of his hand and we both reached to pick it up. I got to it first, he jumped back and I handed it to him. The loose, thin flesh on his arms and on his belly had previously hinted to me of his greater age, yet suddenly, instead of age I saw the sun-darkened skin and rugged muscles of a man accustomed to hard labour.

"Thank you very much, Mr. Hector. I understand. It's a very beautiful gerbera but, you know, if I take it I will have the same problem. It will be in my possession as I walk the grounds and Miss Ramchandin might well be upset. I would really love to have it, but it would be better if you gave it to one of the other nurses or residents."

"Yes, yes! Good idea." He turned away so fast I felt a shrinking inside.

"About the gardening idea," I called out quickly. "I will suggest it. I think it will be a very good idea, myself." He turned and, without stopping, continued to walk backwards. "But give me a little time. She has hardly said any words and it's a struggle to know what she wants."

"You real sensitive to her, eh!" Again he became shy, calling out, "I will keep a place for her. When she ready, it will be there for her."

He could easily have been my father's age — I barely knew my father — and his past kindnesses had struck me as fatherly. But suddenly, Mr. Hector seemed ageless.

I walked the few paces back to Miss Ramchandin. She had come to a complete standstill, waiting for me. I had then yet another feeling toward Mr. Hector. I felt breathless from the excitement of his attentions, but at the same time more than a little nauseous from his discomfort and polite disdain. Discomfort or disdain, they amounted to the same: he recoiled from me and it was his recoiling that stung, made me feel as though my back were exposed, or more pointedly, as though I had been caught with my trousers off, awaiting a whipping with a guava cane. I felt that the entire staff, including Sister and the residents and Toby, had seen our push-and-pull with the gerbera, had seen him walk away, leaving me standing there, humiliated. I took a quick glance at the flower bed he had been tending. He was stooped again, his back to me. I felt dizzy and sick. Why did I want to come face to face with him in some dark room, some dark night? Why did I want to put my arms around him and be in turn embraced by him, engulfing and protecting me? Why did I so desperately want to offer myself up to him and make promises that would cause him to swoon with desire?

At my side Miss Ramchandin cooed like a young bird and took no notice of me. I was a roller coaster of emotions and thoughts, reasoning one minute that if he returned my caresses, he would be as bad, as depraved, as perverse as I, that a man of his age and respect would be complicit, an accomplice — Mr. Hector, whom the staff quite liked, would be just like me — and then reasoning the next that if I did not so loathe my unusual femininity, his rejection of me would not be so devastating. Trying to change him or his reaction might well bring only grief. I decided there and then that I would change my own feelings about myself. I would, I must, cast him out of my thoughts and stand tall.

In moments of despair, thoughts of Cigarette Smoking Nana always reassured me. I remembered the sly smiles, comforting complicity and camaraderie that she and I had shared. But thoughts of Nana were a temporary bandage. I didn't know how to cast Mr. Hector and the incident from my mind. Nana had accepted me and my girlish ways but she was the only person who had ever truly done so. Thoughts of her suddenly lost their power. Try as I might, I was unable to stand tall. I wondered for the umpteenth time if Nana would have been able to accept and love the adult Tyler, who was neither properly man nor woman but some in-between, unnamed thing.

Just then Miss Ramchandin started mumbling. Jumbled,

mumbled words came from her mouth. Her voice was low, hardly louder than a whisper, and hoarse. Slowly I made out individual words and then sentences. She was reciting over and over, a ditty that children sing and play games to:

> Ole lady walk, ole lady fall.
> Hit she belly. "Lord!" she bawl.
> Crick crack, all say oops!
> Brick brack, break she back,
> Le we go tief pom-er-ac.

I decided to do battle against the sinking feeling, and joined in softly. She grew excited, watched my face and laughed wildly, the way children do. I walked lighter and clapped my hands to her chant. I felt like an explorer charting her life in murky, unmapped waters. I was not sure what I was discovering beyond her voice but I felt it would not be long before I would have the privilege, and honour, of entering her world. Across the way another resident was on the path brushing himself frantically. Mr. Phu was often sure that red ants were crawling on him or in his food and was known to dash his plate of food to the floor believing that it was riddled with vermin.

Suddenly Mr. Hector was coming toward us, speaking loudly. He was carrying a full gerbera plant, flowers, leaves and roots protruding from a large ball of soil in one hand, a spade in the other. He focused on Miss Ramchandin.

"Follow me. She will be the first one to put down a plant. Come. Bring her."

The turnaround was faster than I could have dreamed. I grinned. An idea came to me and I excitedly told him to wait right there, not to leave her for a single moment. I ran to her room only yards away and fetched the cereus plant sprouting in the milk can.

Then I followed the sinewy, sun-darkened gardener and Miss Ramchandin, who continued singing the ditty.

At the flower bed Mr. Hector held the succulent cereus up to the sky and examined it curiously. "Why you want to plant this? But it is ugly!" I explained its promise while Miss Ramchandin stood nearby uninterested, distracted by her own mumbling and singing. Mr. Hector shrugged, dug two holes and inserted the plants. He paused, rested his arm on the handle of the spade and began to talk.

"Look. You know every time I see you, my heart does break. I does watch you and, sudden-so, it does feel like something heavy sit on my chest. Is like I recognize you but is a sad feeling. I realize now what it is."

He grabbed the spade and took a few erratic digs at the soft earth. He stopped again. He squinted at the purple hills on the far side of the valley, and his aqueous eyes grew sad.

"I had a brother. He was older than me. Is about — what?— forty years now? More than that since I last see him. He was a young boy. Eleven or twelve, something so. Mammy send him away. Is he you remind me of. Randolph was his name. Randolph Joseph Hector. Randy, we call him. I did love him too bad! And so many years pass and I don't even know if he made it through life."

"Why did your mammy send him away?" My voice was heavy. I wanted to hear the reason and at the same time hoped he would not have the brazenness to say it.

"He was kind of funny. He was like you. The fellas in the village used to threaten to beat he up. People used to heckle he and mock his walk and the way he used to do his hands when he was talking."

That he was brave enough to say it suddenly lifted a veil between us. Unexpectedly, I felt relief it was voiced and out in the open. I had never before known such a feeling of ordinariness.

"Randy couldn't open his mouth in front of Pappy, na. His voice was soft-soft, just like yours, and the way he used to talk, quiet and sing-song sing-song used to make Pappy crazy. You know I can't remember Randy face too good, but I still carry his voice with me. I could hear it plain-plain, like if I had just talk with he this morning. Pappy used to beat him bad-bad, just for talking so. That is why Mama pack him up one day. She leave me by the neighbour while she went away with him. Same day she come back but she come back alone. When I ask where he was, she say, 'Where yuh father can't reach him,' and she tell me not to bring up his name again. I remember Pappy asking where Randy was and Mammy saying she take him to live in a church mission down south, and Pappy never ask for him again. I miss him too bad, but if I talk about him Mammy used to cry, so I stop and as time pass it was like he didn't ever exist. Is like you bring Randy back to me, boy."

Mr. Hector massaged his cheeks with a dirt-covered hand. When he looked directly at my face, his eyes were even wetter and darker.

"I watching you and I want to ask you so many questions but I don't even know what it is I want to know. I want to know something but I don't know what."

My attraction to Mr. Hector, the gardener, subsided like a flame that fell down and died out. I still wanted to gather him up and hug him but only to comfort. He too was tamed, and I felt from and toward him the caring of a brother.

The significance of the previous episode was not to dwell on issues about myself or to relate the bond forming between Mr. Hector and me. He and I had been carrying on as if we alone were privy to our conversation. Yet Miss Ramchandin, in her quiet, invisible way, had heard most of what was said.

After our conversation Mr. Hector departed and I stood quietly for several moments. For how long I can't say but when I looked up and saw Miss Ramchandin approaching, I realized she had wandered off. I thought I had been constantly aware of her in the periphery of my vision. My inattentiveness — irresponsibility Sister would surely have called it — startled me.

She carried something bundled under her arm. Clearly she was hiding it and would not show it until we were back in her room with the door closed. She walked ahead of me excitedly. I turned to wave to my new friend but he just kept tilling the soil. She began to sing in a whisper:

> Ole lady walk, ole lady fall.
> Hit she belly. "Lord!" she bawl.
> Crick crack, all say oops!
> Brick brack, break she back,
> Le we go tief pom-er-ac.
> Ole lady walk, ole lady fall.
> Hit she belly. "Lord!" she bawl.

A bird flew overhead. She laughed and waved. "Poh poh pohpoh," she called softly and then carried on.

> Crick crack, all say oops!
> Brick brack, break she back,
> Le we go tief pom-er-ac.

Once the door was shut she spun around to face me, her bundle now hidden behind her back. I was so buoyed by my conversation with Mr. Hector I did not want to be distracted. But Miss Ramchandin knew how to catch one's attention. I heard something but was unsure what it was, and then I realized she was whispering.

"What? Did you say something, Miss Ramchandin?"

"Asha? You know Asha?" she whispered. Her voice was cracked but she had spoken.

"Yes, yes. I know Asha. I mean I know of her. I heard of her. But I don't know her." She was mentioned in the rumours. No more was said of her than that she was the other Ramchandin child, of no consequence because she had disappeared long, long ago.

"Where Asha?"

"I don't know. I don't know. Do you know?" What a shame, I thought, that her first real communication was to be thwarted by me.

Her question had nothing to do with what happened next. She whipped the bundle from behind her and revealed a nurse's white uniform and a pair of nylon stockings the colour of black tea. She offered me the dress. My first thought was that we would surely get into trouble. Clearly she had taken them from the clothesline in the yard while Mr. Hector and I were talking.

"Miss Ramchandin," I whispered, "what are you doing with that uniform?" She clutched it to her chest. "That belongs to one of the nurses. What do you want that for? I better go and take them back."

She slowly bundled the dress into a ball again and put it behind her back with a look of disappointment and defiance. I dreaded a conflict with her.

"Do you want that uniform?"

She said nothing but now I knew there was more in her head than bird and cricket and frog imitations and childhood chants.

"Well, do you want to wear it?" I asked, using a tone of gentle defiance to match hers. There was no harm in a little indulgence as long as we could get the uniform back on the clothesline before morning.

"You." She looked at the ground.

"Me? Me what?"

"You. You want to wear it." She produced it from behind her back again, shook it out and held it toward me. "You want to wear it."

I stared speechlessly at the calf-length dress and the stockings. I could only guess that she had heard my conversation with Mr. Hector. I felt she had been watching me and seeing the same things that everyone else saw. But she had stolen a dress for me. No one had ever done anything like that before. She knows what I am, was all I could think. She knows my nature.

I reached for the dress. My body felt as if it were metamorphosing. It was as though I had suddenly become plump and less rigid. My behind felt fleshy and rounded. I had thighs, a small mound of belly, rounded full breasts and a cavernous tunnel singing between my legs. I felt more weak than excited but I was certainly excited by the possibilities trembling inside me. I hugged the dress.

"Thank you. Thank you so much, Miss Ramchandin. Yes, I will wear it. I will put it on here so you can see it. Before you go to sleep. Let's eat and get ready for bed and then I will slip it on. All right?"

By the light of one lamp, with the window and door closed, Miss Ramchandin waited patiently for me to keep my promise. I had returned to my room and retrieved a scarf, a little powder and the remains of a rouge cake that had been left in my dresser drawer by the previous occupant. Back with Miss Ramchandin I drew the room divider and stepped behind it. I unbuttoned my shirt and felt an odd shame that my mammary glands were flat. I dropped my pants. My man's member mocked me yet was a delight to do battle with when pulling the stockings up against my thighs. I had no corset to hold them up, but it was enough to see the swirl of hairs on my calves and thighs trapped under the nylon. There was something delicious about such confinement. I held up the dress and slowly stepped into it, savouring every action, noting every feeling. I powdered my nose, daubed rouge on my cheeks and carefully smeared a dollop across my lips. I looked down at my stockinged feet and the dress, pressed it with my flat palms against my body and worried that I might look disappointingly ridiculous to my benefactress. I took a deep breath.

"Ready?" I called out in a loud whisper.

When I stepped out from behind the curtain, I saw that Miss Ramchandin had made herself busy. She was piling furniture in front of the window. She glanced at me, made no remark and kept right on building the tower. I walked over to her and stood where I was bound to be in her vision. At first I felt horribly silly, like a man who had put on women's clothing for sheer sport and had forgotten to remove the outfit after the allotted period of fun. I felt flat-footed and clumsy. Not a man and not ever able to be a woman, suspended nameless in the limbo state between existence and nonexistence. She had already set a straight-back chair on the table in front of the window. On top of that she placed a stool and was now preparing to stand on her bed and place an empty drawer on the pinnacle.

Just as I was hoping the tower would come crashing down and extinguish me forever, a revelation came. The reason Miss Ramchandin paid me no attention was that, to her mind, the outfit was not something to either congratulate or scorn — it simply was. She was not one to manacle nature, and I sensed that she was permitting mine its freedom.

I took the drawer from her, climbed up on her bed and placed it at her tower's peak. I would have to pull it all down before Sister's inspection, but right then every instinct in me wanted to take all the furniture in her room and help her build the biggest and tallest tower she needed. (Sister *was* appalled, sure that Miss Ramchandin was building a deadly trap for the nurses. She made me take it down, naturally, but it became part of my schedule. Every night Miss Ramchandin would build and every morning I would deconstruct.)

I did not even consider leaving her room dressed as I was. I was endowed with a sense of propriety, depended on it, for that matter, for the most basic level of survival. I changed back into my trousers and white shirt, and rubbed my cheeks and lips clean. I stuffed the dress and stockings behind her dresser, deciding to keep if not to wear it again, at least for the memory of some power it seemed to have imparted. It had been a day and an evening to treasure. I had never felt so extremely ordinary, and I quite loved it.

Once Miss Ramchandin was in bed, I sat next to her and smoothed her hair back, reluctant to leave. My hand on her scalp released the sweet scent of yellow potatoes. She sighed pleasantly, with an air of accomplishment. Her breath had the delicate perfume of fresh young carrots. She began to make mellow cricket sounds. When I approached the door to leave, she paused long enough to ask, as if to the ceiling, "Where Asha?" She did not wait for an answer and immediately resumed her faint, perfect imitation of the cricket's one note song.

As THEY GREW older, Pohpoh and Asha would sometimes slip away from their father's house for several hours, fully expecting to face his wrath on their return. The momentary escape, however, was worth any sting afterwards.

One morning Asha awoke so early that even roosters seemed barely awake. Street sweepers were pulling their wide brooms down the road and the swish of their brooms filtered through the tail end of her dreams. She waited quietly and patiently to embark on the outing Pohpoh had promised. When Asha could lie still no longer, she tiptoed across the room and sat on her sister's bed, hoping to nudge her out of her sleep. Pohpoh, forever on guard, suddenly stiffened and awakened fully. Seeing Asha in front of her grinning nervously, she relaxed slightly.

Shafts of dusty light broke through the branches of the pomerac tree outside the open window. Pohpoh stared at the glittery dust particles that rose and fell in waves around Asha's head, partially silhouetting it in a halo of shimmering light. She slid closer to the wall to let the little girl slip under her coverlet. The bed sheets and Pohpoh's pillow held the odour of stale camphor, eucalyptus and turpentine. They clung to each other, inhaling the pleasantly sour blend of their rubbing oil and each other's talcum-sweet scent of sleep, night sweat and stale breath.

They crept out into the drawing room, every moment aware of their father's guttural breathing. The air in the closed-up room was thick with the smell of spilled full-proof babash. When Pohpoh unlatched the window above the enamel sink, yellow light sliced through the opening, hauling in a cold, fresh morning draught. Asha rubbed her bony shoulders for warmth. Pohpoh was oblivious to the cold. One ear continued to monitor her father's sleep. Asha watched her sister prepare breakfast. She stared at Pohpoh's skin, her hair, eyelashes, cheeks and nose, entranced by their change from silhouette dark to brass to gold as she glided in and out of the shaft of dancing light.

"You look like Mama," she whispered reverently.

Pohpoh stared at Asha. Pohpoh had tried to speak with Asha about the day her mother and Aunt Lavinia had left. Asha not only had been unable to remember the day, but her eyes would glaze over and her body would slump with sleepiness and fatigue, making her look, eerily, as though an old woman were about to emerge from her. The only memory Asha seemed to have of her mother came from a photograph hidden in their armoire.

"But you can't even remember what she look like. You said you don't remember her," said Pohpoh.

Asha, hurt, raised her voice, "I do! I do. She look like you." Pohpoh rushed over and hugged her into silence. Suddenly feeling like her mother, like a mother to Asha, she looked into her sister's eyes.

"I believe you, I do," she said earnestly. When Asha seemed comforted, Pohpoh returned to her work.

She quietly tapped a solid nest of cocoa patties with a stone pestle too large for her hand, then melted the patties with molasses and water and ragged slivers of cinnamon bark over high, green flames. The thick liquid bubbled, each bubble bursting and puffing perfumed steam into the room. They ate thick slices of sweet egg bread and drank the cocoa quickly and quietly. The snoring continued. Should he awaken, there was enough cocoa for him too, but the plans for the day would have instantly ended.

Pohpoh brushed and braided her own thick, straight kohl-black hair, then did the same to Asha's. She took more care with her sister's hair than her own, handling and nudging Asha's head this way and that, imitating their mother's manner. Asha winced as her wavy hair was untangled bit by bit until it spread like an undulating fan across her upper back. Down the middle Pohpoh etched a perfectly straight part with the pointed tip of a little wooden comb.

"It have to be real neat and tidy today," she said firmly, "because today you and I going to be leaders, right?"

Asha nodded and then remembered to be perfectly still.

"Yuh hair pretty, Ashie, but I really glad mine not like yours."

"Like how?"

"Curly. Curly-curly and unruly. Yuh hair like Mama's."

Asha tried to turn to look at Pohpoh.

"My hair like Mama's? Is true, Pohpoh?" she whispered.

"Uhuh, curly just like Mama's, like the waves in the sea, crashing and all." She divided the springy handful into three parts, working her hands like lightning. "I could even see little fish and seaweed and seeds from other countries floating in yuh hair."

"And starfish?"

"Uhuh."

"And seagulls?"

"Yep."

"And shells?"

"Yeh."

"And —" but before she could continue Pohpoh tickled her under her arms and said, "and and and." They cupped their mouths and giggled without sound. After tying one braid with a length of red cord behind the ear, Pohpoh began to rein in the wildness on the other side.

"I have bad hair, Poh?"

"No. Is just that if mine was like yours and I had to comb it out every day I wouldn't find time fuh school or to make cocoa-tea for you. It would be plenty work. It pretty, yes, but it take work to see yuh face. An yuh face pretty."

Asha was pleased. "Yuh'd just get muscles from my hair."

"I already have muscles."

"I mean more, Poh."

Asha's scalp stung from all the brushing. As she got dressed she was distracted by the stinging and pain, finding them alternately irritating and exhilarating. Her hairline pricked and itched, and she made exaggerated frowns and raised her eyebrows as high as she could in an effort to pull the hair out of the grip of the cords.

Boyie was nearby, waiting on the corner at Government Alley. He waved. Asha waved back but Pohpoh walked past without looking at him.

"Why you come here?" she said. "I tell you to wait in the park for us. You shouldn't come here."

Boyie grinned at her rebuke. He jumped in line and followed behind the two girls. "Where are we going? What are we going to do? Tell me, na?" he asked.

Their goal, Pohpoh told them as she ran ahead, was to be the first children to arrive at El Dorado Park and to take charge of the day. She had other, secret motives. First, she wanted to pass as much of the day as possible away from her father's house. And she wanted to confront Walter Bissey, a bossy boy from school. He was the most popular boy there, and had recently become territorial in the park, harassing and shooing away Pohpoh, Asha and Boyie whenever they arrived. He led his friends in sneering at her and her sister. Today, she intended to prove to him that she and Asha were not stupid and dirty but were strong and could fend for themselves. But most of all she wanted Walter, not Boyie, to like her.

Rather than taking the cobbled street in front of their house — where people often stared at Pohpoh and Asha and shook their heads in pity — Pohpoh led Boyie and Asha to the paved drains behind the backyards. The drains were already becoming swift-running creeks of soapy suds as the neighbourhood's breakfast dishes were washed. Pohpoh nimbly manoeuvered the splashiest sections and sudden torrents. Boyie, full of admiration for Pohpoh's leadership and agility, tried to keep up. Asha followed in his tracks exactly. The backyards smelled of decaying guavas, uncleaned chicken coops and outdoor latrines. Finally they picked their way through an opening between two houses that delivered them to El Dorado Square, a block away from the playground.

Outside the southeast corner of the square, Pohpoh wedged her face between the ornate wrought-iron railing. Inside was the regular band of stray dogs. Several of them congregated near the bandstand sniffing each other. When Boyie came up beside her she winced, feeling he might be sniffing her too. Two wrought-iron benches were occupied by homeless men sprawled in deep sleep. From the highest platform of the bandstand a wiry old man swung aggressively back and forth on his heels, preaching to the sleeping figures. The three children watched him in fascination.

"... the time is at hand. *The time is at hand!* He that is unjust, let him be unjust still; and he who is filthy, let him be filthy still. Blessed are they that do His commandments that they may enter in through the gates into the city."

Across the road was the playground, in a corner of which were a row of swings, two slides and a climbing frame. Farther along, a few bay-rum trees sparsely lined the playground's edges, leaving the centre bare. Even during the rains, the earth here was cracked and scorched, a pebbly scar from the constant friction of children tearing across it.

Pohpoh planned to take control today and decide what games would be played. Anxiously, conspicuously, they waited in the centre of the playground near a standpipe surrounded by a puddle of water. The early morning sun was hot and within minutes their scalps, faces and necks were covered in a fine mist of sweat. Asha squelched her desire to play on the swings and slide, fearing this distraction would cost them the chance to be leaders. Instead she lifted her hand, pointing a finger high in the air, rocked on her heels and shouted, "The time is at hand! Repent. The time is at hand!" Boyie imitated her imitation. Pohpoh laughed, sitting on the ledge of the standpipe base, but she told Asha, "Girl! You brave yes! What if the man see yuh? Yuh better calm down yuhself."

There was still no sign of other children. Pohpoh got up and impatiently paced. Boyie picked up a large, flame-coloured seed from a mora tree nearby and tossed it to Pohpoh. Suddenly Pohpoh turned away from Boyie and grabbed Asha out of the water around the standpipe.

"Listen!" she said.

They came, seven of them, a band of uncontained wildness led by Walter Bissey. They pranced up the street, announcing themselves with the rapid *thuck thuck thuck* of a guava stick dragged hard against the iron railings that kept them out of people's yards. Three boys and four girls, all in Pohpoh's and Boyie's class. Pohpoh felt a sudden need to relieve herself.

As the troupe arrived on the playground she waved to them, signalling that she had secured their headquarters for the day. Quiet fell over the band while they studied her and her companions. As if predetermined, they huddled together, a tight, impenetrable faction, secrets swishing from one mouth to the next.

"Over here! Come and play with us!" Pohpoh called optimistically. They looked up from their deliberations, almost in disbelief. Walter, the tallest, turned and stomped toward the threesome. His group hesitated then followed him to the centre of the playground.

"Okay. But we want to play blindman's bluff," Walter said gruffly, already waving a red and white neckerchief.

"But who is to be the blind man?" Pohpoh asked, watching his every gesture.

Walter, large boned and intimidating, arranged the group, including Pohpoh, Asha and Boyie, in a circle. He began a chant that they joined in. With an outstretched finger he poked a chest with each word. When the chest was that of Pohpoh, Asha or Boyie he used his palm and pushed hard to unbalance them. Pohpoh winced with each blow but registered no antagonism on her face, a skill she had developed at home. The children bawled:

> Ole lady walk, ole lady fall.
> Hit she belly. "Lord!" she bawl.
> Crick crack, all say oops!

At which they all enthusiastically pointed their fingers in the air and shouted loudly "Oops!" before resuming their chant:

> Brick brack, break she back,
> Le we go tief pom-er-ac.

The rhyme ended here, on one of Walter's group, not on whom they wanted it to fall. So they continued:

> This 'n' that. Tat 'n' tit.
> One two three: you are it!

And sure enough, the rhyme ended on Pohpoh, which seemed to satisfy them. She appeared pleased though she and Asha exchanged discreet glances of doubt. Walter refused to be the one to tie the neckerchief over Pohpoh's eyes. Boyie, watching sadly, scratched the soil with the tip of his shoe. Finally one of the girls accepted the task of blindfolding Pohpoh.

They spun her around and told her to count slowly up to fifty. Then she could begin to try to touch one of them. Pohpoh wanted to catch Walter, but she heard only unclear whispers, giggles, a scuffle, feet scampering in the dusty gravel, and then just the sound of an occasional cart rolling against the cobbled road in the distance, blackbirds twittering in the bay-rum trees, and the high-pitched drone of crickets, her own feet unsettling the gravel beneath her. She stood still listening for the ruffle of clothing. When she opened her mouth to breathe, she tasted the dry grittiness of lime dust risen from the trampled gravel.

Suddenly something poked her in her side. Pohpoh flung herself around with arms extended, grabbing at the air. She tried to open her eyes under the blindfold, but it was tied so tightly she could barely wink.

Whap! She was tapped hard on her head. By the time she had spun around, she again grabbed only hot and gritty air. She listened hard and heard the sound of water gurgling up and out of the standpipe tap. She called out to Asha. No reply. She called Boyie. There was just the sound of running water.

"Walter?" she whispered and picked her way, one tentative step at a time, toward the standpipe. When she got closer, she heard muffled whimpering. Asha. She quickly pried the blindfold off. Her little sister was sitting inside a pool of water under the standpipe, a bandanna tied so tightly over her mouth that her lips were stretched apart and the front of the cloth was wet with spit. Her shoelaces were knotted together, and both her wrists were manacled with a handkerchief untidily hooked to the faucet. Pohpoh gasped, overcome by anger and fear. She looked around for Boyie but he was nowhere in sight. She untied the knots while Asha cried and begged to go home. The other children were near the roadway under a bay-rum tree huddled over a game of marbles in the dry earth. Pohpoh told Asha to wait for her at the standpipe. She puffed her chest and stormed over to the bay-rum tree.

Walter saw her coming, jumped up and stepped outside his group to pick up a stick. With an exaggerated gesture he drew a line between them and Pohpoh. Then he stood with his feet wide apart, his hands on his waist staring at her. The others formed a line alongside him and imitated his stance.

Pohpoh, wasp red, her arms folded defiantly, stood facing him. She hated him yet wished he did not think so badly of her. Out of nowhere words foamed up and took flight.

"You shouldn't do that. Why you do that?" Hardly had the words come out before her eyes filled up with tears that began to run down her cheeks. Angry at such a betrayal from her own eyes, she shouted, "All you too cruel. You stupid! Why you do that?"

Walter crossed over his side of the line.

"This is my side, you can't cross it!" Pohpoh said.

He stared at her in disbelief. He and his friends burst out cackling, hissing and jeering, as though it was the funniest joke they had ever heard. They laughed so hard they doubled over, hitting their thighs and holding their stomachs.

"Is you who draw the line? Or me? I draw the line. I go where I want. Who have stick in they hand? You or me? Go home. Go! Get away from we playground. Get away from us. Dunces. Nothing but a dunce!"

Heavy sweat popped out on Pohpoh's upper lip. She stared ahead but searched for Boyie out of the corners of her eyes. Another boy, hardly bigger than Pohpoh, spurred on by the jeering, quickly added, "Ey, Pohpoh, is true what we hear about your mother? Where your mother, Pohpoh? You giving Boyie or you like girls?"

Suddenly dizzy she shouted, "Boyie!" He was nowhere around. "Boyie! Where is Boyie?"

"Boyie is a little coward," the boy with the stick said. "All we had to do was blow on him and he gone! The three of you cut from the same cloth. He must like boys himself."

Someone laughed. "No, boy, Boyie like dogs." The others howled wildly with disbelief at his bravery to dream up such a thing.

Walter, wielding the stick, spoke again. "Look, this is we park. This park is only for good, decent people. Get away from here and don't ever, ever — you hear me?— don't ever come back in this park." He walked right up to Pohpoh and faced her, inches between the two faces. "Ey. Look here, if we catch you near any girl we go cut ass!"

Pohpoh's breathing turned shallow and rapid. "You so full of big words. You ent worth one word, you little rat face!" Then she lunged and kneed Walter Bissey in his stomach. He doubled over and she smashed her arm down on his back. She swiftly turned and shouted out to Asha, "Run, Asha. Run that way. As fast as you can!" Pohpoh, able to run much faster than Asha, caught up to her and grabbed her arm. They bolted away, Asha leaving the ground as she was yanked along, almost like a kite being launched. They made a direct line toward the road, Pohpoh's speed increasing with each step, like flamingo feet pushing water back just before take-off.

Walter remained on the ground, doubled up, hugging his stomach and screaming in agony. The other children backed away for a moment and then one of them shouted, "Get them! don't let them get away! Cut they ass!" But Pohpoh and Asha were already racing to their safest place, the cemetery a block over and across the road, where the other children never entered for fear of being attacked by people who made their homes under the roofs of crumbling tombs or, worse, of being whisked away by restless corpses to some remote place from which there was no return.

Under the shelter of a roomy stone mausoleum Pohpoh sat cross-legged and sulked. Asha was yanking out knotgrass, rabbit grass and stunted trees sprouting from cracks in the cold floor. She watched Pohpoh pout and mutter what sounded like curse words. She wanted to touch her sister's face and hug her tightly for getting into a fight because of her, and she also felt guilty that Pohpoh was ridiculed and had to endure all those stupid insults. She knew Pohpoh wanted Walter and his friends to like her.

Like the air throughout the cemetery, the spacious tomb smelled of burnt wick and candlewax. On a stone plinth under a plaque with much raised writing, a rusted milk can with cut ixoras and red ginger lilies, their tips turning brown in the heat, rested in a hardened pool of candlewax. Leaf cutter ants zigzagged their way to the flowers, each almost hidden by a little piece of leaf or flower waving like a flag above its body. Asha squatted down to watch them, fascinated by the perfectly cut pieces of plant. She reached down and lifted one. It dropped its umbrella and moved its legs rapidly. She picked up the leaf and tried to put it back in the ant's pincers. When it wouldn't close its pincers, Asha dropped the leaf and tried to get the ant to pinch her flesh. The pincers remained wide open. She put the ant back on its path and it scurried off at a distraught pace. Suddenly the entire line of ants ran off in different directions.

"Oh-oh! Look what I do. I make the bachacs go crazy!" she whispered, afraid to disturb Pohpoh's slump.

Without looking at her, Pohpoh answered, "Don't worry. Is nothing. Just wait one minute. You'll see. They'll get back in their line and carry on."

"Poh? How they know where to go?" Asha jumped at the opportunity to engage her sister. Pohpoh got up from her corner and squatted with Asha.

"They have their way. Look at this." She interrupted the ants' path by rubbing her finger hard across it. The first couple of ants stopped at the interruption and then carried along, followed by the others. "Now watch this." Pohpoh took a tiny piece of blackboard chalk from her pocket. She cut across their path and encircled one of the ants in a line drawn thickly, chalk powder flying. The ants outside the circle marched up to the chalk line and one after the other backed off, refusing to cross. The ant trapped in the circle ran around the inside of the chalk edge, frantically changing course, standing on its hind legs and then crouching on the ground in panic. Outside the circle several ants dropped their leaves and scurried back in the direction they came. Within seconds a new path bypassing the circle had been created, and the ants outside it hesitantly resumed their trek, more cautiously than before. The ant in the circle stood completely still. Pohpoh and Asha watched in silence.

"Why you do that?" Asha finally asked.

"Because," Pohpoh snapped. Then after several long seconds she said, "I hate Boyie. Why he didn't stay with us? I hate Walter. I hate everybody." Wiping tears from her eyes she jumped over the railing of the tomb and stomped off. "I wish Papa was dead," she mumbled softly. "I hate him. I hate him. I wish he was dead."

The cemetery was quiet except for the creaking sounds of tall, old samaan trees weighed down by hundreds of flowering bromeliads. It was too hot for the birds, and they rested in the branches. In the distance came the dull *tock tock* sound of two metal spades hitting stone and shovelling out dirt and gravel for a new grave. The two gravediggers, Pohpoh and Asha were the only ones in the cemetery. Pohpoh, her head hung low, listlessly hopped on and off the cemetery's narrow path. Asha followed at a distance, sometimes running so as not to lose sight of her. On either side of the cobbled path were more tombs, and in the air was the inescapable odour of burnt wax. Pohpoh, with Asha following, left the winding path and exited the cemetery.

ASHA RAMCHANDIN, ASHA Ramchandin, Asha Ramchandin. In quiet moments after a long day caring for your sister, when I would rather lie in my bed in the nurses' quarter and have my mind lie fallow, your name repeats itself mantra-like in my head. At night I fall asleep clinging to the hope that you are happy and well, and you would soon know that it is now safe to return to Paradise.

I often call out Randolph John Hector's name, too. And Sarah Ramchandin's. And Lavinia Thoroughly's. Where are you all?

Today Asha, watching your sister sit in her one-room bungalow stroking a cat she calls "Pohpoh" sometimes and "Asha" other times, I do feel despair. I wonder at how many of us, feeling unsafe and unprotected, either end up running far away from everything we know and love, or staying and simply going mad. I have decided today that neither option is more or less noble than the other. They are merely different ways of coping, and we each must cope as best we can. You see, Asha, I must rationalize your leaving and her staying — and, as many see it — going mad. Otherwise, I must admit to feelings of anger that you left your sister behind. While I don't begrudge your leaving, I wonder if you ever tried to encourage her to go with you. Asha, from the way she calls your name, it is clear that she, more importantly than I, also does not begrudge you.

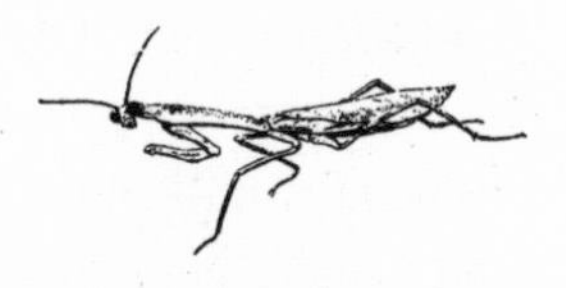

At recess Pohpoh mostly kept to herself, though Boyie still often hovered nearby. She watched the other children as if from the other side of a fence. The boys climbed the hills behind the school looking for snake skins, thriving on the thrill that they might stumble on a snake itself. One day when they turned up neither snake nor skin, they collected handfuls of battimamselles, daddy-long-legs, tree frogs, millipedes and snails that got flushed up in the rains. Pohpoh watched the group huddle in a circle, their heads locked together like a mass of papaya seeds.

"I bet you I know what they're going to do," Boyie whispered, noticing she was curious. "You see, the other day we learned about the reflexes of plants. Teacher said plants respond to gentleness. He told us too that plants could show signs of trauma. Watch this. I bet they are going to do an experiment based on that idea. Want to bet me?"

Pohpoh sneered at him but quietly worried he might be right.

Candlelight flickered across their concentrating faces. Walter Bissey held an inch of candle first about one foot away, then gradually drew it closer to a praying mantis gripped in a pair of lab tweezers. The insect tensed and rubbed its front legs up and down. The boys grew more fascinated. Their bodies seemed to tingle with excitement.

"Ey! Ah tell you, go close na, boy!"

"Slow down, slow down. Doh go so fast, na!"

As the flame got nearer the mantis' body began to arch. The insect twisted its head, its front legs a blur. The instant the flame touched a back leg, the mantis' movements stopped abruptly. It became as rigid as if it had disappeared.

Pohpoh bit her lower lip. She stood perfectly still.

The mantis' chitinous body smoldered where the flame had touched it, crackling and hissing as ruby sparks spat and sputtered. The abdomen took the longest to disintegrate but the boys were resolute. One held the truncated torso with the tweezers as another torched more persistently. When, eventually, the head fell off like the tip of a spent match, one boy reached into his jar and pulled out a grasshopper.

Pohpoh leered at them angrily but she was unable to move. She was invisible to all of them, including the tall boy named Walter.

At school the next day Pohpoh insisted that Boyie accompany her. They followed the crude-smelling, silver trails that led to a colony of periwinkle snails, alive and ripe and vulnerable to the torture squad's delights. One clean blow with a heavy boot or the blunt end of a guava rod could shatter the snails into a gooey green, yellow and pink jigsaw. From Aunt Lavinia, Pohpoh believed such an act would bring down a torrent of bad luck on the boys who committed it, and she believed good fortune would be visited on a protector of the snails. She and Boyie began fervently collecting the periwinkles in the heavy cotton bag she had crudely stitched especially for this purpose. Once the bag was bulging and the thread that held it stretched beyond its capacity, they carried the snails down to the backyard fence. There she turned the bag out over the stone wall and delivered the creatures from the reach of the school yard's bullies.

Nudging Pohpoh away from the wall, Boyie looked expectantly at her.

"Pohpoh Ramchandin," he began to chant as if it were a mantra, "Pohpoh Ramchandin Pohpoh Ramchandin Pohpoh Ramchandin." He guided her to the back wall of the small school building, which seemed to quiver with the shadows of a tamarind tree. Shrieks and screams of after-school wildness floating through half-open wooden jalousies stoked his pubescent desire. Joking and teasing, he leaned his pudgy body into hers, pinning her like a butterfly to the cool jagged wall up which daddy-longlegs crawled. He rubbed his hand up and down the front of her white school blouse. A small club was growing in his pant leg, she noticed, and was starting to press into her thigh.

Pohpoh threw her head back and giggled, more high pitched than usual. She ducked down, spun around and swiftly manoeuvered out of Boyie's clumsy embrace. He waited, unsure yet grinning, for firm refusal or further encouragement. She ran back to him, grabbed his hand, tugging him along with her.

"Leh we go to your house. Your bedroom," she said.

Biting the corner of his lip, he tried to yank her to a halt, protesting that they would be alone, that his mother wouldn't be home until much later.

"Of course, you bachac you," she said half-affectionately. He turned to face the corner of the building, toward a statue of the school's founder, Reverend Ernest Thoroughly. He grazed a shoulder along the length of stubbly brown wall as he limped away from her, his eyes cast on the damp stone littered with pink, wet-weather earthworms.

Pohpoh caught up with Boyie before he rounded the corner. She trapped him against the wall, grabbed his wrist and pushed his now reluctant fist inside her opened white school blouse. The fist disintegrated, weakened by its brush against a small upright nipple under the cotton petticoat. Fingers extended, explored and moulded themselves around the little hump. His other hand groped behind her, discovering with pleasure other mounds. Aroused beyond control he shoved his open mouth, tongue first like a can opener, toward her mouth. The words Pohpoh Ramchandin danced in his mind. Pohpoh Ramchandin thumped a firm palm against his chest. "Not here," she said. "Leh we go to your house, ah tell yuh — I really want to do it with yuh."

Pohpoh and Boyie headed out to his mud house on the outer edge of the Paradise Estate cane fields. They ran in the shallow, fertile gullies between crests of recently planted cane. On the other side of the cane field they came out at the village cricket pitch. Crossing the flat open area, Boyie tried to hold Pohpoh's hand. She squeezed and released it dismissively, plopping her exercise book and dictionary in his arms. She skipped ahead of him past the roughly hewn bleachers and improvised pavilion and down through a row of poui trees.

He followed her over rickety boards that lay across a ravine of foul-smelling water. They beat through curtains of mosquitoes and black flies to the back of the whitewashed ajoupa where he and his mother lived. Inside the yard of lepayed clay she deferred to his lead. Boyie dilly-dallied by the fruit trees and insisted on showing her his brood of rabbits penned up in a decrepit hutch under the sapodilla tree. He nervously explained how he had constructed the hutch himself. Pohpoh tugged at his shirt sleeve, insisting they go inside straight to his room.

Standing before the heavy cotton curtain that cordoned off his room, he held a trembling hand up, signalling to her to wait while he checked just to make sure that, even though it was much too early, his mother had not already returned home. In the centre of the sparsely furnished room Boyie stood motionless, listening to the sounds of the evening, expecting any minute to hear his mother calling to him from the yard.

The already dim interior was made darker by the fading evening light. Pohpoh waited, watching him impatiently. Slowly parting the curtains she slipped into the sliver of space that he called his room. He followed reluctantly, brushing his body deliberately against the curtain to separate it again. Pohpoh turned and yanked the two sides tightly together. On this side of the flimsy partition, amber-coloured evening light streamed through a square window recently cut out of the mud wall. An overturned crate fit snugly against the wall between the curtain and Boyie's bed. Neatly pressed and folded school shirts rested on the crate in a sternly perfect pile. At the foot of his low and narrow bed was another crate, also overturned and raised with stilts. Dog-eared, tattered books and a jam jar full of pencils were arranged on it. Two more jars sat like trophies. One contained the remains of a single green and black locust with a chalky white underbelly, the other a monarch butterfly. Pohpoh picked up the jar with the butterfly and turned it around, tracing the fat, unbroken black lines of its wings. "Well, is better, I suppose, than leaving it to rotten out there," she said dismissively.

Boyie, unsure of himself, sat on the edge of the bed facing the homework crate-table and busied himself twirling a compass. Pohpoh stood behind him, not at all caring for any sense of his body but intent on keeping him attuned to what had now become *her* goal. She inched forward and quietly stopped just behind him. He could feel her body blocking the breeze through the window.

Pohpoh braced herself and slid her fingers through his greasy hair. She walked the tips of her fingers up and down his damp, hot neck, flitting one in and around an oily ear.

"Did you know, uh, you see Stanley and Deo?" he muttered. "Did you see them copying from each other? In class today? Teacher could have caught them, yuh know. What would happen if they were caught." To deny the sounds of her undressing, he rearranged the tattered books stolen from the school library. At the edges of his vision, just above the rim of the table, he saw bare skin and the soft, yellowed cotton of her bloomers. He turned, mesmerized by the deep cinnamon swirl of her navel. Slowly he adjusted his eyes to rest first on one pinkish-brown breast, then on the other. Pohpoh Ramchandin Pohpoh Ramchandin Pohpoh Ramchandin. He stood up and faced her. She held his hand and pulled him to the bed while he glanced at the drawn curtain. His eyes flitted to the orange sky through the window as though he expected to see someone peering in. He was stricken with panic, yet aroused.

Pohpoh lay down. The mattress was lumpy, thorny. Coconut husk fibres protruded through the rough cotton top sheet. The cot had the musky smell of sweet-talking schoolboys and coconut. Still clothed in his school uniform and shoes, Boyie climbed on, guided by her, hovering and trembling and frightened and bumbling over her near-naked body. He stayed elevated on his knees and elbows. When his fear succumbed to the urgent lowering of his pelvis, she grabbed his waist and firmly pushed him back up into the air. She held him there until he understood that this was where he should remain. He brought his mouth awkwardly down to peck, flit, pry at hers, tongue first again. She stopped him, turning her face sharply away and pushed his head down toward her breasts. She locked his head with both her hands so that his mouth was placed where she intended it, on a breast. She lifted her nose toward the ceiling to escape the schoolboy sweat trapped in his thick, oily hair. Without looking at him she whispered, "Suck them."

He instinctively grabbed her waist with his hands and did as he was told. His eyes, wide as dinner plates, remained planted sideways on the closed curtain. He was terrified of being caught, yet half hoped his mother would return.

Suddenly he felt her entire body writhing and her hand clutching at his head. The curtain now forgotten, he dropped off of one knee and angled his crotch between her widening thighs. He fidgeted and fumbled to undo the belt of his pants, dropping his other leg and letting his full weight fitfully thump against Pohpoh. She pressed up against the hard shaft that seemed to have found its niche even through his smelly khaki shorts and her wet panty that she knew very well would not come off. She used this hardness to arrive at her intended destination before he could even unbuckle his belt.

Instantly, her body dissolved into an entirely different mode.

"I have to go, it getting late," she blurted out, pushing him off to the side of the bed. She pulled her clothing from the floor and began to dress. Boyie lay on his stomach, not breathless but airless, his deflated face propped in his hand. Confused and hurting, he studied Pohpoh as she fumbled, turning her petticoat inside out and yanking it over her head.

And without notice Pohpoh Ramchandin was gone, as though it were nothing at all.

Clutching her school satchel like armour against her chest, Pohpoh hustled home. She wanted to beat her father's arrival from the rum shop where he often spent his afternoons. Sometimes Pohpoh imagined that if she could gather up enough speed, she would be able to take off, flying above all the walls and gardens, above the topmost branches of the tallest trees around and even farther — a frigate bird soaring with other frigates until her town below was swallowed up, consumed in an unidentifiable fleck of island adrift like a speck of dust in a vast turquoise seascape.

She unlatched the high, latticed gate to her father's house. She didn't want to think about the smell of someone else's saliva on her breast, or that scrubbing off such evidence meant preparing her body for him. Inside the unlit, musty wood cubicle in the backyard, she filled an enamel basin with water. She decided it would be best to scrub herself with a concentrated solution of borax and rub her body with an unction of eucalyptus oil, camphorated oil and turpentine, and then to complain of a stomach ache and sore muscles.

The staff and residents of Paradise Alms House were growing less afraid of Miss Ramchandin. Some were even beginning to doubt the rumours, which in the presence of her quiescence and pleasantness, began to seem ridiculous. There was talk that I had "performed miracles" with Miss Ramchandin. When I resisted such praise, knowing the change in Miss Ramchandin was only a result of humane treatment, I would be cut off with protestations that I was far too modest — for a man. Initially I felt flattered at being finally included in conversations and being missed if I didn't show at meal times. Now, whether I had parted my hair this side or that, or wore a new scarf at night, I was no longer pretentiously fawned over. The change was delightful if not daunting. Then Sister asked if I would take over the care of Mr. Phu, a resident who had no rest and allowed his caretakers no rest because he was sure his room had been taken over by an army of red ants. She thought I might be able to wrestle that idea from him and calm him down. Although Sister asked and did not demand it of me, I could not refuse the transfer. Her asking was a sign of growing respect.

That night I mentioned to Miss Ramchandin that I would not be spending as much time with her in the future. She didn't respond. I returned to my room but kept one ear open all night waiting, expecting, wondering. As the hours passed and there was no commotion I became more and more despondent. I imagined that she too felt it was time for me to move on, that she looked forward to a fresh face. I thought of the dress stuffed behind the dresser and felt my chest cave in with grief. I slept in the early hours of the morning only because being awake, alive even, had become too painful.

Delivering her breakfast was still my chore, and the next morning yielded another sign of how amicable everyone suddenly felt toward Miss Ramchandin. During the first weeks of her stay, I used to go into the kitchen and prepare her a meal without animal or fish products. Every morning I would have to listen to the cook rant and rave that I was making more work for her, that I was spoiling the old woman, giving her preferential treatment.

This morning, I followed a trail of scrambled eggs into the kitchen, intending to make Miss Ramchandin her breakfast as usual. All the trays were lined up, each one looking just like the others with a mess of mashed eggs and a slice of buttered bread, a cup of cocoa and an unpeeled banana. I opened a cupboard and reached for the loaf of bread and bread knife when the cook silently handed me a tray: a mess of mashed avocados, a slice of bread, cocoa and a banana. I should have seen the offering as the cook's and Miss Ramchandin's accomplishment but instead my heart sank. I felt cheated. My spirits seemed perilously low, dragging on the floor several paces behind me like a reluctant shadow.

I approached Miss Ramchandin's bungalow with a dry mouth. My legs had become leaden and I wanted nothing more than to go back up to my room and fall deeply asleep. I knocked as usual, and as usual did not wait for an answer. When I entered I almost dropped the tray. The centre of the room had been made bare. Three dresses, a slip, two nightgowns, panties, four pairs of socks, a pair of shoes, a night potty, brush and soap were neatly lined up along the edges of the room. A roll of toilet paper had been dissected, sheet by sheet, each sheet pinned to the wall. The dresser lay flat on its face in front of the window. The bed frame, balanced on its side, sat on the dresser. It was straddled by the eating table atop which lay the mattress, which itself lay under four drawers, neatly arranged side by side. Two chairs faced each other with their feet symmetrically placed in the drawers. Straddling the two chairs was the stool and in, or rather on the stool sat Miss Ramchandin. She was close enough to the ceiling to pluck old spider web threads from the wood boards. I was grinning but she carried right on plucking. She made a low buzzing sound, like a neon light about to expire, punctuated by a single interjection, as if to the ceiling: "Where Asha?"

I stayed by the door, leaving it open and feasting my eyes. To make certain she had seen me appreciating her grand statement, I gasped loudly. A crowd gathered. Sister came running. She gasped too, after which her only words, spat out and laced with frustration, were "Well! At least there are only imaginary ants to clean up in Mr. Phu's room!"

And I got to keep my full-time job caring for Miss Ramchandin.

To everyone else, Miss Ramchandin appeared to have a limited vocabulary or at least to have become too simple-minded to do more than imitate. However, I knew for a fact she was able to speak and had volumes of tales and thoughts in her head. She rambled under her breath all day and all night, as long as she and I were alone. Seconds before someone else approached, as though she were trained to hear the stealthiest footfall, she would become flatly silent. I came to realize that no response was required yet I knew it was no accident that she chose to chatter only in my presence. For a while I considered this to be merely an honour. Then I began to recognize in her mutterings elements of the legendary rumours. I had Mr. Hector run me the errand of acquiring a notebook, and I started to jot down everything she said, no matter how erratic her train of thought appeared to be. When she saw me awaiting her next word and writing it down as soon as she uttered it, she drew nearer. I soon got the impression that she actually began to whisper in my direction, that I had become her witness. She spoke rapidly and with great urgency, in a low monotone, repeating herself sometimes for hours without end. There was little doubt that I was being given a dictation, albeit without punctuation marks or subject breaks. I scribbled and when she took to repeating parts, I caught my breath and rested my cramped fingers. It became apparent that the question "Where Asha?"—usually asked without emotion or nuance — was not idle rambling. There was a purpose to it and to all the chatter, and finally a purpose to my listening and to sifting, cutting and sewing the lot.

One day a nurse arrived to announce that Miss Ramchandin had two visitors. I put my book and pen away quickly. The visitors, the nurse said, were the same ones Sister had turned away earlier — a Mr. Ambrose Mohanty and son, the ones who had left the cereus clippings. Miss Ramchandin's eyes flickered. I had already run across the name Ambrose among her ramblings.

Accustomed to reading, as if by Braille, her twitches and gasps, it was fortunate that I sensed to spruce her up first, for her visitors were dressed to the hilt. The old gentleman was a spectacle. From a distance he seemed to totter and shake and had to be supported by the younger man. Miss Ramchandin walked slowly alongside me. As we approached the visitors waiting in the garden she became mildly agitated. She did not look toward them but glanced from side to side, picked her fingernails, looked up at the sky and dawdled. I encouraged her with little nudges. Her nervousness could have been infectious were I not made curious by the visitors' unusual attire. The old man wore a black top hat, a formal white shirt with a bow tie, and heavy black coattails and trousers, unusual at any time in Lantanacamara but especially odd in the heat and humidity of the season. He held a polished cane yet he shook so much that the cane was of no practical use. The young man at his side was tall and slim. At one glance he had the angularity and sprightliness of a girl reluctantly on the verge of becoming a woman, and at the next the innocent feyness of a young boy who would never quite grow into the glove of manhood. He too wore a hat, and though it was a straw fedora, it also drew attention, for in spite of the heat, head-coverings in Lantanacamara were reserved for funerals, church and state functions.

Positioning himself behind his father, the younger man put both hands on the old man's shoulders. It could have been either a gesture of restraint or protectiveness. The old man trembled. He covered his mouth with one hand, as though holding back his emotions, and shuffled forward. Miss Ramchandin focused on a wispy cloud on the far horizon, off to the side, but she too began to shuffle.

"Pappy, is she," the young man said. "You all right, Pappy?"

The old man, still with his mouth covered, started sobbing. His shuffle quickened toward us.

"Oh, my-my, Mala Ramchandin, Mala Ramchandin, Mala Ramchandin. It is you, indeed, it is you. Oh, my-my. My Mala Ramchandin." His voice was low and seemed riddled with remorse.

Miss Ramchandin skirted around them and headed for the nearest park bench. I said hello awkwardly and continued to keep pace with her. The two men turned and followed. She sat down, calmed suddenly and looked across the valley, swinging her legs. Her face would have appeared expressionless to them, as though she were unaware of their presence.

The old man walked up to her and his son moved discreetly around to the back of the bench. I found myself stealing glances at his unusually soft and hairless skin. He caught me staring and held out his hand.

"I am Otoh Mohanty. Otoh. This is my father. He has known her for a long time," he explained. "They were friends."

His hand was tender yet his grip so secure and present I was compelled to look directly into his eyes. I can think of no other way to express myself — even superlatives would be useless: simply stated, he was breathtakingly beautiful. He saw me gasp. My hand went limp with embarrassment and shyness. He held it a moment longer and smiled. I had to clear my throat to introduce myself.

Mr. Mohanty hesitantly sat down beside Miss Ramchandin, his palms pressed together and tucked between his legs. He stared at her, shaking his head. Deep emotion contorted his face as he allowed his tears to fall freely.

"Is he all right?" I whispered.

Otoh Mohanty shrugged his shoulders.

"He hasn't seen her in many years. How is she? Is *she* all right? Does she know we are here?"

"Yes, she knows. See how she is swinging her legs? You might not be able to tell, but I can. She is happy."

Miss Ramchandin's face may have seemed expressionless but to me it was clearer and calmer than I had ever before seen it. I could not help my curiosity. "How well did she know your father?"

Otoh gave me a look that said that he would explain later.

The real question desperately wanting to slip off the tip of my tongue was, "Does he know her sister, Asha?" Confident that I would see these men again, I refrained from asking for fear of toppling the moment.

The two gentlemen did become weekly visitors. I looked forward to their arrival as much as Miss Ramchandin did. Admittedly, my anticipation was in no small part due to my growing fondness for the most alluring Otoh Mohanty. Over the course of their visits Otoh explained just how well Miss Ramchandin and his father knew each other. From both him and his father I was able to fill in gaps and make sense of things she mumbled. One day, for example, she would go on and on about some gramophone or other, the next day about spiders, then about peekoplats or snails. As much as I had learned not to discount her mental fitness, I must admit there were times when I believed her words were fanciful imaginings. I wrote everything down though, just in case. You can therefore imagine my giddiness when Mr. Mohanty and the uncommonly lovely Otoh related tales in which the very same gramophone, spider, bird or snail were featured.

II

The temptation to digress from my mission and to relate every scintillating detail of the romantic blossoming of my knowledge of Otoh Mohanty is overwhelming. And every detail, at least in my estimation, because this was the first experience I had that actually occurred outside the realm of my fertile imagination, seems nothing less than scintillating. I must remind myself, however, that Mala Ramchandin's story is my prime purpose here. Asha, if you are reading this, all I will say is that, thanks to your sister, my own life has finally — and not too late I might add — begun to bloom. Enough said. Now, I will exercise restraint. You will hear little more of me as I apply myself to the story of Mala Ramchandin, fashioning a single garment out of myriad parts . . .

IN THE KITCHEN of a house in Government Alley, Otoh Mohanty was being closely watched by his father, Mr. Ambrose E. Mohanty, who slouched in a bentwood wheelchair. Otoh Mohanty pried three paper-dry fillets of heavily salted cod from a barrel and wrapped them in sheets of brown paper. Before washing the salty grit from his hands he nestled his face in them and inhaled the concentrated scent. Mrs. Elsie Mohanty sat at the kitchen table, shelling a basket of pigeon peas. Her motions conveyed her displeasure at the task. She grudgingly noted her husband's every gesture as he directed their son. Finally, under her breath but making sure to be heard, she grumbled, "I suppose you will take the peas I shelling too. It is too many years now that every month without fail, I sit in this kitchen and watch you pack up food, my family food, to send to that woman. I going to go to my grave and be reborn before you wake up to think of anything else but that old lady. If I had known the spell that Bird put on you, I would've study my head good before I say I do to you, yes!"

"And our son, our great joy, would never have been born," said Ambrose Mohanty. "Mrs. Elsie Mohanty, wife of mine, Mala is mad. She is as mad as a brainless bird. Crazy. Do you understand

I am saying? From whence would she obtain the essentials of life, dearest? We are entrusted with her care. You might simply consider charity toward such a creature as insurance toward positive retribution. Truthfully, she has no mind for me, or anybody else in this town, as a matter of fact. There is no need, I assure you, for you to confuffle your tender brain." He turned to his son. "Now the rice. Don't forget the rice. And take a pack of matches, son."

"Pappy, I ever forget the rice yet?"

Elsie shook her head with frustration. "Well, I never! Entrusted! By whom, pray? You say she mad and you sending matches for she? For what? For she to burn down house and town?" Once upon a time Elsie had been enraptured by the silken petals that fell from Ambrose's Wetlandish-affected lips. Now she wished that he would either shut up or talk simply and plainly with her again.

On the first Saturday of every month Otoh heard the same conversation between his parents. It was indeed the only one they really ever had. When he was a child the two hurled insults and accusations at each other, like people playing a game of ping-pong — each, however, with a different ball. Their tone had become duller and their pitch lower over the years, and the vociferousness of Elsie's complaints lessened as she realized that they were absolutely in vain. Besides the occasional, under-the-breath mumblings calculated to reach Ambrose's ears, she confined herself to drawn-out, carefully arched sighs.

The first package of dried goods had been sent just before Otoh was born. From the beginning every delivery was accompanied by varying degrees of wrath from Ambrose's new wife. She had in her enough compassion and sense of civic duty to appreciate the idea of sending food to a helpless bird, but she could hardly bear Ambrose's insistence on preparing the food himself. He performed the task with such attentiveness that Elsie's heart wept and her spirits became blistered. In the days before their marriage, rumours had spread that the bird up the hill had gone crazy but even if that was so, the fire of Elsie's jealousy could not be easily extinguished. It was, in fact, jealousy that had driven her to marry this man.

Ambrose E. Mohanty returned from study abroad to become the most eligible young man in Paradise, a foreign-educated fop with the airs and speech of a Shivering Northern Wetlandsman lord. It seemed a waste to the townspeople that such a catch would be so preoccupied with a woman whose father had obviously mistaken her for his wife, and whose mother had obviously mistaken another woman for her husband. It would have been a matter of pride to reform the eligible bachelor but Elsie herself had little to do with the transformation. It was only after Mala Ramchandin shoved Ambrose out of her life that he noticed one Miss Elsie Smart, who, looked at from a particular angle, with her hair pinned up in a high bun, quite resembled his beautiful Mala in the days before she turned into an untamable creature. He turned to the eager Elsie for solace.

From the first days of their marriage all altercations between Elsie and her inert, non-confrontational husband concerned her jealousy — and his fixation on The Bird's well-being. Their antagonisms took place mostly in the hardening of their eyes and hearts, becoming audible only around food delivery days. It was in those early days of marriage that Ambrose mastered the art of side-stepping his wife's fits of rage against what she called his mental infidelity. He never missed a month's delivery.

Hardened hearts having little to do with conception, the couple had a child. Elsie gave birth to a girl. Her arrival in the midst of one of his (*her,* then) parents' regular tirades profoundly affected all three. Ambrose never raised his voice again. He developed a propensity for month-long slumbers from which he miraculously awakened only long enough to replenish Mala Ramchandin's supplies. Elsie refused to sleep or to even blink her eyes in case she missed the longed-for occasion when Ambrose might awaken and desire her and a family life at last.

By the time Ambrosia was five, her parents were embroiled in their marital problems to the exclusion of all else, including their child. They hardly noticed that their daughter was transforming herself into their son. Ambrose slept right through the month, undisturbed until the first Saturday of the next, and Elsie, hungry for a male in the house, went along with his (her) strong belief that he (she) was really and truly meant to be a boy. Elsie fully expected that he (she) would outgrow the foolishness soon enough. But the child walked and ran and dressed and talked and tumbled and all but relieved himself so much like an authentic boy that Elsie soon apparently forgot she had ever given birth to a girl. And the father, in his few waking episodes, seemed not to remember that he had once fathered one.

The transformation was flawless. Hours of mind-dulling exercise streamlined Ambrosia into an angular, hard-bodied creature and tampered with the flow of whatever hormonal juices defined him. So flawless was the transformation that even the nurse and doctor who attended the birth, on seeing him later, marvelled at their carelessness in having declared him a girl.

Ambrosia's obviously vivid imagination gave him both the ability to imagine many sides of a dilemma (and if it weren't already a dilemma, of turning it into one) and the vexing inability to make up his mind. Ever since the days of early high school, where he excelled in thinking but not in doing, this trait of weighing "on the one hand" with "but on the other" earned him a name change. He began, though through no choice of his own, to be called Otoh-boto, shortened in time to Otoh, a nickname to which he still answered.

One rainy Saturday morning, Otoh lay shirtless on his back in his ground floor bedroom. A woman lay at his side. The woman was attempting to arouse him by drawing circles and figure eights with the tips of her fingers on his delightfully hairless chest. He was silently perplexed, examining the sensation as her hand made sly and furtive contact with the nipples atop his muscled breasts. The sensation of his body being played with was far more arresting and pleasurable to him than was the woman. In spite of himself Otoh was suddenly so overcome with yearning that he turned to face her and began a sensuous caress along the bare leg strewn provocatively across his half-naked body. She slid her hand around to the small of his back, nestling into the gully of his spine. She played in the gully, riding up the sides and dipping back down. Then she slipped her hand inside the waist band of his trousers. He was suddenly beside himself with desire. He was just about to extend his caress higher up, toward the back of her thigh, just about to start unzipping his trousers, readier than ever before to risk the wrath of Paradise, when he was launched out of bed by a dreadful commotion. Ambrose Mohanty, still groggy from the previous month's sleep, carelessly hurried past his wife's grumbling and went thumping on his backside down the flight of slippery back stairs. The sack of rice he carried in one arm and the bag of onions in the other broke apart before hitting the bottom stair. Rice was strewn about as though a wedding had just occurred. The ambulance men's path proved quite treacherous.

As Ambrose was locked into the emergency vehicle he made Otoh swear on his disassembled pelvis to immediately prepare and deliver a new package. This was the first time Otoh was dispatched with his father's package to Mala Ramchandin. Ambrose's slow-mending pelvis provided him with his most unarguable excuse to lie all day and all night in his bed. And Otoh, intrigued by his father's devotion to a woman whom he had not seen in more than thirty years, accepted his inherited task.

Back in the kitchen in Government Alley Ambrose told Otoh to wheel him out to the front porch. Out of his wife's sight and hearing, he took Otoh's hand and pulled him down.

"If fortune sees fit to grant you the pleasure of an audience with her," he whispered in Otoh's ear, "may I impose upon you, my treasured son, the honour of conveying to her wishes for an incomparably good day from one Mr. Ambrose Mohanty, otherwise known to her as Boyie."

"Pappy, I take food up there so many times that I lose count now and to this day I never yet see she. I only know she up there because the food does disappear before I reach back down to the roadway."

His father, refusing to give up, kissed Otoh's cheek. "*If* is all I can ask and hope for."

"Month after month you does ask me this same thing — if, if, if — but she never yet let me see she face. Nobody see she in years, Pappy, nobody. What does keep you thinking and hoping so, month after month, that I going to glimpse she? Is a long time now even the children in town give up waiting to see she plant snail shells in she front yard."

"If, son, simply if."

"Otoh!" Elsie called from the kitchen.

Otoh knew what to expect. Unknown to Ambrose, Elsie had lately taken to adding one more package as *her* civic contribution. She slapped a pound of cold salted butter against his chest.

"She don't have no fat to cook with. That lunatic! How she will cook? Look, make sure and leave the things where she could see them, you hear? Is no point our good food going to waste. Lord! What I doing, tell me, na, child, in my old age looking after a old woman you father used to be romancing up? Tell me this, na."

"For better or for worse you said, Ma, and things could be plenty worse."

"But listen to you, na, child. Children really don't understand the needs of they parents, na. For your information we gone past the stage of 'plenty worse' long time now. Things already plenty worse. That woman zap your father of all his passion, and what I end up with is a month-long corpse and a once-a-month man. The man ent got no passion. He like a chipped marble come to rest in a soup bowl. A marble that can't pitch. In his mind and heart he just like all them other men. Even when you see him there, sleeping alone in that chair, he unfaithful-unfaithful. He does only wake up to think about her. Your father foolish, Otoh. If even she was to see him, she wouldn't know him from Adam. The man is a chipped marble, in truth, yes."

"The thing is, Mammy, I can't make sense of what you does stay in this house for when you could have a life somewhere else."

"Hmph! What you know about marriage to be advising me so?"

He embraced her. Smelling the familiar mustiness of her hair he was overcome with soft-heartedness. He pressed her against his body and kissed the top of her head. She held on to him, cherishing the touch and smell of another human.

"Well? What it is you waiting for? You don't have enough to carry?"

"But, Mammy, is you who call me back to give me the fat to take. This thing will melt in the heat before I make it up the hill."

Everyone in the village seemed to have finally forgotten about Mala. The generation of children who harassed her by calling names and pelting her with mango seeds had grown up. Their children preferred to chase each other within the confines of their own yards, playing games of cops and robbers, cowboys and Indians. They occasionally noted the ever-widening, ever-lengthening rows of bleached white snail shells planted along the inside of her fence. But they expressed no curiosity about this or about her rare, unpredictable appearances out of the impenetrable sea of brambles and stinging nettles that barred a view of her house. When they had to pass by, the children walked on the other side of the street, glancing through her fence — not to see her but to make sure she did not see them.

According to their parents, she possessed the ability to leap her fence, track an offending child into its hiding place and tear out its mind. No one had experienced such a fate but the children feared it as if it were proven fact. Their parents used her legend to their advantage, as though she were a whipping cane. Should she suddenly appear while the children were walking along the road they would fall silent, conceal themselves behind the twelve-foot-high poinsettia shrubs, pray feverishly and make noble promises. They watched as the tall, upright, wire-thin woman with matted hair the colour of forgotten silver emerged from the bramble patches, carrying a silver bucket of snail shells. They saw her gather up her ankle-length dress, stoop and place the unusually white shells in a neat line, now three rows deep, pressing them hard into the earth and adjusting the ones dislodged by the rain. Without her eyes ever crossing the fence, she would turn and disappear again into the brambles. The children ran off, each willing to swear on the Bible that she or he had seen the woman, and their sightings became the substance of frenetic dreamings at night.

THERE WAS NO need to kill a thing to relieve it of a drop of its own blood. A pin prick would do. Mala's hands trembled yet she was swift with the pin. A tear-size bead of maroon, velvet blood fell on the yellow saucer. Before the pigeon could feel and respond she pressed it against her chest and swiftly rubbed the spot on its belly. The bird shivered with surprise, giving off a strong, sharp smell. She pursed her lips and touched the top of its head. Very softly, from the back of her throat came a cooing sound. When its heartbeat returned to normal she loosened her hand. The pigeon looked solemnly at her. Mala looked back with no judgement. The bird hopped off her hand and fluttered to the floor. She leaned back quietly, holding the saucer. The outside edge of blood had begun to dry. The enamel pot on the wood stove in the kitchen began a slow rattle, and a smelly cloud billowed through the porch. She returned to her kitchen with the saucer.

The backyard was overrun with periwinkle snails, glossy mucous trails crisscrossing the milky brown clay as they crawled from one juicy plant to the next. At the rear of the house near the drain was a patch where they went to die. The cemetery was littered with upturned shells, each one empty except for any raw, fishy remnants of its inhabitant mixed with lumps of garden soil.

Every few days, a smell of decay permeated the house. It was the smell of time itself passing but lest she was overcome by it, Mala brewed an odour of her own design. She collected and boiled six empty shells at a time. After an hour, the shells lost their pink and yellow. The house would fill with the aroma of a long-simmering ocean into which worm-rich, root-matted earthiness was constantly being poured and stirred. The aroma obliterated, reclaimed and gave the impression of reversing decay. Mala needed only a pinch of salt to start the waves of steam, and a pin prick of fresh blood to sharpen the snails' scent and make it almost tangible. The odour hung, rejuvenating the air for days. It wove itself through Mala's hair and penetrated her pores.

Wobbling unevenly on the back porch in her bentwood rocking chair, Mala closed her eyes and lifted her face to the breeze. The trees in the yard purred and rippled. Iridescent purple and grey pigeons danced in the water trough where they nested. They hopped on and off, from the trough to the rusted eve that overhung the verandah, and back again. Mala opened her eyes. She couldn't see the birds but she noticed that a grapefruit tree and several pepper plants had sprouted in the dirt and rust of the roof. The roof already squeaked and sagged under their weight. The edge would break away any day. She told herself that she must remember not to be under it when it fell.

She looked at her yard. Fruit trees and hot pepper trees had sprung wherever birds and insects dropped their seeds. A patch of bright orange, sweet-smelling roses and a profusion of night-blooming cereus plants were the only ornamentals in the yard. The roots of the cereus, like desperate grasping fingers, had bored through the damp wood of the back wall of the house. It was no longer the wall that supported the succulent but rather the other way around. The yard was a jumble of different greens: the bright yellow of the lime trees, the silver of the eucalyptus, the dark blue of the mango.

Under the bodice of her dress, inside her petticoat, was a handkerchief bundle. The knotted 'kerchief was limp with sweat. Inside was a crumpled sepia tint photograph, also sticky and damp. She carefully opened the photograph, carefully studied every detail as though seeing it for the first time. The wide expanse of sea behind the two women. The white crests on the small waves that lapped the beach. The cloudless sky. The pelican soaring overhead. She stared at the women. The shorter one partially obscured the dress of the one standing close behind. They wore ankle-length skirts and long-sleeved white blouses. The woman at the back was larger. Her skin was white and her hair, which appeared to be white also, was neatly tied atop her head. She smiled broadly but her eyes were cast downward as though looking at the woman in front of her. Her hands were not visible. On her feet were heavy black shoes laced past the hem of her skirt. The woman in front was shorter by a good head. Her hair, a curly mass of the darkest tint possible in such a photograph, was tied in a single braid that hung in front of her, reaching well down the middle of her long skirt. Her skin was barely a shade lighter than her hair. Her hands were clasped in front at waist level. She stared at the camera, perhaps at the photographer. Her pupils were the most commanding detail of the picture. They were as dark as her hair and seemed to stand out from the whites of her large eyes. Whatever other detail one might notice, her eyes pulled the viewer like a magnet. Mala looked at the women's shoes, at the closeness of their feet. She rubbed the spot where their shoes met, the ball of her index finger tenderly covering them. She raised the photograph to her nose. She smelled only her own sweat and the earthiness of her fingers. She carefully refolded it and replaced it in the handkerchief.

Rocking harder in the chair, she shoved the bundle back inside her petticoat. A cooling breeze passed and coconut tree branches dipped and scratched against the galvanized roof. The pigeons took off in a frenzied flutter, flying outward in a tight, parallel formation. When the breeze and the scratching subsided, they swerved sharply one after the other and returned to the gutter.

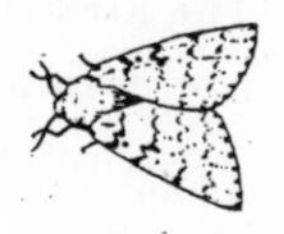

IT WAS BARELY midmorning yet already the sun offered no mercy. The air above the paved road quivered in the heat. Otoh fanned himself with the package of cod and butter as he scuffed up the road. Few people dared brave such heat but Otoh had pledged to carry out his father's mission.

In all his deliveries to the house on Hill Side, not once had Otoh seen the woman who so obsessed his father. As he neared her house he became anxious, wanting desperately to see her yet hoping she would not show herself. He had grown up hearing all the rumours, even the ridiculous one that claimed she turned into a ball of fire and whipped across the sky at night. His skin tingled as he approached the gravel path leading up to her chicken-wire fence. The path was strewn with discarded oil drums, old machine parts, tires and other debris. He set the parcels in a cool spot near the fence, then walked away slowly, his head to the side to catch any movement.

"All right, Mala Ramchandin, show yourself," he shouted. "If you don't come and fetch my parcels fast, my mother's butter will surely be nothing but a useless sludge." He hid behind the deteriorating tractor parts, propped up on his elbows with his face in the cup of one hand. He peered through a chink in a large piece of garbage. Otoh had decided that this was the day he would get a glimpse of Mala Ramchandin.

The sun pelted down and the package of butter began to shrink. Pebbles under his elbow bored into his skin but Otoh was determined. An hour passed. Finally an ache in his back forced him to readjust his cramping knees. The movement took no more than a few seconds but when he looked back, the parcel was gone. Otoh jumped up. Not even a bush shook. She had obviously been observing him all the while. He barely moved, afraid now that he might find her standing behind him, ready to scold him for his prying ways.

Eventually Otoh gathered up the courage to scramble up and bolt from the property. Back on the road, he sat on a shaded curb trembling with fear and excitement. For a moment he was deliriously happy and anxious to tell his father that Mala had made her presence known to him. It was almost as good as seeing her! But why had Mala "introduced" herself to him in this way? Why to him and no one else? Why today and not before or later? He stood up, shook his limbs loose and calmed his breathing.

He walked slowly home. He wished he could take his shirt off but there were some risks he preferred to avoid. Several ideas pawed at him, each one contradicting the other. On the one hand was his desire to make a more substantial bond with Mala before reporting to his father. On the other was a passionate desire that raced across his mind like a shooting star, imploring him to imagine how much happiness and hope he could give his father if he were to break this auspicious news today. Imagine Ambrose being able to stay awake for days and his mother to sleep at last — or to rage decisively! These last thoughts, however, brought a sobering fear, a sudden resistance to the tremendous change in the order of his family's affairs that a sighting of Mala might cause.

He decided to hold off giving his father the news. True to his nature, however, Otoh began to deliberate not the decision itself but the origin of the decision, and the authenticity of its birth. A memory soon fixed itself on his retina.

He was no more than eleven years old, dressed in a long-sleeved white shirt, blue-and-black striped schoolboy's tie and long, white trousers. Spotting the silver-haired recluse in her yard, he and some school friends had darted behind a shrub across the street from the Ramchandin house. They watched the woman, whom they knew from sources as reliable as their Sunday school teachers to be madder than a naked chicken at midnight and wilder than a leatherback in laying season. She stooped by her fence and dipped her long, twig-like fingers into a rusted, enamel bucket. She retrieved snail shells, white as chalk and as large as cricket balls, and wedged them, one by one, into the earth along her fence. The following day he walked again on the far side of the road, curious about the neatly placed decoration that lined her fence. Otoh waited the month for his father to awaken. Then he blurted out what he had seen, the strange ritual of the woman to whom his father delivered food.

A smile of recognition crossed Ambrose's face.

"Now isn't that interesting!" He said no more but slowly nodded his head and grinned. He seemed to slip into a distant reverie.

"Tell me, Pappy, why she was doing that?" Otoh shook him. "She trying to grow snails or what?"

"Snails, eh! She and I, she and I — we used to have this little ritual when we were students together. We were about your age." He drifted off.

"Pappy, I want to know —"

"We fancied ourselves protector of snails and all things unable to defend themselves from the bullies of the world. The school grounds were littered with snails in the rainy season. Is your schoolyard still crawling with the helpless creatures, Otoh? They would be crawling up the walls of buildings, shinnying up tree trunks, dragging themselves across the concrete paths and lawns, exposed and thoroughly tempting to a group of heartless boys who liked to stomp on them and watch them shatter and splatter. Bissey. Walter Bissey — he's now a judge — was at school with us. He was such a bully as a boy, catching and torturing and killing anything that crawled. Do you know Bissey?"

"I don't know any Bissey. What about Mala Ramchandin and the snails?"

"Mala and I used to be the first ones out of the classroom at recess and lunch time. We would race through the schoolyard with a bag and collect all the snails before Bissey and his gang could get to them. Then we would take them and release them safely over the fence. Mala had this idea that snails were good luck. She wasn't one to harm an ant. Protecting those snails was our mission. So she's still looking after the little creatures, eh?"

"So you used to save the snails, too, eh, Pappy?"

"Well, the truth is that she was the one who initiated the whole thing and I went along until it became something I looked forward to. There was an urgency to the whole business, you know."

This was the only time his father ever mentioned details of his connection to Mala Ramchandin.

Otoh realized he had never possessed a clear idea of who Mala Ramchandin was, except that she had collected snails with his father as a child. Yet he went against his mother's wishes and delivered food to her for his father, who came alive only for that single purpose.

The old bird's snail-planting rituals must be an extension of her childhood kindness, Otoh mused. One thought led to another. He wondered about the gentleness and compliance his father exhibited during the snail-protecting activities, and tried to think how his father manifested such traits in the present — besides delivering food to a helpless bird. His sleeping seemed to be a passive smouldering, a withdrawal from Otoh and Elsie, a rebellion.

Not for the first time Otoh found himself desperately wanting to know what caused that rebellion. It was as though his father was cowering under a veil of sleep. A torrent of frustration swept over him. He stopped at a standpipe that gushed sun-heated water into a basin. He bent close to the spout and splashed the hot water on his brow, then put his mouth to the faucet and drank. Where on earth had his father been? Otoh wondered. Not with him or his mother, and not with Mala Ramchandin. He had neglected everything. In the middle of a brilliant day Otoh's world spun and grew dark. He sat on the rim of the basin and hung his head.

That night Otoh could not sleep. He stared restlessly out his window into the thick, still blackness onto which he projected a full-colour image of the Hill Side property, the fence and the rubbish-strewn yard. Before he had time to assess his actions he rose and went into the backyard, yanking one of his mother's dresses off the clothes line. Back in his room he removed his clothing and stepped into the dress. In the mirror of his armoire he watched himself pull on the blue-and-white-flowered garment, half expecting to resemble his mother, but there was no resemblance. Without knowing why, he wanted to share his secret with Mala Ramchandin, even at the risk of being caught walking the streets dressed like a woman.

Wearing a dress made Otoh carry himself gracefully. He left the house. The hem of the skirt swung from side to side with each pointed step. Every house along the route to Hill Side was in darkness, and the only sounds were electric fans and frogs hidden in the bushes on either side of the road. He glanced from balcony to balcony.

When he reached Mala's backyard fence, he gathered the skirt of his dress in one hand and tied the cloth in a knot high up his thigh. The house was in total darkness as usual. Otoh began to think things that had never crossed his mind before: Perhaps after her light bulbs were spent she had never had them replaced. Surely her electricity source would have been cut. He had never taken pitch oil or gasoline or coals, and unless someone else was delivering these to her, what on earth had she been using for fuel, for cooking? How did she cook the salt fish?

With an uncharacteristic brazenness he clasped his hand around a fence post. As he readied himself to leap over, the post trembled in his hand and came away. Otoh shrieked. A snake glided slowly past. He jumped up and, clutching the loosened knot at his thigh, bolted away from the fence. When he reached the road, he glanced back and saw what appeared to be a person waving to him. The harder he looked the more confused he became.

Heading home, Otoh was still so shaken by the idea that he might have seen her and that she might have seen him — and in a dress — and by the post that came alive in his hand, that anything moving — leaves on trees, flying moths, a swooping bat, buzzing mosquitoes, a noisy breeze, a dog in its yard — made his heart leap. He raced home with much less grace than he had set out.

POINT NUMBER ONE: The Paradise Alms House is not en route to anywhere. To get here one must leave the main road, cut through a cane field and carry on up a lane that ends at the top of a small hill. The home with its excellent view of the cane fields is in the shallow valley below. There is nothing beyond.

Point number two: At their age, residents in a home such as this, in this kind of heat, tend to take naps after lunch. So when Otoh Mohanty arrived without his father one hot afternoon, mumbling that since he was in the area he thought he might just stop and say hello, I blushed even as I apologized that he wouldn't be able to see Miss Ramchandin just then because she was sleeping.

"Oh, that's too bad. Well, I could come back later. That's what I should do then, eh?" It would be foolish to deny that I read uncertainty in his response. As though he had never before strung two words together, he continued, "But, uh, well, you know — uh, hmm." Finally he confirmed my hopes about whom he had come to visit. "I mean, look. I am already here. You know what I mean? You, you busy? You have a little time? I mean, you could show me around the grounds if you could spare the time. They are nice grounds. Since I am already here, na."

I had not received a visitor since taking the job. My heart fluttered and the soles of my feet tingled wildly. I gave him a tour of the grounds and Mr. Hector's gardens. Lost in conversation we wandered outside the property and ended up on a trace in the cane field. From then on Otoh became a regular visitor. Sometimes he came twice in a week, always during my off-hours. We would meet away from curious eyes on the periphery of the grounds. Propriety restrains me from detailing just how alluring cane can be when a falsetto trill long trapped in your heart is bursting forth. Although Mala Ramchandin was by no means our sole topic of conversation, I will dwell mainly on those discussions concerning her.

On one visit, after a long walk we came to rest in shade among the exposed roots of a wild mango tree. Otoh tended to be self-reflective and philosophical, even mildly morose at such times.

"You ever feel like something come and tief your mind from you?" he said. "You ever feel like you have no control over yourself? You know that feeling?"

"Often," I teased, "ever since meeting you. You have cleverly invaded my mind, Otoh Mohanty, and occupied all the territory there." He was kind enough to respond to my flattery with a wary half-smile. But I had the feeling that what he was thinking had to do with Miss Ramchandin. After all, if it weren't for Otoh, Miss Ramchandin might still be thriving in her own home on Hill Side, and this fact tormented him. I reminded him often that if it weren't for his intervention, as unfortunate as it may have seemed in the moment, she and I, *and* he and I, would likely not have met.

He tried then, as he had several times before, to explain why, following a compulsion stronger than a riptide, he had entered her yard. Even though I felt that I understood his need to come face to face with her, Otoh seemed never completely satisfied with how he expressed himself on the topic. Some fragments seemed to elude and frustrate him.

"Everybody used to fraid Miss Ramchandin —"

"They still do," I interjected.

"— but I was the only one who used to go up into her yard, not to torment the lady, but to take food for her, and I wanted her to know that I wasn't frightened and I didn't have a bad mind for her. I didn't want her to think I was like everybody else."

"You really aren't, you know," I said.

Encouraged, he carried on. "I felt as though she and I had things in common. She had secrets and I had secrets. Somehow I wanted to go there and take all my clothes off and say, 'Look! See? See all this? *I am different!* You can trust me, and I am showing you that you are the one person I will trust. And I am one person, for sure, for sure, that you can trust. I will be your friend.'"

"Otoh, that is exactly how I feel about her. I am certain — I can't express how certain I am — that she holds no grudge against you."

"I never cared what anybody else thought or said about me, but somehow I cared so much about what Mala Ramchandin thought. I needed her to know that it was my father, Ambrose Mohanty, who was sending food for her. And that I was his son, Otoh Mohanty. You know what I mean, Tyler?"

"I feel protective toward her too —"

"Deep in my heart, Tyler," he interrupted me, whispering as though he were saying something heretical, "is he, is Pappy, I hold responsible for all the rumours spread about her. I blame him for her barred-up house." I raised my eyebrows. "Yes, blame. I don't know why exactly but is he I blame."

I thought of Mr. Mohanty, dressed up especially to see Miss Ramchandin in his coattails and top hat, and of the gleam in his eyes when he sat next to her on the garden bench in the evening. I could not imagine him spreading rumours about her.

"Instead of sleeping he could have done something to prevent children from harassing her and tiefing from her fruit trees. I blame him for them pelting her and her house. For all the jokes and horror stories. I still didn't know what his real connection to her was, yet if anybody could have helped her it was he. That is why I wanted to come face to face with her. I wanted to go up there, to meet her and apologize for him and say that even though he was my father I wasn't a coward like him and that I would take care of her."

I thought of Otoh walking beside his father, lovingly clutching the old man's arm as they approached Miss Ramchandin. I was filled with a new admiration for Otoh. I thought him daring to want to search inside the cavernous areas of his soul and to speak out loud his feelings toward his father. I do not believe he feigned affection for his father: his love was deep and genuine, and perhaps that is why he was so tormented.

Then I thought of Asha.

"Do you know anything about her sister?" I asked.

"She had a sister? I never knew that." Otoh was oddly unmoved by the news.

"Asha. Her name was Asha. She left home in her teens. Your Pappy would know her. Do something for me, Otoh, please. Could you ask him about her. About Asha Ramchandin? Whatever happened to her, please?"

He squeezed my hand, nodded and then returned to his preoccupation.

"It's as if I wanted to redeem my father's name, to rescue her and be the Romeo he never was. It's a funny thing, yes, but I was never so protective to my own mammy."

It was the most he had ever spoken on the subject. The fear of discovering his anger toward his father made his body shake.

In spite of what Otoh thought of his father, I myself was partial to him. The old man was delightfully indiscreet.

"Mr. Tyler appears to be painting his face more diligently as time goes by," I heard him whisper — albeit loudly — to Otoh. "My boy, I think Mr. Tyler fancies you, wouldn't you agree?"

Then he whispered much more softly, "He is a Mr., isn't he?"

Mala Ramchandin, as usual, did not talk in public. She made gurgling sounds. It was unclear to the Mohanty gentlemen whether she really knew or cared that they visited. When I assured them that on days they did not visit Miss Mala was noticeably irritable, the lovely old gentleman winked slyly at his son. "I would wager that it is not Mala who gets irritable when we don't visit!" he declared. I blushed even as I pretended not to hear. I could sense that Otoh was delighted, even though he feigned irritation and said, "Shhh, Pappy! Shhh!"

"Why should I shhh? I am an expert in the field of passivity," chuckled Mr. Mohanty.

Another time while sitting on the bench next to Miss Ramchandin, he squinted at Otoh and me and said amicably, as though talking about nothing more than fishing, "I know what I am saying: don't let a good one get away, is what I say."

How can I possibly condemn him for the sluggishness of character that has so saddened his son?

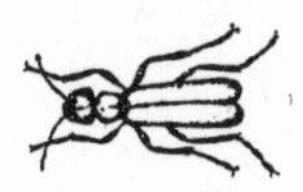

MALA SAW SOMETHING crawling on her verandah. She had never seen such a thing before. She got down on her hands and knees and crawled alongside the iridescent, winged and multi-legged creature.

In the phase just before Mala stopped using words, lexically shaped thoughts would sprawl across her mind, fractured here and there. The cracks would be filled with images. Soon the inverse happened. A sentence would be constructed primarily of images punctuated by only one or two verbalizations: a noun tentatively uttered in recognition, a descriptive word confirming a feeling or observation. A flock of seagulls squawking overhead might elicit a single word, *pretty.* That verbalization, she came to understand, was not the feeling itself but a name given to the feeling: *pretty,* an unnecessary translation of the delight she experienced seeing the soaring birds. Eventually Mala all but rid herself of words. The wings of a gull flapping through the air titillated her soul and awakened her toes and knobby knees, the palms of her withered hands, deep inside her womb, her vagina, lungs, stomach and heart. Every muscle of her body swelled, tingled, cringed or went numb in response to her surroundings — every fibre was sensitized in a way that words were unable to match or enhance. Mala responded to those receptors, flowing with them effortlessly, like water making its way along a path.

Many of her sounds were natural expansions and contractions of her body. She grunted when lifting something heavy. She dredged and expelled phlegm. She sighed melodiously. Cried and belched unabashedly. She coughed and sneezed and spat and wiped away mucus with no care for social graces. She laughed, sometimes as quietly as a battimamselle flapping its wing tips against water in an old drum, or as raucously as a parrot imitating her imitating it. She farted at will, for there was no one around to contradict her.

There was a time when Mala would hum two-note and three-note melodies. The number of notes soon decreased and she settled into a monotone whose pitch varied, harmonizing with whichever insects' shrills prevailed on a particular day. She started cooing, rasping, gargling — the sounds made by the pigeons on her roof.

She did not ascribe activities to specific times. When doziness pawed at her, she responded regardless of the time of day or night, curling up in the yard or on the verandah. If she awakened in the height of the night's darkness, she did not force herself back to sleep but arose as though it were daytime. She fed herself when she needed to, voided when and where the impulse knocked. She manoeuvered her half-acre world intuitively, withdrawing, smiling, laughing, fighting, crying, sulking.

Mala's companions were the garden's birds, insects, snails and reptiles. She and they and the abundant foliage gossiped among themselves. She listened intently. With an ear pressed to the ground she heard ant communities building, transporting food and breeding. She listened to worms coiling arduously from place to place. She knelt on the ground and whispered to the grass and other young plants, encouraging them to grow, and then she listened as they stretched up to her. She did not intervene in nature's business. When it came time for one creature to succumb to another, she retreated. Flora and fauna left her to her own devices and in return she left them to theirs.

At first Aves, Hexapoda, Gastropoda and Reptilia burrowed instinctively into nooks and crevices. They realized eventually that they had no cause to hide. Mala permitted them to roam boldly and to multiply at leisure throughout her property. She provided them one service. Every season she rummaged through the yard for carcasses of those fallen prey to natural causes and, with ritual grace, she facilitated an honourable disposal.

She noted the position of the sun. When it reached a particular spot on the horizon she would finish her collecting for the season. Before that day, she routinely descended the back stairs with a bucket in one hand. One morning she came upon a shiny honey-brown beetle. Her heart soared and she reached into the pocket of her flower-print dress for the item she had once called *tweezers.* Before she made it to the foot of the stairs she had plucked carcasses of a bachac, a spinner ant, two red ants and a black-red cockroach as long as her thumb. She placed them gingerly in the bucket. By the time she had picked every visible corpse off her property, the heap included ants, beetles and cockroaches, different kinds of spiders, some bees, flies, a wasp, two fetid lizard skins and the brittle remains of their skeletons, six butterflies, a stick insect the length of her forearm, two dragonflies, a handful of crickets and other creatures that in the world of naming remain untitled. The collection measured a full hand deep. She paid no attention to the odour rising out of the bucket. The scent of decay was not offensive to her. It was the aroma of life refusing to end. It was the aroma of transformation. Such odour was proof that nothing truly ended, and she revelled in it as much as she did the fragrance of cereus blossoms along the back wall of the house.

Separating the kitchen from the rest of the house was a partition she had built of furniture piled several feet thick. The network of armchairs, rockers, side tables, dining table and high-back chairs was locked together by the ramming and jamming of protruding limbs into each other and age-old cobweb threads. The whole thing smelled of time and dirt. The individual shapes of the furniture were all but obliterated by the density of dust. The wall was so precariously balanced that no one but Mala could have detected the precisely obscured entrance.

She lifted away an old web and tugged at the legs of a straight-back chair. She slid that out first and then a hat rack. Next came a tall, ebony pedestal that she jiggled and pulled to unlink its long legs from the filigreed brass panel on a side table. Finally, she shoved a caned footstool forward, excavating a narrow passageway to the other side. She tucked her bucket against her body. Only one as nimble as Mala could have shimmied through such an opening without bringing the whole arrangement down.

On the other side of the furniture blockade was a spacious room that had once served as drawing room and dining room. The space was now empty. All that remained was a cut-glass chandelier. Disturbing not a speck of dust more than necessary, Mala stepped into old footprints that she had previously left in the carpet and headed to a bolted doorway.

Holding the bucket in one hand, she used the other to unpin an iron key from the hem of her petticoat. She struggled briefly with the old lock and then the lopsided door scraped open. Mala reached into the darkness behind the door for a hurricane lantern. With the unlit lantern she descended the darkened stairway.

At the foot of the stairs was another door. She hung the lantern on the doorknob, reached up and extracted a key from a dusty wooden ledge. She unlocked and opened the door. Mala greeted the stink of decomposition in the room with aristocratic grace, her head and the unlit lantern held high. She set the lantern down on a table.

She was delighted with her timing. Termites had gnawed at a board barring the window and sunlight beamed through, throwing a brilliant gash on the opposite wall and illuminating the insects that were pinned there. Mala walked along the wall, negotiating webs and nests, pinning her new cache to the remaining spaces. The insects that had fallen crunched beneath her bare feet. They were fodder for a vibrating carpet of moths, centipedes, millipedes, cockroaches and unnamed insects that found refuge in Mala's surroundings. Death feeding life.

The tenor of the vibration shifted as she passed. Those with wings fluttered. Those with legs crawled. Those on their bellies slithered a pace or two away. Mala finished her task just as the light was sucked back out through the chink in the board. She picked up the lantern and bucket and retraced her steps, taking special care to lock both doors behind her.

In the former drawing room she planted her feet carefully in the dusty footsteps and walked, backwards, to the hole in the furniture wall.

She enjoyed the smell of rotting, water-logged wood. It had been at least a decade since the eaves trough came away from the roof over the back stairs. Rain now cascaded onto the stairs and the top steps were coated in a dangerous green and black slime, especially thick in each depression at the centre. Holding the slippery banister with one hand, Mala pulled her skirt up and spread her feet to avoid the slimiest areas. At the bottom of the stairs, standing on a concrete slab that had risen out of the washed-away dirt, she scooped rainwater out of a barrel and splashed her feet clean. Before her was the wall of climbing cereus, foliage scaly with age and striped with the mucous trails of buff-periwinkles. The succulents, half a dozen plants in all, had raged over the side of the house, further concealing the boarded-up window of the room downstairs. Scattered over the network of spiny, three-sided stems and fleshy leaves were countless buds, each larger than her fist. The sight of the buds made her giddy. She so looked forward to the night of their opening that she decided not to sit idly and wait but to enjoy every moment until then.

Upstairs on the back porch, sitting low on a peerah, she completed her preparation. On a slab of stone she ground a handful of peppers. The large, concave rock turned brilliant red. The lining of her nostrils became raw and singed and she squinted her eyes against tears. Mala scraped the slab clean with a flat stick and pushed the pepper sludge into a glass jar. She continued grinding handfuls of peppers, throwing her head back as the burning increased, her eyes mostly closed now. The jar was soon two-thirds full. Sweat ran down her face. She cleaned the stick on the banister, leaving a coating of seeds and red flesh behind for the pigeons.

On the stone slab she chopped limes into eighths. She topped the jar with the fruit and juice, and then held it up, tightly covered, to the blue light of the sky. Mala exulted in the medley of colours she had composed. She placed the jar at one end of the porch in a bleached area that received sun most of the day. There the jar would sit, for weeks, until it was well fermented.

It stopped raining long before the sun came up that morning. The dripping continued off the leaves, off the stairs, off the roof. Run-off in the back drain, frightening at times, sounded as though it would rise and spill into the yard. And rising from the soggy earth was a brown, ammoniac smell.

During the dry season, the hour of ten o'clock in the morning came and went without her taking notice. But in the rainy season that same hour was unbearable. The elements seemed to pull together in perfect imitation of another moment, long ago, just after a heavy rainfall.

It was the light. It was the blueness of the sky. It was the colour in the trees and shrubs in the yard. The dankness of the house. Everything so opaquely saturated with moisture that the sun couldn't shine strongly enough to soak it up. The time of day would come upon her and deafen her with the noise of insects screaming, *Pohpoh, Pohpoh, I want Pohpoh.* Insects spawning in pools of water, their drones shouting, *Sarah!* The suffocating pervasiveness of stagnant water.

At ten o'clock in the morning Mala knew the sun would catch on a jagged edge of the back porch roof where the iron was torn. The spot would dazzle white like a blinding star. A beam of silver light would pierce the hole in the roof, targeting the porch floor.

Time would collapse. Every inhaled breath was a panicked tremble sustained and each exhale a heavy sob. In anguish Mala would clutch her blouse, petticoat, handkerchief into a ball in front of her breast, her harried breathing punctuated with fits and spasms. Her skin and bones, especially her upper arms and the back of her neck, would become chilled, unable to dry out or warm up.

One such morning, a good hour before ten o'clock, she began strategizing against it. She armed herself with a bottle of bird-pepper sauce and a spoon, and lay down on the bare floor of the porch. The sun had begun its ascent to its highest point. All around her the quality of light signalled the approaching collision of sun and roof. Lying on the floor, looking up at the crack in the roof, she breathed slowly. For a while, staring up at the slit, all she saw was sky in various shades of hypnotic blue. Gradually the slit darkened. The edges turned harsh silver. Mala sat up. Her heart began to gallop, the beat crescendoing in her temples.

She opened the bottle. She raised it toward her nostrils and tentatively sniffed the flaming red sauce. The pungency, cultivated by the sunshine on the porch, startled her. She tried to stay calm but her pounding heart made her breathless. She closed her eyes and inhaled deeply from the bottle, feeling the flames leap out at her upper lip and lap into her nose. She opened her eyes just in time to see the jagged piece of galvanized iron ignite like a brilliant sparkler. The cacophony in her head resounded. Insects shrieked. *Mammy. Asha. Pohpoh. Lavinia.* The rumbling of a buggy.

A shaft of harsh light poured through the gash in the roof. Crickets began to screech, the running water grew torrentially loud. Mala shook her head. A wave of nausea washed over her. She raised the bottle to her face, shoved the open rim against her face, her nose deep inside, a wet, red ring imprinting across her nose, cheeks and lips. Her tear-filled eyes fluttered but she fought the exhaustion. Her sinuses released a flood against the fire trying to break through.

The shaft of light had grown so strong it blinded her. Her body suddenly, fitfully fastened itself to the ground. Her arms and back became cold. With effort she lifted herself off the ground, pulled in her chest and thrust her shoulders forward. She cried out the only words she had spoken in ages. "Oh God. I beg you. Please. Doh leave me, I beg you, oh God, oh God, doh leave me, I beggin you. Take me with you." The pigeons on the roof hopped around frantically.

Mala looked down at the cerise blossoms of the pomerac tree and braced herself. She thrust her finger into the bottle, scooped out a heavy clump of raw pepper and shoved the finger into her mouth. She scooped up more and then more, wiping her finger on the sensitive tip of her tongue, and then again, scooping more, shovelling it into her mouth. The skin underneath her fingernail tingled. She didn't swallow, keeping the fire on her tongue, by then so blistered that parts of the top layer had already disintegrated and other areas had curled back like rose petals dipped in acid. She pressed her tongue against the roof of her mouth, dispersing the slush to the tender pink flesh on the sides and under her tongue. The roof of her mouth bubbled. Pepper mush oozed out past her clenched gums and spilled into the sides of her cheeks. She gasped for air. A torrent of sweat washed her continuously, her body trying desperately to cool itself.

An eruption of pain spread into her ears. A thousand bells clanged. Then all sound stopped. She squeezed her eyes tight and stomped her feet. She couldn't feel her legs or the ground beneath her feet yet she pounded the floor and beat the wall. She heaved, trying to find cooling air but the air entering her mouth sent her lacerated flesh into further agony. A tide of peppery saliva cascaded over her lips. She ran to the balcony and spat, salivating and expelling sauce and pepper flesh and seeds. She waved her grotesquely enlarged tongue in the air but this brought little relief. Exhausted and dizzy from breathing so rapidly she collapsed on the balcony floor. Glancing up, she noticed the light had changed. There was no trace of the silver beam.

The cerise blossoms of pomerac swayed in the breeze. She shut her eyes and listened. The pigeons had calmed down, their feet scratching faintly against the galvanized iron. Mala's mouth remained open, her lower jaw dropped partly in exhaustion, partly to release heat and let air in. Her flesh had come undone. But every tingling blister and eruption in her mouth and lips was a welcome sign that she had survived.

She was alive.

IT WAS ONE of the brightest moonlit nights Mala had ever witnessed. Every evening for the past week she had descended to the cereus patch and checked the state of the buds. Their time had arrived, and the long-awaited event coincided, as she interpreted it, with another blooming, that of the moon. As night fell she dragged her rocking chair down the back stairs and into the yard under the fringes of the giant mudra tree. She sat upright like a concert director in front of the wall. As the night unwound she witnessed the slow dance of huge, white cereus buds — she counted sixty-two — trembling as they unfolded against the wall, a choreography of petal and sepal opening together, sending dizzying scent high and wide into the air. The moonlight reflected off the blossoms' pure whiteness and cast a glow over the yard. Mala basked.

In Lantanacamara when the moon blossoms, so, traditionally, does love. The monthly occasion is anticipated and prepared for even now, and no one, including the older people who tend to stay indoors, wants to be caught without a companion for the evening.

In the week prior to this event Otoh had been visited in his downstairs room in Government Alley by at least one young woman a day inviting him to the moonlight stroll in the lovers' garden. He turned all offers down because he had a mission of his own. As the days passed, however, he worried his suitors would see him outside that evening and take offence that they were not good enough. After tortuous deliberations he decided to accept the first suitor's invitation.

He was so preoccupied by Mala that he had forgotten his suitor's name and had to check his diary. It had always been this way for Otoh. Unlike the other men in the village, and much to their envy, he had long been the object of desire of almost every Lantanacamaran woman, regardless of her age. (It is also noteworthy that a number of men were shocked and annoyed by their own naggingly lascivious thoughts of him.)

Mala heard the footsteps of people ambling down the road. She knew that when the footsteps slowed it was because someone was sniffing the heady perfume. It was a change from the odour of age, filth and rot that normally permeated her yard.

On this cool bright night Otoh strolled arm in arm with the elegant Mavis. At the front of Mala's house, mesmerized by the smell, his companion, thankfully, was curious. The pair stopped to see what it was that so perfumed the entire neighbourhood. The air was full of bats swooping and swishing, diving and darting. Otoh and Mavis ducked to avoid the ugly creatures. He was still shaken from the scare on the night when he tried to enter Mala's yard but in the company of another he found the courage to approach the fence.

He tiptoed close to the wire, bent down and looked for a crack in the foliage. Peering intently into the bushes he momentarily forgot his companion. He was convinced that Mala would show herself to him again. Mavis disturbed his concentration with a polite tug on his arm.

"Come, Otoh, boy. Look how many people going up to the park. If we don't hurry we won't find a nice place to sit and enjoy the evening, you know. Come, na?"

"Right," said Otoh limply.

A scented breeze came gushing through the bushes and whipped itself around Otoh, nabbing him like a lasso. Taken aback, he closed his eyes and breathed in slowly and deeply. He took Mavis' arm and pulled her to a stop.

"Mavis, the park will be full by now. Look, I know another place, a better place. Come with me."

"What you mean another place? Is moonlight night. El Dorado Park is the place to go."

"Smell the air, Mavis. That park never smells so good. You don't want to see what flower could make such a scent? This could be our moonlight adventure . . ."

"But Germaine and Pauline and Radha and everybody else going to the love garden in El Dorado Park . . ."

"If we go to the back of this yard we would get a good view of the blossoms and be able to smell them better. Come tomorrow, you could tell them about our unusual adventure. I know how to get up into the yard. Come with me, na."

"Otoh Mohanty, you are adventure enough, yes boy!" said Mavis, shoving her arm under his. "It smelling good, is true, but I don't too much consider *that* yard to be romantic. Is moonlight night, boy! You really adventurous, yes, but come let me teach you about romantic."

She whispered the word, drawing it out reverently. She gripped him close to her and ushered him onward. Mavis, given to babbling and convinced that Otoh knew Mala's yard through involvements similar to her own, began to babble.

"Otoh boy, you know what we used to do when we was children? You remember Jason and Jacob? They married now, you know. Well, the three of we and some other children used to climb this fence and go and tief whatever was in season and come back out, suck the meat of the seed dry-dry and then the fellas them used to pelt the house with the seed to try to get the old lady —"

"Mala. You mean Mala."

"Yes, she self, to try and get she to show she self. I remember them even using stone to pelt at the house, yes. Ey. But when I think about it now, them boys was bad, yes. But they grow up good and the two of them married as I say just now. Mammy hoping I would marry soon too, you know."

Otoh did not respond. "You know, now I remember," she continued. "Sometimes when the fellas and Jason and Jacob used stones, windows did break, yes."

Noticing his unresponsiveness, Mavis became pensive. She hadn't thought of these childhood escapades in years, and hardly anyone in the neighbourhood, she realized, made mention of Mala any more.

Otoh was amazed at how stealthily, like an insidious, long drizzle, his sadness had turned to drenching anger. Forever a gentleman, he checked his reaction and managed, with only a margin of hesitation, to pull her closer, a gesture intended to comfort him more than her. Why had he never engaged in such callousness when he was a child? he wondered. Out loud he assured her that such actions were the natural stuff of childhood. Assuming that his voice had deepened in anticipation of their arrival at the lovers' garden, Mavis pressed her cheek against his chest and smelled his gentle body odour, highly unusual and so very welcoming from a man. Otoh released her and leaned toward the misshapen fence. He wanted so dearly to see Mala that he believed that any second now he would catch a glimpse.

His companion, now impatient, tried again to coax him up the hill with a little teasing. Otoh reluctantly followed. On the way to the garden he was untalkative. And Mavis, sensing the evening might come to an abrupt end, held her tongue. Otoh let go of her hand and clasped his behind his back.

Behind them pairs of lovers strolled by on their way to the garden. Inspired by the dizzying scent of cereus they were compelled to stop in front of Mala's house to caress and steal probing kisses.

Close to midnight the buds had opened fully. They intensified their scent, steadily pumping it into the air, an urgent call to insects and bats to find and pollinate the flowers. One by one the moths came. They slid from cracks in the walls of Mala's house. They bored through and wriggled out from every moth-ridden enclave in the neighbourhood. They unbound themselves from sticky webs nestled in dents of rocks and from cocoons that dangled from leaves. They migrated in swarms from the lime tree in her yard to the wall of expectant cereus. The arrival of thousands of moths, already drunk from the smell alone, held Mala spellbound. The sound of a thousand pairs of flapping wings drowned out the screaming crickets and created a draft. Mala rubbed her arms for warmth. Crazed bats swooped by, crisscrossing each other's flight en route to suckle the blossoms. They disturbed the swarms of frantic moths. They brushed their hairy bodies against the blossoms to sample the syrupy, perfumed juices. Then, thirst and curiosity satisfied, they darted off. By two o'clock in the morning, every moth was thirstily lapping sweet nectar, bruising and yellowing its body against the large stamens that waved from the flowers.

The smell in Mala's yard drenched the air and flowed across town. Neighbours in deep sleep stirred, suddenly restless. Some were pried wide awake but were soon pleasantly besotted by the perfume and swept back into deep sleep.

The moon lifted higher. Mala herself felt intoxicated and finally, deliriously tired. She must have dozed off because suddenly there was only a handful of moths lilting heavily and precariously in flight. She hadn't noticed the swarm leaving. She slumped in her chair. The scent was indeed more pleasant than the stink that usually rose from behind the wall.

FROM THE MOMENT his companion admitted she had tormented Mala, Otoh found himself awkwardly distanced from her. Not wanting to upset her, he allowed her to return to his bedroom in Government Alley. Mavis immediately lay on the bed. She might as well have been alone, though, because he seemed oblivious to her. Throughout the night she cooed at him. She tried tossing and turning with much drama, hoping he would hold her to calm her. It was futile. When he did not respond she became more direct. Mavis reached for him, caressing his belly, chest and shoulders, and, through his shirt, his nipples. They hardened and she coaxed off his shirt. When she began to work on the belt of his trousers, he became aware of her in his bed again, and he rolled over and feigned deathly exhaustion. She sulked long and loud and then, resigned, dozed off. When he heard her steady breathing, Otoh turned over and lay on his back wide awake.

He was still full of the night's perfume. What was it about Mala, he wanted to know, that his father so utterly adored? Had she rejected his father and if so, why? He suddenly wondered if Mala would reject him if they were to meet. Perhaps he might be able to hold her attention in a way his father had been unable to. It was still dark. Above him in the kitchen his mother, fully awake, paced with a studied shuffle that by now had become an integral sound in his family's house. Cocks in the distance were just beginning their hesitant pre-dawn crowing. Otoh drifted in and out of sleep.

Mala faced her wall of faded cereus blossoms. She was content. Oblivious to the dew that drizzled from the mudra, she rocked and dozed lightly. Scent, as though too shy for light, no longer trickled from the blossoms but Mala was not yet ready to leave the yard. Her eyes would flicker open and catch a glimpse of the day that was beginning to split the black sky apart. In that first orange light the flowers hung limp, battered and bruised, each one worn out from the frenzied carnival of moths.

Mala refused to sleep.

Otoh awakened to a stillness in his sun-heated room. His companion was no longer with him. In the unanchored moments between sleeping and awakening, ideas came with unshakable conviction. One such idea was an image of how his father might have appeared as a dapper, young man on his way to court his lady.

Several years earlier Otoh's mother had packed up two boxes of clothing and other miscellany, including a damaged gramophone and some recording disks — things that a man who was awake for only one day a month would hardly require. She was reluctant to do away with the boxes. This would have been akin to giving up hope that her husband would resume a day-to-day existence, so she stored them for safe-keeping in Otoh's room.

Otoh had the gramophone repaired and for a while he played the recordings constantly. Since then he had paid only scant attention to the dust-covered boxes, the tops of which were resting places for his shoes.

He got up now and opened the boxes, pulling out a few items of clothing, the gramophone and records.

Otoh A. Mohanty dressed himself in front of the mirror on the door of his armoire. There was no question in his mind this morning that he would not be wearing one of his mother's dresses to make the monthly delivery. He dressed instead in the heavy, black, pleated dress pants of his father. They fit him as though they had been custom tailored. He angled himself in front of the mirror and, with both hands in the pockets of the slacks, widened his stance, rhythmically rocking back and forth. He looked at his slender three-quarter profile, tilted his head downward, squinted and thrust his jaw forward to give a sculpted line to his soft face. He puffed his chest and lowered his shoulders to turn his torso into plates of muscle. He ran his palms across his two tight, little nipples. He held the nipples between his fingers, squeezed and rubbed them until they puckered into little squares, trying to imagine what Mavis might have felt when she lay next to him and touched his shirtless body. He was grateful for such small breasts. As long as his tightly belted trousers were never removed he had nothing to worry about.

He pulled on a dress shirt made of fine Irish linen. From years of storage the shirt was no longer white but unevenly cream-coloured. Fastening the long row of pearly buttons he wondered on what occasion his father might have worn such a shirt. Buttoned all the way up to his neck it hugged his body and showed off his leanness. He took a red, white and black-striped silk tie and knotted it loosely around his neck. Next, a black jacket and fedora. He posed. In all this black he might have passed for a pallbearer if it weren't for his colourful necktie and elegant posture. In his father's get-up, Otoh looked more like a dancer.

Closing his eyes and tucking in his lips Otoh shook a few drops of sweet-lime *3333* after-shave cologne from its bottle. Having nothing on his face to shave, he used the cologne entirely for its smell. The toiletry reminded him of the compelling perfume of blossoms that had filled the air around Mala's yard the previous night. This morning he would find out what flower turned the air so sweet and take a clipping of that plant, even if it meant entering her yard.

Anxious to meet the woman who controlled the lives of both his parents, he forgot to match his footwear to his clothing. Otoh still wore his red rubber thongs, which exposed the pink edges of his soles.

LONG INTO THE morning Mala remained in the yard. The sun had warmed her arms and legs, chilled through the night. Every so often a breeze nudged her rocking chair. She kept her eyes closed. Fortified by the night's display she wove memories. She remembered a little and imagined a great deal . . .

Pohpoh's shivering was not a response to the cool night air. No blanket of any thickness could have warmed or calmed her. Any weight, even that of a thin sheet on her body, would have stifled her. She stared wide eyed in the direction of the pomerac branches swaying in the night wind outside the window at the foot of her bed. She had to fight the temptation to indulge in yearning—yearning to have her mother back next to her, to feel her mother hugging her against her breasts with one hand resting on wet cheeks, absorbing Pohpoh's tears. But if she did not stay strong, if she succumbed to her longings, she would not be able to look after Asha. It had become Pohpoh's mission from the first day her father put his mouth on her little body to prevent Asha from experiencing the pain of his touch. For the most part she had succeeded. Her stone-blank eyes concentrated on the blackness of the night outside her window.

Mala wished that she could go back in time and be a friend to this Pohpoh. She would storm into the house and, with one flick of her wrist, banish the father into a pit of pain and suffering from which there would be no escape. With piercing eyes she would pull the walls of that house down, down, down, and she would gather the two children to her breast and hug them tightly, rock and quiet them, and kiss their faces until they giggled wildly.

Except for a silver-edged harshness there was not the slightest suggestion of emotion on Pohpoh's face. In the corners of her eyes, however, a saline spring slowly welled up and bubbled out. The tears fell in spite of her stoniness.

She lay still, waiting for anything that might be a cue. It arrived after some moments of prickly silence. The pomerac tree swayed and rocked in the wind, washing like the ocean across her body, a roar so encompassing it seemed to absorb every other sound. Commanded by the tree's creaking in the wind she mechanically rose from her bed. Her body had so stiffened she had to make a conscious effort to loosen it with long, slow breaths.

On relaxing she was overcome by the rage that seeped into her veins. At times like these she felt inflamed to the point of wanting to tear and scream into her father's room, of screeching so piercingly that she disabled him, of punching him in his stomach over and over until he cried like a baby, admitted how loathesome he had been and begged hers and Asha's forgiveness. But at such times her rage was usually muffled by a sudden injection of good sense. The success of an adventure like the one she was embarking upon depended on the control of all her faculties. Anger, hatred and even fear could very easily trip her up. Pohpoh worked on finding that perfect balance between being rigidly alert and dangerously relaxed.

She covered herself with her darkest clothing, olive-green trousers and a dark brown vest. She glanced over at Asha, who slept on her back with her arms stiffly at her sides. She looked like a corpse. Mala listened and heard her father's snoring. Asha was safe. She pocketed her silver stopwatch and after a farewell glance back at Asha, exited barefoot through the window as effortlessly as a moth.

WHAT IS IT about you today that seems so familiar, my son?"

"What exactly you mean, Pappy? As far as Mammy is concerned, I am your son. And unless your memory is on its way out, you are right, we have seen each other before."

Ambrose E. Mohanty chuckled. "No, no, no! One might call you impertinent but charming is more apt a description I am sure. I mean that you seem to be a reincarnation of a past familiarity."

Elsie Mohanty shook her head and snapped, "For the love of Jesus Christ in heaven, speak plain words, na, man!" She too was taken aback by her son's choice of attire on this once-a-month morning but she sensed that, as usual, she should probably not ask too many questions in case she received answers she didn't want. "Look here! Even with red 'kerchief tie up round his neck he look like he going to funeral," she muttered.

Otoh rested a sack of rice, a bottle of coconut oil and two bottles of sweet drink by the door. Wheeling his father out to the porch he had a sensation of being both mother and father to his own pappy. He patted Ambrose's head affectionately, rubbed his cheek and ran a hand under his chin. He almost wanted to say out loud the thought that played in his head like a mantra: "I'll win her back for you, Pappy. You just have to know how to do it." But he stopped himself because deeper than this thought was one less benevolent that said, "How could you not have looked after her?"

Before Otoh turned to go his father whispered, "I remember now, son. You are indeed a reincarnation but not of a person per se, merely of a forgotten memory. You are a perfect replica of me in my prime. I have never seen you look so stunningly like myself before." Then he pulled Otoh close and lowered his voice further. "If I am not mistaken, you are wearing my clothing."

Otoh began to apologize.

"Shhh. I am only too pleased," Ambrose interrupted, "for by appearing in front of me like this you have given me the gift of remembering. I am sure I cannot thank you enough. You are wearing the very same clothing I wore whenever I visited my dearest Mala. We used to dance together. She and I. Did I ever tell you? I used to be a very good dancer, you know. Are you a dancer, son? My clothing looks very good on you, but I must say you are so much younger looking and rather more tender than I was in those days."

Otoh blushed.

"If fortune sees fit to grant you the pleasure of an audience with her," Ambrose continued, "may I impose upon you, my treasured son, the honour of conveying to her wishes for an incomparably good day from one Mr. Ambrose Mohanty, also known to her as Boyie?"

Otoh smiled. His father said the same thing every month.

"Mr. Ambrose Mohanty, also known to her as Boyie."

Otoh nodded and smiled again. His father reached up and touched his face, rubbing it more intently than his usual perfunctory father-to-son pat. "Son, perhaps if you were to use a razor on your face, you might encourage the growth of some hair. It is unusual, and not very nice I might add, for a grown man to have such soft and smooth skin." After a heavy pause, he whispered, "Have you a Mala of your own?" Without waiting for an answer he continued. "She was quite a dancer too, you know, and she dressed so beautifully, always in the same simple dress, but, oh, so beautifully. We used to dance together." His voice trailed off.

Otoh squeezed his shoulders, remaining quietly with him for a while longer and then left. On his way out his mother shoved a biscuit tin full of coconut drops against his stomach. She had baked them yesterday along with other savory and sweet dishes in preparation for her husband's awakening.

"Your father think I don't know. I hear how he used to dress up and go and visit she when he was young. And that he and she used to be dancing up, dancing wild-wild in the house up there. I even hear he and she used to go to a dance club in town. He ever take me anywhere? How many years now we married and I ent leave the house? That woman loose too bad, yes! I should be so wild and loose! If I had wild blood in me and I was loose, he wouldn't now be sleeping-sleeping so.

"And you self! Listen to me, Otoh, it is morning. It don't have no dance happening this morning. What you dress up so for? You go and make death restless dress like that today, and it will be on your head for you to deal with, you hear!"

Otoh made his way down the stairs quickly. Before heading out he stopped in his room to pick up the portable gramophone and one of the recording disks.

HER ROUTE HAD been calculated long before Pohpoh jumped out the window, an effortless leap to the moist grass below. She had never yet hurt herself, perhaps because on such nights she tended not to feel much of anything.

With catlike sure-footedness she made her way to the edge of the garden. A small wind rustled the neighbourhood's shrubs and trees, masking her sounds. She parted a break in the hibiscus and the wire fence and crawled out to the grassy sidewalk. Dew from the shrub hedge drizzled over her clothing and hair but she was so tense she was unaware of the wetness or the cold night air that crept under her vest and clung to her skin.

Pohpoh paused. The ditch running down the side of the fence provided enough of a gurgling to cover the sound of her steps. Up above, dark clouds raced each other and were soon blown far away, leaving the sky crisply cold and clean. There was no moon, making for a perfectly pitch-black night, the kind that permitted Pohpoh to roam without concealing herself in shadows. On the outermost edges of the sky was a display of suspended stars that made the heavens twinkle and shimmer.

Like a crane pondering flight Pohpoh stooped low on one leg, the other bent at the knee. In gracefully flowing motion she lifted her arms, ready to shield her chest should it need protecting. She spun around, her eyes searchlights surveying the quiet street and the neighbours' yards. She did not look back at her own. Only a sharp breeze here and there stirred. Occasionally a dog's whimper sliced through the background pulsing of crickets and hiccuping of frogs. Pohpoh thrust her jaw forward and, like a cautious night animal, bounded across the road.

A lantern always glowed in the front hall of the house opposite her father's. She knew the yard well. The guard dog, a plump boxer named Tail, knew her too. Tail heard Pohpoh scuffling in the ditch and, curious, sniffed his way over to the fence. He began jumping against the wire, growling, scratching up the garden soil and barking, igniting the other dogs in the neighbourhood. Every dog for miles around seemed to have been awakened and Pohpoh's disappointment changed to fear. She knew better than to try to calm Tail. She leapt up the ditch, slipped on the mossy side and landed face down in a tall grass bush. This would be a good place for her to burrow for safekeeping. She squeezed her eyes shut and prayed that if she were perfectly still Tail would lose interest. She tightened the muscles between her thighs against an urge to pee. She heard people swearing at their dogs to be quiet, and then front doors slamming shut. The pulse in her temples thumped with an exhilaration she loved, and she grinned in triumph. Pohpoh waited another few minutes until she was confident the neighbours had gone back to bed.

Her eyes had learned to see so well in this outdoor darkness that she picked out a dead and perfectly intact harlequin bug lying in the grass. She lifted, sniffed and pocketed it.

When she was again able to hear the crickets and frogs, she

pulled her trousers down, avoiding crushing her little find, and relieved herself in the cold air.

TLIP-TLAP TLIP-TLAP TLIP-TLAP. With every step Otoh's rubber thongs slapped the road. Cars went by, each driver slowing to look at him, curious as to why in a town the size of theirs they had not heard about the event that would warrant the wearing of a suit. One car pulled over, keeping pace with him. The driver, an out-of-towner who regularly visited for some unknown reason, leaned out of the window and chatted him up. He had admired Otoh from afar. Seeing him today dressed so beautifully, sauntering up the road with unsurpassed grace in spite of the hot sun, an untidy load in his arms, the stranger had a reason to accost him.

"Psssst! Young man, where you going? You want a ride?"

"Not far," said Otoh, "but thank you all the same."

But his voice, unusually silky for a man's, intrigued the out-of-towner more. Shaded by the brim of his fedora, Otoh's black eyes and long, full eyelashes made the man even more desirous. Flattered by the attention, Otoh was both amused and bewildered at how much the man assumed.

"Don't be so shy, na. I might be going your way. As a matter of fact, I will even go out of my way — for you — and take you right where you going. But, look at that load you carrying in the hot sun, na. It must be heavy for so. What you say?"

Otoh grinned. "No. Really. Thank you. I going to see a friend and is better I take my time and walk there."

"Who is this lucky friend you dress up nice-nice so, goin' to see? Tell me, na? Why she — is a she you going to see or is a he? don't mind me asking, you know. Why she so lucky and not me? A nice fella like you need a friend to show you the ropes. Let me give you a ride, na? Is a gramophone you have there? You like to dance?"

"But you does ask a lot of questions," laughed Otoh. "Really, I don't need a ride, thank you kindly. I don't have far to go. And is a lady friend I going to visit."

"Oh. Well, let me take you by she. You could make your visit and I go wait for you. Then you could come back with me. You didn't answer. You like dancing? Because I —"

"No, thank you again. I spending the morning with she."

"Okay, spend the morning and I'll come and meet you back by noon. Then we could set up the gramophone. What you say?"

The proposition amused Otoh. He enjoyed the flirtation and was reluctant to end it. But since there was no point in carrying on in this vein, he dribbled water on the desires of the amorous out-of-towner.

"You are very kind, but I am not sure how long this will take. You see, you could say that I am courting her."

"Oh, you courting her. You? You courting a woman! I see. Is a lady you courting, eh. Uhuh. Well, I better not keep you back, because I have to go and meet my wife to take she to matinee. And my children coming with us too. What I was asking you was to come to the pictures with my family. You understand, na."

The man drove off, his brick-red face sweaty. Otoh smiled and picked up his pace.

He had decided that his delivery that day would be made at the front gate. On arrival he used the top of the biscuit tin to check his hair and scarf. He pushed the gate, expecting it to open. Instead the entire fence made one long creak, like the sound of a misplayed violin, and lethargically tilted backward. Otoh almost lost his balance and the goods. He looked around. He felt foolish to have damaged the fence when his intention had been to project the epitome of debonair. He would return later or first thing tomorrow and repair it, he promised himself. The only way to enter the front yard now was to hop over the fence.

The yard did not seem cared for. He studied the terrain searching for an easy route to the front door. He spotted a clearing among the brambles and carefully bent over the fence depositing his goods and the gramophone on the other side. Holding the record album, whose sleeve was damp from sweat, he retreated several paces. Sizing up the fence, he took wide strides toward it and leapt over. He landed in the midst of row upon row of shells, some whole but mostly all shattered and partially buried in the hard-packed earth. He tiptoed around the brittle pieces.

On this side of the fence, the world seemed quieter, as though time had slowed down. The soil smelled damp and rich with earthworms. He gathered up his armful of offerings and headed through the break in the brambles. As Otoh went further into the yard, sounds that he took for granted — the pounding of hammers, the swish of cars and barking of dogs — receded. Rather there was the buzzing of insects, the flutter of wings and the sounds of a breeze circulating earthy odours.

Otoh arrived at what were once the front steps. Before him, obscured by overgrowth, were the remnants of an old-fashioned gentility that was unapparent from the roadway. Leading up to the verandah was a wide, flagstone stairway, from whose many cracks pepper and orange trees protruded. The verandah's banister was of simple wooden posts, many missing or about to fall. Looking up, he saw stranglers growing out of the roof, their thick roots clutching the sides of the house.

Otoh wanted to be polite and present himself by knocking at the front door but after negotiating the first, treacherous steps he realized the stairway stood precariously alone, separated several feet from the house. He stepped down and stood awkwardly in the centre of the walkway, wondering whether to advance or retreat. Disappointed but undeterred, Otoh resigned himself to a more pedestrian entrance around the back of the house.

Mala had not had a human visitor in at least a decade. The last ones to enter her yard were not even visitors but vandalizing youngsters who tormented her and her plants so callously she was obliged to chase them out. One time she saw blood spurt from a boy's head when she angrily threw back at him the leather-bound cricket ball that had missed the mango tree he was pelting and had broken her window instead. The last of that kind of problem took place a very long time ago and it no longer occurred to her to watch for trespassers or visitors. It was difficult to remember who her last visitor had been, probably Ambrose, just after he returned from the Shivering Northern Wetlands.

With Otoh so close but unknown to her, Mala returned to her memory...

Finally feeling in control of the night's possibilities, and having relieved herself, Pohpoh relaxed. Even though her eyes had adjusted to the darkness, they were of little use. To negotiate her way Pohpoh had to experience her surroundings, become one with the trees, shrubs, weeds, fences, thorns, water and mossy ground. She stood in the ditch and lifted her hands into the blackness before her, meditatively feeling the shape of the moist air, inspecting and greeting the space. Her heart drummed with excitement.

She was ready for the sprint up the ditch. Her legs spread apart, Pohpoh took a long, slow breath and then, like a soldier running for dear life, bolted up the slope. On either side of the ditch, overhanging foliage and slimy fronds slapped against her body, sending ripples of fear and excitement through her limbs. In seconds she had reached the top and stood among several houses. Her clothes were dew-damp and her teeth shivered, but her mission was of such importance that she could not allow it to be thwarted by mere physical discomfort.

The yard on the left had neither fence nor hedge, just a few unmanageable clumps of razor grass. This yard, she decided, was no challenge for her. All through the bushes a discordant chorus of bullfrogs belted territorial warnings. At such a late hour she was surprised to see a light in a bedroom window of the house. A man passed in front of the window and then back again. She crouched lower, just in case. On the other side of the ditch was a hedge of boundary shrubs, easy to get through but too close to the insomniac.

At the top of the incline lay another backyard as familiar to her as though she had planted it herself and watched it unfold leaf by leaf, insect by insect. Pohpoh felt an uncanny communion with the fruit trees that had sprung up from thoughtlessly spat-out seeds: lime, pomerac, cherry, dongs, orange, two common prickly-mango trees and a fat nutmeg, all conspiring to make the night even darker than it already was. In the pomerac tree slept several fowl. Pohpoh was aware of them yet their snores and ruffles sounded to her as though someone else was also in the yard. She became even more alert. The acidic smell of bird droppings contrasted with a stronger, very sweet odour. Among the bushes was a single cereus plant. Pohpoh saw its large white and crimson flowers, gleaming like stars. With the force that comes from a broken fire hydrant, the cereus blossoms spewed heavy perfume in the air, luring the thousands of moths and flies whizzing by, colliding and humming so loudly that an ominous drone hovered in the air around Pohpoh's face. The air was full of floating moth powder. The scent of the cereus with its two edges — one a vanilla-like sweetness, the other a curdling — so permeated the air that she could taste it on her tongue as though she were lapping it from a bowl.

OTOH AVOIDED BEING clawed by the patch of stinging nettles. He walked toward the back and through the thick grey-blue mudra stilts that propped up the front of the house, and then around a room, positioned like his bedroom, underneath the house. He noticed that, unlike his room in Government Alley, this one had no doorway and would only have been accessible from the top floor of the house. What was once a window was now completely boarded up and covered by a thick plant.

He sniffed, trying to ferret out the scent that had captivated him last night. The sun never shone under here. He came upon dank pools, thick layers of rotten water that had seeped into crevices and settled under thin slabs of broken concrete. A pungent stagnancy rose up in bursts. Otoh held his goods close to his chest and tiptoed, afraid to disturb whatever thrived there.

A handful of steps farther and another perplexing odour washed over Otoh. He gasped on the crest of each wave delivered by the innocent morning breezes wending amid the mudra posts. It appeared to be the full-bodied foulness of an overflowed latrine. From the back fence, far away from the house itself, where he had made deliveries on mornings past, nothing prepared him for such sensory assaults. Certainly his dreams of meeting Mala had been filled with the scent of frilly herbs and potions, potpourri and balms, and nothing so oppressive as what choked him now.

Otoh forgot for a moment his reasons for entering the yard. So appalling was the odour — and thick, like a miasma he had to wade through — he expected to see some kind of spillage. Yet as much as he was repulsed he was again overcome by curiosity. He was also prompted by memories of a similar smell — the memory of an outdoor latrine far behind his grandmother's house, down by the edge of the cane field. He used to think of it as a hut, a hut big enough for only one person at a time.

The putridity under Mala's house, Otoh noticed, was strongest close to the downstairs sewing room. He walked with a measured pace, absorbing every detail of the outer wall of the room before him: decades of dust; clumps of matted cobwebs; old cavities eaten away by wood lice; lazy, unperturbed daddy-longlegs clinging to the siding, motionless; stout cloud-white moths polkadotting the wood; remains of snake eggs, lizard eggs, hatchlings lurking, squirming squishily as they sought the warm sunlight. An old glass aquarium lay on its side.

He made his way from underneath the house. His eyes felt fragile in the sudden brilliance. Warming shivers rippled up and down his arms, and he started to perspire. He lifted an arm and wiped his damp brow and upper lip on his shoulder. Nothing in the yard stirred in the claustrophobic morning heat. There was still no sign of Mala.

Probing farther around the back of the house he gasped when he came upon the wall of cereus blossoms, every one of them completely wilted. He had forgotten about the flowers. Their blooms, brown-splotched by the stinging sun, hung limp. Even so Otoh was amazed at their size. The heads were larger than any flower he had ever seen before, much too heavy for the small, stunted stems from which they dangled. A ghost of scent hovered close to the blossoms, remnants of last night's fullness now souring in the heat. Replacing the perfume was an even more startling one that seemed to emanate from the wall behind the blossoms. The smell, like those under the house, quickly grew nauseating. Within seconds the contents of his stomach rebelled, rising, twisting and turning. The combination of odours and the heat made him dizzy. The stench made him want to drop his package, gramophone and all, clasp his stomach, hold his breath and run as fast as he could back out of the yard. But he was determined not to give up. Otoh scurried like a distressed mouse noisily past the wall. In his haste he raced past Mala, who was sitting under the mudra tree.

And she, totally entranced by her day-dreaming escapade, didn't hear the bees buzzing around her ears or feel them slurping the salty sweat trickling down her neck. Neither did she hear the peekoplats in the mudra tree when they suddenly stopped trying to out-whistle each other and joined forces to warn of Otoh's approach.

He turned to look for the birds. They fluttered and squawked in the uppermost branches of the old mudra tree. Otoh marvelled at the sight of the magnificent mudra, knowing that such a specimen might be seen only in the heart of an old-growth forest on the other side of the island. With its yard-long, bean-like purple pods, the mudra had taken over the side of the yard, completely blocking out the road beyond and glimpses of the town. It took generations for a mudra tree to grow so large. The peekoplats hopped to the edges of the branches and their whistling subsided as though in curious and worried anticipation. Otoh noticed the quiet and looked up to see the tree covered in sleek, brown-grey birds. Never before had he seen this kind of bird in the open. They were usually associated with money, with gambling and singing competitions. Men from Paradise often went into the deep forest and returned with cages crammed with rare peekoplats. A single bird of that species would fetch a large sum of money, an investment paid out willingly in the hopes of higher earnings and prestige in singing competitions. Otoh was astonished that in his own neighbourhood, unknown to catchers and gamblers, there existed a tree laden with hundreds of peekoplats. He suddenly felt himself a trespasser, an awkward voyeur. Surprised that in all his deliveries he had never seen the huge tree, he looked around, trying to locate the back fence.

He came to an abrupt halt. Right there, directly in front of him, was the reason he had come. Mala Ramchandin. She sat in a rocking chair beside the tree, her eyes closed. Her figure was all but lost in the blueness of the mudra's trunk. She wore a petticoat, greens and browns and light blues, that blended into the background of leaves and gnarled, twisted limbs. Otoh's face burned. He stood and stared. He was seeing the woman for whom his father awakened. She was no bird, he thought. She was thin, indeed, but her height, dwarfing the rocker, surprised him.

Without taking his eyes off her Otoh squatted and deposited his load on the dusty clay ground. He moved slowly. He could so easily have missed her, mistaken her for a shrub. He was again aware that he was trespassing on this woman's land.

She was unlike any woman he had ever seen. It was as though he had stumbled unexpectedly on a lost jungle, and except for the odours he would have sworn he was in a paradise. Making sure the gramophone was safely settled on the ground, he untied his bandanna and wiped his face and neck.

Dankness hung heavily. The air close to the ground bristled with the natural fragrance released in the blackest period of night. The aroma of grapefruit, lime and orange trees lay like a fringe on the edge of the darkness. Pohpoh began to tingle with a sensation of delirious omnipotence — she was able to find her way, to survive in the dark, to name plants and insects with only their scent or a brush against them as her clues. She sprang out of the ditch, landing elegantly in a crouch. Inching her way along the narrow bank of overgrown razor grass, she gravitated toward a ragged opening in the wire. Like a moth, she breezed through the hole and out the other side without a scratch.

Crickets and tree frogs sang out among the trees. She listened for dogs. Hearing nothing, she decided that if there were any in the yard she would have by now smelled the evidence of their presence.

Darting across the lawn Pohpoh arrived under the skirt of a citrus tree. With fewer bushes to conceal her, she exercised care, peering out at the large two-storey house in the centre of the grounds. The ground floor of the house was washed in dull yellow light from garden lanterns planted in a bed of thick, low shrubbery and flowering plants.

This would be her target tonight. Pohpoh cupped her ears and aimed them at the house. She heard nothing. She imagined bedrooms with a happy family, a fairy-tale family in which the father was a benevolent king. There would be a fairy queen for a mother, and enough little cherub siblings to fill a very large shoe or pumpkin carriage, their fat, pink faces smiling even as they slept. In the wash of garden lanterns she could see curtains on the ground floor drawn behind ornately wrought-iron bars. High up on the second floor she saw curtains pulled back, windows open and no bars.

The old samaan tree around the back wasn't hard to climb. Near the tree's top, a branch extended like the palm of a hand to an open window. Pohpoh had seen four-foot-long iguanas crawling along the branches of other samaan trees, and she decided to descend to the window slithering on her belly. Midway down the branch she stopped. Pohpoh swung her head from side to side looking down at the yard and up into the branches that crisscrossed the star-laden sky. Closer to the window she waited for the wind swishing through the branches to cover the sliding sound of her body.

There was a light on in the hallway just outside the room she entered. She perched like a gargoyle on the window sill, her eyes still unused to the light. Pohpoh imagined herself invisible, sitting there and thwarting monsters and demons who tried to lay a finger on the little baby in whose room she found herself.

A baby's room is a good clue to how near the parents are, Pohpoh thought. Imagination could cost too much. She put herself back on track, shaking her finger sternly at herself. She pinched her eyes tightly shut, squeezing out the friendly gargoyle, iguana, monkey and fairy, and returning to the concentration of a night prowler at work.

"Two minutes. I *can* do this — I *will*— in two minutes, not a second more." She activated her stopwatch, then slipped off the sill.

Pohpoh glided gracefully across the smooth teak floor. The door of the parents' room was wide open. Her eyes followed the shaft of light to see a large bed, too large for the two adults asleep in it, facing apart and joined in deep sleep at their backs. She passed another bedroom. Her eyes now accustomed to the reddish light, she made out the figures of two children asleep in a large bed high off the ground. On a wide window sill sat stuffed toys and rag dolls.

The hallway led to a landing at the top of a wide, winding stairway. The banister was inviting, its wood warm red. She would have loved to mount it like a horse rider and slide down backward. She held fast to her determination to touch nothing. Pohpoh moved toward the panelled wall, pressing her back against it as she descended. At the bottom of the stairs she wiped fine sweat off her upper lip and forehead.

The downstairs room was lit only by the feeble, blue light of the night sky entering a pair of windows on the far wall. Another wall was lined with bookshelves. On another were framed pictures. One in particular caught her attention. It was larger by far than any of the others and sat in the centre of the wall. She could make out a full-length portrait of two adults and two girls. The mother had one hand on a girl's shoulder and the father had one hand on the shorter child. Pohpoh had never been in the house before but she had seen the family passing on the road in front of her home.

She passed into a corridor. Pages of children's drawings were tacked to both walls. The pages rustled as she passed. At the end of the passage was an archway. She knew the route that she had to take lay there. During these night-time adventures she had learned that the layouts of houses were predictable, depending on the social status of the dwellers. It thrilled her to have guessed correctly which room followed which.

Her eyes brightened with triumph as she stood at the entrance to the living room. Across it was her destination — the front entrance. She headed straight for the door. There was a long mirror, the largest she had ever seen, in a carved gold frame on the wall, and as she hurried by she saw a tiny, ragged girl.

Pohpoh stopped. She had never really thought of herself as tiny or mangy before. Her confidence slackened. She looked closely at sunken eyes. She had never noticed that they were so large and set so far back in her skull, shadowed in comparison to the rest of her features. Pohpoh wondered which was her true self — the timid, gaunt, unremarkable girl staring at her, or the one who dared to spend nights doing what no one else ever dared to do. The image of her father about to lower himself on her body charged at her suddenly, complete with smells and nauseating tastes. She gasped loud enough to startle herself and pinched her arm hard, an admonishment that she dare not lose her concentration. Pohpoh swiftly navigated around the ornate furniture to the entrance hall. She opened the door and faced the familiar darkness. Success so far was giddying but she knew the adventure was not over until she was once more back in her own bedroom. The air outside was comfortingly warm compared to the cool dampness of the house. She pulled the door softly behind her. There would be no hint of a stranger's presence, no trace of entry.

She gave the yard a perfunctory survey before bolting across the lawn and into the background of a fat grapefruit tree. She felt triumphant. Avenged. The image of her face in the mirror was forgotten.

A smile of triumph lit up Mala's face. She had relived this scenario so often that even she did not remember how much of it actually took place — whether it took place in the day or night, whether she was accompanied by Asha, whether she actually entered a house, whether she was ever caught. Her eyes stayed closed. She was not yet ready to enter the day with its cutting brightness.

Otoh had managed to get the gramophone out of its box, inserted a disk and wound it up without disturbing her. When he lifted the needle's arm the turntable began to spin with a fine whir. Mala opened her eyes. When she saw the young man in front of her she gasped.

A Dixieland quartet began to scratch along. Otoh and Mala locked onto each other's gaze. Otoh rose up from fiddling with the device. The music was too loud but he could not bring himself to stoop again to turn it down. He retreated a couple of paces.

Mala's lips moved but the din of jazz drowned out her words. Holding the arms of her rocking chair she pushed herself up, then reached a hand out to the young man before her. As the music came to an end she breathed, "Ambrose."

Otoh was awed that she recognized the resemblance to his father. The needle arm retreated with protesting squeaks to its rest position. In the stillness Mala mumbled his father's name several times. It was then that Otoh realized she had mistaken him for his father. He was about to say, "I am Otoh. Ambrose is my father," but stopped. She might not know that Ambrose had a child or even that he had married. Right then, he did not want to bear such news.

The arm of the needle automatically lifted up and moved once more into position and lowered itself on the record. Mala shuffled toward Otoh in time to the music. She laughed like a giddy child yet all at once her face contorted. Her gaunt eyes were large and glassy with expectation. Otoh's first instinct was to flee but he was wary of making abrupt movements or of turning his back on this woman whose wiliness he had witnessed in the past. Besides, he wondered in which direction he would run to escape the yard. He was completely disoriented.

Mala approached, humming and dipping and sliding to the fast-paced melody. In a strong clear voice she sang not only the main tune but the buoyant *wa-wa wa-wa* of the clarinet. She closed her eyes, gave an exaggerated tremble of her head and mouthed two soulful *wa-wa's*. Nearing him she became feverish with excitement, cast her arms rhythmically sideways and executed fast-paced dance steps in perfect time to the drum beat and banjos.

She reached a hand out to him again. He took it, an angular parcel of flesh and bones. The pale skin of her face and hands was finely wrinkled, as textured and colourless as a young albino lizard. He was mesmerized by her green-brown eyes and complied. She suddenly pulled him toward her grinning face and just as swiftly pushed him away at arm's length. She spun them both around and around her yard to the accompaniment of her imitation clarinet solos. The music stopped again yet she continued to hum and sing out *wa-wa* and twirl him around. All the while she peered intently into his eyes.

Otoh stepped outside of himself and imagined he was watching the scene from the roadway. In light of what the townspeople had assumed about this woman over the decades, and of what he had known of her through his deliveries and his father's yearnings, he was amazed. He was actually in her yard, holding her hand. They were whirling about. Unaware that her own voice had long been a stranger even to her, he was still awed that he should be privy to its sound, and a witness to her past.

They moved to the foot of the back stairs. Mala slowed and pulled Otoh close to her chest and whispered, this time pleadingly, "Ambrose?"

Otoh brought them both to an abrupt halt.

"It's all right, Ambrose. It's all right. He won't hurt you," Mala whispered in his ear.

"Who won't hurt me?"

"He can't hurt you now, Ambrose. Come, come." And she took his hand and led him up the stairs. Mounting the weathered boards he imagined himself retracing his father's footsteps from decades back. He reminded himself to observe every particularity so that on his return to Government Alley he could recount the minutest details as proof that he had indeed been a visitor in Mala's house.

At the top of the stairs Otoh was startled by the sound of pigeons scurrying on the roof. Mala giggled at his timidity. She stood on the verandah, pleased to have him in her house again. One edge of the porch, he noticed, was lined with rows of small jars of what looked like pepper sauce. He recognized the jars. He had delivered them to her full of condiments and spices.

On the verandah the redolence of the yard had diminished and was replaced by another: the sea-like freshness of dark dirt, earthworms and, oddly, garden snails. The smell, this high up, baffled him. Mala stood next to him and clasped her hands behind her back, not wanting to disturb what she thought were his reveries. Humbled with appreciation for his return, she once again longed for him to be the king of her garden. Seeing him looking in the direction of a spider web she became very excited.

"Spiders. There are enough spiders nowadays, Ambrose," she whispered. Getting no response, she looked up at him hopefully.

"More than enough spiders now, Ambrose."

"Oh, that's good. That's good. Spiders. That's good."

His words encouraged her. She held his arm and led him into the kitchen. He opened his eyes wide trying to see in the dark interior. He realized that the kitchen window had been boarded up with scraps of wood, cardboard and galvanized iron. On the other side of the room was a mound of furniture piled into the shape of a dust-and-cobweb-packed wall. A mustiness tickled his throat. He coughed and his eyes filled up with tears. Mala began to disassemble the wall. Worried it would come crashing down but unsure what to do, he watched in resigned awe as she pulled items from the bottom. The structure didn't cave in. She stopped only when an opening, large enough for them to both creep through, appeared. She tugged him through and they emerged into a vacant space Otoh thought might once have been a drawing room. There were three closed doors leading from the room. Two, judging from the thick layers of dust on the floor, had not been opened in years. Reaching the third, Mala took a key from the pocket of her dress. Before inserting it in the keyhole, she looked up at Otoh, placed a thin finger to her lip and said, "Shhhh." She turned the key and opened the door.

An odour far more intense than that under the house burst out like a gaseous belch, knocking him back onto the carpet of dust. Mala helped him up. She was far stronger than she looked, Otoh realized. The foulness was suddenly recognizable. It was a combination of organic rot that has reached maturity and stale adult urine. He gasped, unable to breath. His stomach felt as though it were work-ing its way up to a somersault. He sputtered and coughed.

She ushered him into the darkness at the top of some stairs. When his body resisted she slipped behind him and pushed him forward. With one hand on his back for assurance, Mala held up a bundle of weeds.

"Jenghie, shandolay," she explained, waving the weeds under Otoh's nose, "baby bonnet and shado-beni. Keep it by yuh nose. It will help with the bad-feeling. I accustomed to it long time now." The bouquet had lost its aroma. He gave it a harsh rub, hoping that some sliver of scent might have remained trapped in it but he only broke the brittle twigs. The leaves crumbled into dust. She locked the door behind them.

"Is better not to take chances, you know. We'll keep it locked so he can't come out."

She took his hand and pulled him down the flight of stairs. His legs wobbled. The smell intensified as they descended. Halfway down the stairs Mala stopped, let go of his hand and lit a lamp. The glow revealed moths as large as a hand, fluttering about disoriented as though too abruptly awakened from a stupor. At the foot of the stairs was another door. Mala retrieved a skeleton key from a ledge above the doorway and opened the door only wide enough for them to slip in. She moved about the room swiftly, confidently. Otoh stayed close behind her, afraid to be left alone.

Farther into the room, through the haze of dust, Otoh made out a high platform the size of a single bed. A long, uneven bundle of clothes lay upon it. Something black protruded here and there. Mala walked right up to the bed frame and stared at the indecipherable mass. Otoh looked at her.

"He can't hurt us now, Ambrose," she smiled and whispered. "Look, come and see." Otoh walked closer, sick to his stomach from the smell and terrified at what he was about to see. She held the light high above the bed frame so he could get a good look.

Opening his eyes Otoh realized he was collapsed over Mala's shoulder, watching the back of her legs as she mounted the steps to the drawing room. He was too weak to demand to be put down. She pulled the door shut behind them and locked it again. She then carried him, still on her shoulder, through the space in the wall of furniture, out through the kitchen, and set him down to rest on the verandah floor. Kneeling over him, fretting, she chanted, "Shhh, don't worry Ambrose, shhh, shhh, shhh."

Her face was uncomfortably close to his. She tenderly kissed his forehead. His temples throbbed. He closed his eyes in terror only to be presented with the image of what he had just seen down below.

"You want water?" Her voice was soft and caring. She got up and disappeared through the kitchen door. When she was out of his sight he jumped up and bolted down the back stairs. Before he reached the bottom Mala was on the verandah again. So distraught was she to see him running off and leaving her again that her cries froze in her chest. Her face appeared fully composed yet tears ran down her cheeks as she watched Otoh navigate her yard.

He headed for the front fence, passing the wall of dead cereus blossoms that covered the room he had been in minutes before. His strides widened so he was able to leap over shrubs. By the time he reached the road he had lost his thongs. Both feet and his face were scratched with slashes from twigs, sharp grasses and fine thorns.

When he reached the other side of Mala's tilted fence, Otoh felt overwhelmed. He shivered in the heat, entirely unsure of the reality of anything he had just witnessed. The farther he got from the house and yard the weaker his legs became. He felt faint, as though the frenetic spell on which he had been riding were falling away. He slowed down, swerving from side to side before unravelling in a heap in the middle of the narrow road. Within seconds people began to gather around him.

"But ent he is Ambrose son?"

"He name Otoh."

"I thought he name Ambrosia."

"Doh be stupid. That is a girl's name."

"But that is Ambrose son self. Look how he looking. He looking like Ambrose self. You can't see a trace of he mother in he. But what he doing dress up so and lying in the hot sun in the middle of the road?"

"I see everything. The boy fall. He was running and he fall down. I see he fall myself."

"He must be get heart attack and fall down?"

"A young boy so? Don't be stupid. Young people doh get heart attack. But look how white he gone, na. Take off the 'kerchief from round he neck."

"I see he running out Miss Mala yard, pelting down the road like if he just see ghost."

"Miss Mala yard? You sure? But this boy crazy like he father or what?"

"What he was doing there, pray? Take off he jacket. What he doing wearing black jacket in the daytime for?"

"Ey, what wrong with all you? Stop talking so and call police."

"He don't need police, he need doctor."

"Somebody call doctor."

"He is a slight fella, eh!"

"Talap, run and get the doctor, na."

"Somebody go with Talap and get doctor. Fast-fast. The boy trembling in this hot sun. Look how he shaking. Take off he shirt. Talap, you gone yet?"

"My daughter like this boy, too bad, yes. But I don't want her with no weak man. Go and tell Mavis lover-boy fall down and hit he self. Mavis. Where Mavis? Talap, go and call Mavis. Tell she . . ."

"Talap, forget Mavis, boy. Go and call doctor."

"Ah tell all you, call police. Doctor too, but police too."

"Jojo, shut up your mouth about police, na, man. Why you need police for a fella who running and trip he self?"

"I agree with Jojo. I say call police too. And leave he shirt on, that boy trembling with cold."

But they did not have to call the constable. He was inside the house opposite, visiting a woman friend while her husband was out for the day, when he heard the commotion. Peeping from behind the edge of a heavy curtain he recognized the call of duty. Much to the woman's annoyance he dropped her and scurried out the back of the house. He leapt over the backyard wall and made an ungraceful trek down the ditch at the back of the house and onto the road, confident that his arrival would be unnoticed. Everyone's attention was on the boy on the ground.

Otoh opened his eyes. A halo of heads and countless eyes peered down at him. At the centre of the halo was a sliver of cold, sharp silver sky.

"A body, it have a body in she house . . ." he managed to say before he again fainted. He couldn't stand another smell, and surrounding him was a collection of bodies that had melded into a choking odour. He closed his eyes and allowed himself to slip away.

"What is that he say?"

"He say he see a body."

"Lord, oh, Lord! Look here, we have real trouble in the town now, yes."

"What is that?"

"Police, call police, he say it have some body in Miss Mala yard."

"Somebody gone in Miss Mala yard."

"Eh-heh! So how he know that? What he was doing up there, inside the woman yard?"

"Well, he must be was in she yard trying to catch tief, na."

"He say it had a tief in Mala yard."

"He say tief gone in she yard."

"It doh have nothing to tief in that house. The tief must be gone to murder she!"

The constable forced a clearing in the crowd and peeped down at Otoh. He arrived just in time to hear, "What is that? Some tief gone to murder Mala?"

"Mala? Mala Ramchandin?" he said to no one in particular.

"Yes, he say he see somebody trying to murder she," he heard the nearest one say.

The constable took off toward the police station. It was not often that any of the force got a chance to show off their training in physical endurance and, conscious that he was in full view of the townspeople, he made good use of the opportunity.

Hearing the town suddenly astir, women, children and men started pouring out from their houses. Every dog for miles, aroused by the unusual din, commenced barking. There were two streams of people: those leaving the spot where Otoh lay to race through town crying, "Murder in the Ramchandin yard," and those rushing toward the scene, almost trampling one another in their haste.

Ambrose E. Mohanty sat low in his wheelchair on the verandah waiting for Otoh to return. Hearing the din in the streets Elsie came onto the verandah.

She saw Pilai, the old grocer, edging under the strain of lumbago toward the scene.

"Ey, Pilai. Pilai! Mornin' Pilai. How your madam?"

"She good. She good, yes. She real good. Thanks, Mrs. Mohanty. So you hear news?"

"No, I ent hear nothing. What happening that everybody running so?"

Pilai knew of Ambrose's and Mala's interest in each other in their youth. He had even played a small role in getting them together or so he liked to think. Realizing this moment held great importance he stopped and faced Elsie, for he could not see Ambrose. He took off his hat, held it reverently to his chest and spoke with appropriate solemnity.

"Some fellas gone in the Ramchandin house and they tief everything and murder the old woman dead-dead! Yes, somebody say they catch one of them already. He lying in the road near she house. It still have about five of them loose. I going to pay my respects." And he nodded and walked slowly onward. After a few steps he picked up speed again.

"Oh God!" said Elsie, "Oh God, I hope they didn't kill Otoh too. Oh God, Ambrose, I feeling weak. My son dead. Is you who send my only child to his death. Oh God, they kill my only child." And as she slipped down to the ground in an unsightly crumple of panic and uncontrollable wailing for her son's supposed death, Ambrose rose like heat out of his wheelchair.

"He has seen her. He has. I just know that he has. That son of mine. Otoh has seen her!" Ambrose E. Mohanty was standing upright for the first time in decades.

Elsie, still on the floor, did not notice when her husband, attired in his moth-eaten, camphor-smelling, wrinkled black suit, stood behind his wheelchair and pushed it down the stairs. He held the railing and lumbered after it, his elegance belying the pain caused by such an ordinary act. At the bottom Ambrose sat in the wheelchair to catch his breath. Re-energized, he rose, moved behind the chair and with decorum pushed it out of the yard and onto the roadway.

How Paradise has expanded! he thought. It had never occurred to Ambrose that, while he slept, the rest of the town was busy. Paradise, he noticed with bewilderment, had grown from a village with a house here, plots of raw land there and then another house way over there, to a town with houses crammed against each other and hardly any wild land in sight. To get to Mala's house he relied on habit and a homing instinct.

Eventually he arrived at a corner, a vaguely familiar spot, in the middle of which sat his discombobulated son. Most of the crowd that had surrounded Otoh had surged away when it became evident he was no longer in any danger. The real story was unfolding up the hill at Mala's house.

One would think Otoh would have been shocked to see his father out in the world, not in but accompanying his wheelchair, standing tall before him. But Otoh was too stunned to be shocked by anything. He also now understood his father so well that he fully expected Ambrose E. Mohanty to spring back to life the minute he heard that his son had made a meaningful connection with Mala. Nor was Otoh at all surprised at how swiftly the news of his adventures had travelled to Government Alley.

Otoh had never before looked up at his father. The new angle revealed an aged face with a fleshy, sagging chin and tangled nose hairs. He was quite tall and startlingly unfamiliar, standing up. Ambrose attempted to stoop down beside Otoh, but instead tumbled to the ground. This view of his father was more familiar and gave Otoh much-needed comfort.

"Ooh! A little stiff!" Ambrose giggled nonchalantly.

Otoh put a hand on his father's thigh. They remained quiet until the last of the onlookers had rushed up the hill. Only then did Ambrose lean closer.

"Does she remember me? Did she ask about me?"

"She remember you very well, Pappy. I think she waiting for you."

Ambrose made grand gestures to raise himself from the ground. "Well then, let's go. Here, let me help you up, my gallant son." When he realized he wasn't able to get himself up, he giggled with jovial embarrassment. Otoh smiled wearily and put a firm arm on his father's elbow to keep him on the ground.

"Pappy, it have something I have to tell you."

"Oh, my son, are you all right? Tell me, she didn't try to use a cleaver on you, did she? Did she wield a cleaver at you?"

"A cleaver? God! No!"

"Oh. Good. That's good. Then tell me how you are. I should have asked after you sooner. How negligent of me. Tell me. Tell away. You know you can tell me anything. How can I be of assistance to you?"

"No. No. Wait, just listen a minute . . ." Otoh told his father almost everything that had occurred and all that he had seen that morning, omitting only the parts about the gramophone and dancing. When he told about the sickening odours and the room beneath the house, Ambrose remained studiedly composed. He wrapped his fingers around one of his son's hands. He sighed and in apparent desperation breathed out, "Dearest, dearest!" several times. Otoh had the sense that his father was awakening to much more than he had, in all his years of sleeping, ever dreamed about.

"Son, did you tell anyone about all of this?" Ambrose whispered even though there was no one nearby. Otoh said that he remembered running out of the yard but had no recollection of falling in the road. He vaguely remembered opening his eyes, perhaps even trying to say something, but had no memory of speaking.

"Why does everyone then think that a band of murderers have been in her yard and that she was murdered?" Ambrose gestured toward the people running by. "What did you say to them? You must have said something that became exaggerated. Did you perhaps use the word *marauder*? Have you no memory? Try, son, try to remember what you might have said."

Otoh, fearing he might have exposed more than he intended, shook his head. "Pappy, I really didn't mean to cause she no harm. I just wanted you and she to be able to meet again."

"Well, how else can one look at this rather unfortunate turn of events? Clearly you did not cause trouble. It seems that trouble was lurking like a diseased phantom, waiting to be revealed, and you had the misfortune to have come upon it. Ultimately, I suppose, one is led to fulfill every iota of one's *raison d'être.* And you have just so done. It was your duty, my unfortunate son, to be the man who unleashed the business of an ugly, lurking phantom."

Ambrose looked directly at his son. Seeing on Otoh's face a look that Ambrose mistook for despair but was actually befuddlement at his father's ramblings, he smiled sheepishly.

"Our relationship to each other, yours to me and mine to her, serves only to make the waters that we travel interestingly murky," said Ambrose. "Cheer up. There is no point trying to undo what can't be undone."

Otoh glanced at Ambrose. His father's eyes were downcast. Even though he tried to be optimistic and philosophical about the situation, the old man was in fact pained.

"You know, my son, to all appearances, current circumstances are rather dire. But our thinking exhibits both the ignorance and shortsightedness of mere mortals. Mala and I will meet again, as you wish." He grinned and looked straight at Otoh. "Endings are but beginnings that have taken to standing on their heads. Come. Let us, you and I, go to her house now."

"Pappy, I hear you. But I want to know what really happened. You sound like you know. Who is Mala, Pappy? What happened between you and her?"

"Oh dear. Where should one begin? Even beginnings have their own beginnings. What a daunting task."

He paused, took a deep breath and turned to Otoh.

"Shall we just trek on up to the house? Since she has not been murdered off, as all these folk in this town might have relished, we might ask her ourselves. Come on, son, get up, get up. Come along, now. You're dilly-dallying. One might be inclined to believe, from the example of your tardiness, that it is you who has slept life away."

As Otoh and his father, pushing the wheelchair up the road, approached the house, they could see uniformed policemen whacking at the brambles in the front of the house with scythes and machetes. A path wide enough for a car had already been cleared. There was a good view of the dilapidated house.

Ambrose halted. He stared at the house. He covered his open mouth with his hand and tears began to fall. They reached the crowded front gate, which had been completely mowed down by the police, but were restrained by a young officer with a baton. Otoh was puzzled that his father allowed the police to hold him back.

"Pappy, tell the officer you know she. Tell him."

Ambrose thought for a long moment.

"Pappy, why you don't tell the man, na? We have to go up there and take care of she."

Ambrose shook his head. "I have never been very good at this sort of thing, have I?"

Otoh did not smile back. He felt an unusual anger and loathing rise in him. There would be no *on the one hand . . . but on the other* now.

"No, son. What has been done has been done. I believe that it would be in our best interest to stay here and wait."

Otoh stared at his father in disbelief. Then he tore decisively through the little crowd, intending to make a break for the yard. The crowd parted. The officer attempted to intercept him but Otoh pushed ahead. The officer reluctantly whacked him on the head with the baton but only hard enough to stun him. Ambrose remained where he was and covered his face with his hands. Shaking his head he whispered, "I should not have risen today. I suddenly feel so sleepy."

As soon as Otoh bolted out of her yard, Mala had sensed that trouble would follow. She wrung her hands in desperation and sadness, wondering if what she thought was a visit from her beloved Ambrose was simply a memory, as vivid as her daydreams about Pohpoh's adventures.

She looked with longing at the bottles of pepper sauce that surrounded her. The pain of a teaspoon of the fiery sauce on her tongue would surely dull the despair that threatened to swallow her up. It all seemed so real. She sniffed her hands for a trace of clove oil, cardamon and bayleaf — scents she associated with Ambrose. There was an unfamiliar smell but not what she remembered. She decided that if trouble was indeed on its way her first duty was to save and care for Pohpoh. Hardly anyone, in her estimation, ever cared for Pohpoh. Now that she was grown up, she herself would take care of little Pohpoh. She made her way down the back stairs and toward the mudra tree and her rocking chair. She sat there and waited.

Before long she heard the police siren. When the siren fell silent at the front of her yard, she leaned back in the rocker and closed her eyes.

Now where was she, she wondered, before Ambrose — it was Ambrose, wasn't it?— entered her yard. Ah yes! Pohpoh had just exited the strangers' house successfully and was out in the yard. Over the last few years Mala had grown fond of this particular Pohpoh. She had rather disliked her many years before when they were one and the same. But these days she wished that she and that Pohpoh could have been two separate people, that they could have been best friends, or even that she could have been the mother of Pohpoh or at least her older sister. She would certainly have lifted her up in her arms, held her, hugged her and protected her as well as Pohpoh had protected Asha.

Yes, Pohpoh was out in the yard behind a grapefruit tree. The stars in Pohpoh's sky had receded. Isn't that so? Isn't that where she left Pohpoh? she wondered. Yes. The stars were much less bright than when Pohpoh had first climbed through the neighbour's window. And there was a wisp of pink cloud, a little wisp, like a scribble, visible as the first light broke. It streaked across a corner of the sky. And, that's right, there were roosters. In the distance a rooster here and there, the earliest risers among them, gave the morning's first hesitant crowings.

A man's voice called out. "Miss Ramchandin. Miss Ramchandin. You there, Miss Ramchandin?"

She did not answer. She thought harder of Pohpoh. She ignored the sounds of her fence being torn down.

"Mala will take care of you, Pohpoh. No one will ever touch you again like that. I will never let anyone put their terrible hands on you again. I, Mala Ramchandin, will set you, Pohpoh Ramchandin, free, free, free, like a bird!"

The grapefruit tree trembled. Cold dewdrops flew like a sudden rain shower. Pohpoh was startled. An old man, the night watchman, whipped around the shrub brandishing a broomstick and attempting to shout. Shaken by the appearance of a stranger in the yard, his voice was thick with the fear trapped inside his chest.

"Who is that? Who is that?" he asked gruffly then took off, nervously beating the air in front of him with the stick. Finally able to shout, he screamed at the top of his voice, "Tief, tief, tief in the yard!" and headed toward the house.

Through her dreaming Mala could hear that her yard was crawling with police. Like Otoh, they were unable to spot her in the camouflage of the mudra tree. They had surrounded the house where they would concentrate their search for murderers and a corpse. She rocked a little and thought of Pohpoh's dilemma.

Pohpoh decided to make a dash for the hole in the fence. As she was about to spring out from behind the grapefruit tree, the dogs in the area started a frantic barking. Her first instinct was to stand frozen, to will herself to disappear into thin air.

Lights in the house went on, room after room. Pohpoh grasped her chest. With the speed of a terrified hare she darted to the opening in the fence. Less graceful than her entrance, she scrambled to get through. As she somersaulted into the ditch she noticed lights in every house in the neighbourhood. She tumbled down, slipping and sliding on the mossy bottom. She peeped out from the ditch, preparing to sprint to her house across the road.

The light in her father's room was on. The front door opened and he came out shirtless and paunchy in his pajama pants. He stood on the top front step trying to make sense of the commotion with his alcohol-saturated mind. Running down the street were two neighbours in pajamas and brightly coloured rubber thongs, wielding sticks in their hands.

Pohpoh dropped low in the ditch. She listened but her head reverberated with her own breathing, which was shallow and rapid like a cornered animal's. She began to feel what she was normally oblivious to: her face and neck, wet with sweat and tears, bruises on her legs, skin that felt as though it had been torn off her back in thick chunks. Her lower stomach ached.

Fear was breaking her, was unprying her memory. She was reminded of what she usually ignored or commanded herself to forget: her legs being ripped apart, something entering her from down there, entering and then scooping her insides out. Her body remembered.

Mala remembered.

She heard the voices of the police. She reconfigured what they said to match her story of how she saved Pohpoh that day.

Pohpoh, remembering her father's invasion, put her hand over her mouth and nose to stifle her panic and the nauseating smell of fear that rumbled from her insides. Pressed against the bush, she bit the inside of her lip and willed herself to think.

Mala bit the inside of her lip and willed herself to think. She squeezed her eyes tightly and ignored the people trampling, destroying her yard. She put all her efforts into protecting Pohpoh.

Pohpoh squeezed her eyes tightly, inducing a red and silver fireworks explosion inside her eyeballs. She scolded herself sternly, insisting that she would never ever give up or get caught or allow herself to panic. She never had before and now would not become the first time. It had always been this way for her: just as she was about to succumb, an irrational strength would surface, taking control, propelling her toward feelings of invincibility. Yet this time there was a difference. Pohpoh felt, for once, that she was not alone.

With a determined bolt she raced back in the direction of Mala's house. Mala's yard appeared, strangely, to come toward her as she moved toward it. As though emerging from a stupor she realized that this was the yard she knew best.

With all the activity and excitement in the road, the neighbourhood dogs were still barking and neighbours were still shouting out to each other.

"They get caught?"

"They ain't find the killers yet?"

"They find the body?"

"Is true the old lady dead?"

"They should let go the dogs loose in the yard, quick quick."

"But what them police waiting for, pray tell?"

When Pohpoh arrived at Mala's fence she knew she had reached a refuge. She grabbed one of the rotting fence posts and scaled it with magical speed. Instead of landing in the stinging nettles she was caught by a soothing mess of aloe vera. This yard was different from the others. The plants were not arranged in any order and no path seemed to exist. She made her way through papashy and toolsie, the sharp medicinal smell clinging to her clothing. Pink morning light was too weak to illuminate the trees and plants in the chaotic garden but Pohpoh didn't care. She knew the yard better than any in her neighbourhood.

The policemen in the yard thrashed at the shrubs and bramble trees. In her dreaming Mala whispered as though to Pohpoh, "Oh my God! They going to mash up my plants. And they talk so loudly and roughly."

"God, this place have plenty bush."

"Look at this cactus, na. The blossoms on this thing so big! I wonder if it will catch if I break off a piece and take it home?"

"Shit. What dis is? It have a smell back here, foul-foul. Yuh smell it?"

"Fuh true. But what dat could be, boy? She does pee-pee in the yard or what?"

"Oh God. It smell like something rottening, something dead."

"Well, to make a smell like that it have to be something big like a cow, yes."

One voice broke out in a song. "Ole lady walk a mile an a half an she taylaylay." The men laughed and he sang it again.

"Ey! All yuh. Look over here. It look like somebody was in dis yard, yes."

"It could be children from down the road come up to harass she. I could remember years aback when I was a child comin round here to tief dongs and plum, oui. It was de best dongs, from dat same tree."

"Yuh know why it did taste so good?"

Again there was laughter. "Good manure, well-fertilized soil."

"Ey, all yuh, shut up yuh mouth and get serious, man. Ah tell yuh somebody was in dis yard not long ago. It wasn't a band of fellas. Only one person was in the yard. De aloes patch in de back mash-up-mash-up. It oozing fresh. It have fresh footprints here by the steps. One set small-small. That must be she footprints. And one bigger. And look at the footprints in a circle here and over here and over here. It look like . . . it look like . . . like, hmmm, dancing? Take a look, na."

"Is best to bring in de dogs, I say."

"Dem dogs ent go want to come an sniff in dis yard, na. De children always saying how back here does smell bad-bad in truth, oui!"

The prickly orange flowers of the shandolay scratched at Pohpoh, and as her lower legs rubbed against shado-beni, their bruised leaves gave off the smell she loved in raw, seasoned meat. Closer to the house, concealed in the foliage of broad banana fronds, she waited. The peekoplats in the mudra were silent, hopping nervously, afraid to call attention to themselves and their ward beneath. The chickens in the pomerac tree had become restless and clucked with worry. Call-and-answer cock-a-doodle-doos across the village were fast paced and urgent, like warnings.

The chief constable had arrived. The men became more serious when they saw him coming down the recently cut path. The farther into the yard he penetrated the more disturbed his face became. He took a white handkerchief from his breast pocket and covered his nose. In his other hand he gripped a baton, thumping it anxiously against his thigh. He passed barely glancing at the wall of cereus cactus.

"Rotting. Death. Old death," he whispered. It did not take him long to spot Mala in the rocking chair under the mudra tree. His men watched him and wondered what had attracted him to the huge tree. Then they too saw her.

Mala heard him approach. She kept her eyes closed, rocked with more agitation, determined to continue her dreaming. She imagined she was inside the house, looking down at Pohpoh from a bedroom window.

Crouching down and peeping out from behind the ixora bush, Pohpoh saw what she first thought was a giraffe, then a bird flapping its wings. She realized it was Mala, her eyes prominent like an owl's. Mala waved urgently and pointed beneath her to a wall of cereus plants outside a boarded-up window on the lower level. Pohpoh nodded in perfect understanding and headed for the cereus. Mala disappeared.

"Miss Ramchandin? Good day, Miss Ramchandin." The chief constable waited but there was no response. He raised his voice.

"Uh, Miss Ramchandin, good day. Can you hear me? Hello."

He called one of his men and ordered him to check her wrist for a pulse. Determining that she was alive, he told two of the men to lift her by the arm and take her up to the verandah.

The men were surprised when she brushed away their hands, rose up and walked toward the house by herself. Even as she walked she stayed close to Pohpoh. To her, Pohpoh came first.

Nearing the house Pohpoh noticed that the white cereus flowers were tinged with colour, as though they had been washed in a laundry that contained red clothing. Each blossom was larger than two hands side by side, and in the dawning of the day they were closing themselves against the onslaught of light. Their intrusive perfume waned. As Pohpoh approached the house the sweetness turned bitter and sharply foul.

Standing on the verandah the chief constable stared out at the mudra. He slowly shoved the baton back into his belt and walked over to the jars of dazzlingly coloured pepper sauce. He shoved a bottle with the toe of his heavy boot.

"Excuse me, Constable, sir," one of his men said. "There is no sign of foul play in the yard. A lot of foulness, sir, but no foul play."

The chief constable ignored the humour. "Call the men out of the yard. That boy, Mohanty, he saw something, yes, but it was no murder — at least not a recent one."

"Sir?"

"Just follow my orders. Call the men out of the yard."

"Yes, Constable. At once."

The chief constable squatted next to Mala, who sat on the top stair of the verandah.

"Miss Ramchandin, we are worried about your safety and would like to take a quick look through the house."

"You never had any business with my safety before." Although her voice was gritty, she spoke with such force that the chief constable drew back involuntarily. "Why now for? You taking advantage of a ol' lady, that is what you doing. Besides, yuh think I stupid or what? I know you can't search people house without search papers."

"Miss Ramchandin, well, we ent actually searching your house." He chose his words carefully. "We got a complaint that some fellas running around and making trouble in the neighbourhood. They hiding somewhere. And we checking every house in the area. Every house."

"At dis time of mornin yuh wakin up people. All yuh have no shame." Mala felt herself drifting back to Pohpoh.

"It's well past afternoon now, Miss Ramchandin. We are going to look through the house." He ordered one of his men to wait with Miss Ramchandin, adding in a whisper, "Don't let her out of your sight."

The chief constable entered the kitchen and shone his large flashlight slowly around the room. He came upon a mound of snail shells rising knee-high from the floor and poked that too with the toe of his boot. He aimed his light at a strangely shaped doorway. It was an opening in a wall constructed of dust-covered furniture. He sent a reluctant officer through the opening and called other men to dismantle the structure.

When Mala heard the wall being pulled apart, she bit her lower lip and stared out across the yard, losing herself in the shapes of the mudra tree. *Save Pohpoh,* she chanted. *Save Pohpoh.*

In the midst of the cereus Pohpoh trembled and waited. She was fearful she would be spotted by angry townspeople before Mala reached her. Moments later the slats of wood over the window downstairs were quietly removed one by one. As soon as the space was big enough Pohpoh nimbly hoisted herself up to the ledge. Mala grabbed and pulled her in. The stuffiness and smell of the room astonished her. She coughed momentarily but quickly adapted. Mala replaced the slats swiftly and the room became as black as blindness. Without a word she wrapped a musty dressing gown around Pohpoh, her bony fingers squeezing Pohpoh's shoulders once. A chorus of flapping wings surrounded Pohpoh, moths reluctantly prying themselves from the long-unused gown. Their stir created the only movement of air in the room.

When the furniture wall was dismantled, the police trekked into the old drawing room. A carpet of dust rose in billowing clouds. As they checked the two unlocked rooms that had served as bedrooms, the house filled with a chorus of sniffling, coughing, sneezing and nose blowing.

They arrived at the third door to discover it not only shut

but locked. The chief constable told an officer to bring in Miss Ramchandin. Once again Mala refused to be touched. She knew what the policeman wanted and, without fuss, followed briskly on his heels. She regarded the door defiantly, then whipped a key from her pocket. When she pushed the door wide open the smell assaulted them. She was quite pleased that they all, including the usually composed chief constable, retched.

"Sir. That smell —" One of the men whispered.

"What smell?" Mala blurted out. "If you have no search papers, doh bother to insult me. No respect."

The chief constable, holding his handkerchief to his nose, pointed sharply toward the stairs. When he signalled that she was to accompany them he saw her look off to her side and nod, as though in agreement with some imaginary person.

Mala prodded at Pohpoh to move farther into the room. With one hand pressed on her back for assurance, Mala held up a bundle of weeds to Pohpoh's nose. "Jenghie, shandolay, baby bonnet and shado-beni," she said. "Press to yuh nose. It will help with the bad-feeling. Even you safe down there, as long as you stay close-close to me."

The men cautiously descended using a single flashlight for guidance. Suddenly an officer shrieked and spun around, jabbing the air with his elbow. They all jumped back snapping, "What was dat? What happen?"

The chief constable, who had positioned himself behind Mala, lurched backward, himself startled by the man's cry.

"Get control of yourself, man," he snapped angrily. "If a moth going to frighten you and make you make a fool of yourself so, it doh have no room in this force for yuh."

At the foot of the stairs they arrived at another door. The officer in front looked back to the chief constable. The chief constable nodded. The officer tried the door. It was locked.

"What it have in dis room?" the chief constable asked Mala. No answer. "Miss Ramchandin, you could save us some trouble if you would just tell us if anybody in that room."

Mala defiantly folded her arms across her chest. She closed her eyes and pursed her lips. Finally she said loudly, "Eh-heh, it have somebody in there. But is okay. He does live there. Is my father."

There was a moment of silence. Then a young officer spoke. "Eh. Yuh father. What yuh mean yuh father? Which father?"

"I only have one father." Mala was piqued. She mumbled a few sentences, almost inaudible to the men nearest her and totally incomprehensible.

"Mr. Ramchandin?" the chief constable asked. "But he disappear long, long time back, not so?"

"Exactly," Mala replied. "He does just lie there, not sick or nothing, just old and wear out, an I still looking after him all these years now. Is a daughter's duty, Constable."

"I think you better open up de room for us. Please."

She dealt with his insistence with an insistence of her own. She rocked from side to side and started to hum an old Dixieland tune. Then Mala raised a hand and pointed to the ledge. One of the men reached up, gathering a handful of dust before finding the key. She grabbed the key out of his hand and unlocked the door.

The officer gave the doorknob a twist and a hard shove. An emission of nasty gasses belched out at them. They twisted as though the odour had physically assaulted them. The front man turned around and, shoving aside the others, bolted up the stairs.

The chief constable shone his flashlight about the room. A swarm of bewildered moths flapped about. There was a tall cupboard against one wall and a rusted-out sewing machine. In the centre of the room was a high, wrought-iron bed.

Pohpoh saw a high, wrought-iron bed. Under sheets that glowed dark red from the lamplight lay a motionless stick figure. Skin, which looked grey one minute, red the next, stretched across the hairless cranium, clung to the forehead and cheekbones, defined the contour of a mouth cavity and fell off the precipice of a jawbone. From parted black gums a thin purplish tongue flickered as though attempting to lick its lips every few seconds.

The constable saw Mala look to the side again, as though talking to someone.

"Father, Pohpoh," she whispered. "Remember him? Doh go near him. Even now, he still like to try and touch too much." Mala sucked her teeth, making a drawn-out sound. "Behave yuhself," she said to the bed, "or else yuh ent go get no light fuh two-three days." Turning to the invisible figure at her side, she said, "Stay here by me, child, and everything will be awright. Doh frighten. I ent go leave yuh here with dis wretch and all these other ones who disturbing the peace so. Just stay close by me. Doh frighten."

From the figure's throat came a faint noise muffled in cobwebs. Pohpoh leaned back. The figure expelled another mangled groan, this time with more force.

"Come, child, come," it said.

Pohpoh darted toward the bed and slid underneath, bursting through a wall of thick cobweb fibers. She peeled the sticky cords like plastic wrapping off her eyelids, away from her nose and lips. She trembled.

The constable approached the figure on the bed uneasily. "Mr. Ramchandin," he muttered. Hearing himself he gave a good cough, then expelled his words with the authority expected of a chief constable. "It must be old man Ramchandin, in truth!" He walked around the bed to inspect the level of decomposition, then commanded an officer to remove the white sheet that partially covered the corpse.

When he hesitated the constable bellowed, "Your days numbered, man. Get de hell out a here."

Another policeman came forward and grasped the crumpled sheet with the thumb and index finger of one hand and pulled it back tentatively. He had the sensation that the corner of the sheet trembled between his fingers. As he pulled it back farther it began to unravel. Suddenly entire patches of the white sheet broke away and turned into a rising haze of reluctant moths. The terrified officer pitched the sheet out of his hand. It hovered, then broke apart in a flurry of activity. Thousands of tiny white moths had so tightly packed themselves side by side that the tiny hooks on the edges of their wings had locked together, linking them to form a heavy sheet that was slowly devouring the corpse underneath.

The policemen and the constable grabbed Mala by the arm and rushed out of the room to avoid being smothered by the cloud of moths. One officer tried to close the door behind them, but Mala broke back into the room. As she bent to look beneath the bed, they heard her call out, "Come, Pohpoh. Come, quickly. Run!" Mala extended a hand and pulled her from under the bed. Pohpoh nestled her face between two dried-out breasts.

"You smart, child. You real smart. Dey ent go come back here. Come." Pohpoh's body shook like leaves in a wind.

To Mala's mind and ears alone, the figure in the bed grunted again. The bed creaked as though the body had managed to shift itself. The occupant made another effort to speak. Mala swiftly pushed Pohpoh out of the room.

"I does watch you. I does always watch you. Whenever you go out. At night, you know. I see everything, *everything* you does do, *every* house you does enter. But tonight your plans get a little mess up, eh? Things bad at home, child? I understand. I understand everything. *Everything.* Today is the last day that anybody will ever be able to reach you. Oh, you so cold."

Mala hugged the taut, stiff child.

"I old but I not stupid. I don't have to go far to see everything. I does see how your father does watch you. His eyes just like my father own. You resourceful. I wasn't resourceful. You do for yourself better than me!"

The chief constable, fearing that Mala was becoming totally mad, approached her stealthily. He flung his arms around her upper body and one of his men grabbed her legs. They were surprised that she did not resist as they hauled her up the stairs.

"Run, run, fast, Pohpoh, run," Mala mumbled.

Pohpoh nimbly passed the officers on the stairs and reached the drawing room first. At the top of the stairs the officers put Mala down and watched her tip her head in the direction of the verandah.

"The verandah," she whispered. "You could take off from the verandah." Mala, followed by the curious officers, hobbled out onto the verandah.

In the drawing room the chief constable made arrangements for the inspection of the body downstairs. "From the way it decomposing I would guess the old man was trapped down there alive for a long time before he died. Or was murdered. Make arrangements for Dr. Datt to inspect the body and for Inspector Moroze to check out the scene."

"Constable, a body in that condition? They could do autopsy on a body in that condition?"

The chief constable glared.

"All right, all right," said the officer, "but I can tell you right now that Dr. Datt gone away for the weekend. He take Mrs. Datt and the children for seaside holidays. I could try and get in touch with Dr. Ottley but he wouldn't be able to make this place today."

The chief constable pondered the situation. "Well, that body ent going no place. One more day wouldn't hurt it."

He looked over at Mala. She was on the verandah gripping the banister railing and gibbering excitedly.

"See how that child could run? Look how she running, boy!" The officers mocked her. One of them shouted out, pointing to nothing in particular. "Look! She gone over the fence. Behind the tree . . . where she? Lord! She is lightning in truth —"

"They coming after you, run, run!" Mala shouted to the child who, in her imagination, had already escaped the yard's confines. Her mind filled with sounds of voices and footsteps following Pohpoh. "Yes, Pohpoh, you take off and fly, child, fly!"

One of the police thoroughly enjoying egging Mala on, grinned and said to the chief constable, who was finally somewhat bemused, "Wha de ass! She flying or what! Constable, she leap over dat fence — even the dogs can't do that, sir!"

At the top of the hill Pohpoh bent her body forward and, as though doing a breast stroke, began to part the air with her arms. Each stroke took her higher until she no longer touched the ground. She soon found herself above even the tallest trees. High enough, calmed, she glided, dipping to the left, angling to the right. She made a wide circle trying to make out familiar gardens, to pinpoint the cricket pitch and the yard with the rabbits' hutch. Before long her village was swallowed up in an unfamiliar coagulation of green, brown and yellow. She did three more breast strokes and soared higher before gliding again, basking in the cloudless sky. She practised making perfect, broad circles, like a frigate bird splayed out against the sky in an elegant V. Down below, her island was soon lost among others, all as shapeless as specks of dust adrift on a vast turquoise sea.

The crowd gathered outside saw the officers wrestle with the wriggling old lady. One grappled with her arms and the other with her feet. The onlookers fell silent as a member of the force opened the back door of the police car. They watched as she was deposited in the care of an armed officer. Word spread fast that she was a murderer and had killed a man. From one officer, who was eager to reveal what he knew, it was determined that old lady Mala Ramchandin was being taken in for questioning about the death of her father. On hearing the gossip Ambrose sat down in the road, buried his face in his knees and cried.

Even before the crowd had dispersed Otoh, still smarting and stunned from the baton blow, saw a band of men with bird cages, four each, approaching the back fence. Following them were three men with saws.

As the bird catchers passed he heard them talk. "In a pinch ten birds could live for about two, three days in one cage."

"You know how much one peekoplat fetching these days?"

"Divide up, a third each, a mudra that size would make each one of us a rich man. I myself putting in a bid for the lower third of the base."

Otoh squatted down next to his father.

"Pappy, if they decide that she kill him, what would happen to she?"

Ambrose shook his head in disbelief. "Impossible. Impossible."

"Tomorrow they going to inspect the scene."

Still his father said nothing.

"Pappy, say something! Why you don't say something? Why you don't do something? You just going to let them take she so?"

Then out of the blue he asked his father, "You have any matches on you?"

That night, after the rasping sawing of timber had stopped, Ambrose stood on his darkened verandah and leaned on the banister railing. In the darkness he watched men carrying piles of the heavy timber from Hill Side to Government Alley. They struggled several paces with one load, rested in the middle of the road, ran back for another, and so they inched their treasure along. There was more to come from the house on Hill Side.

Otoh was nowhere in sight. Elsie Mohanty, feeling tired for the first time in decades, had finally dozed off. Ambrose had not the slightest need of sleep. He stared blankly toward the house on Hill Side, grimly contemplating his life-long inability to act decisively. He stared morosely, wondering what was to become of the woman whom he had loved since he was a little boy, wondering if there was something that he could do, something that would spring to mind if only he meditated long enough, something that he dared to do. He could think of nothing, really.

Suddenly, emanating from exactly where he estimated Mala's house to be, a flare of brilliant red and yellow light shot into the sky. Within seconds the hissing and spitting of a fire could be heard. Flames leapt up and licked the heavens. Ambrose's heart raced. He stood on tiptoe, as though doing so would help him to see better. For the second time in twenty-four hours, excited neighbours filed into the street. The fire truck arrived but the firefighters' efforts to get to Hill Side were hampered by the piles of mudra blocking the street. As they worked to clear a passage, a brilliant display of embers spit up into the sky as old, dry timber went up in flames. The intoxicating fragrance of burning mudra wafted through the air. The fiery sky swarmed with crazed bats and moths. *Fwoop. Fwoop. Fwoop.*

Otoh appeared. Behind his back he clutched clippings from a cereus plant. He stood beside his father and, buoyed by the scent in the air, they watched the luminous sky until dawn. In the early hours of morning the flames and the scent subsided.

For almost a week, however, until a day or so after the presiding judge had reached his decision, the house and the trees and shrubs and every bit of live and dead matter that had thrived on the Hill Side property remained floating through the town in an irritating dust, suspended in a thick, black cloud above the town and blocking out the light of the sun.

III

THERE WAS A time when Ambrose E. Mohanty was not in the least interested in sleep. He used to laugh and say that he would sleep well enough and long enough when he was dead. These were the days when he and Mala hoped and dreamed together, the days well before he had married Elsie.

Ambrose had spent several years studying in the Shivering Northern Wetlands. He returned a natty, foreign-accented bachelor full of dreams. Mala heard that he was returning. She went to buy salt fish and ground provisions from Pilai's Dry Goods and Pilai dropped the news on her. He waited until they were alone in the store.

"Ey, Pohpoh-beti, how you doing? What you come for today?"

"I am good, thanks, Mr. Pilai. I come for cassava, yam, green fig and plantain."

"I have plenty. Take a basket." And then he came closer to her. "So, Pohpoh, you hear news, girl?" he said in an excited whisper.

"Mr. Pilai, please, you keep forgetting, please don't call me Pohpoh. I am no longer a child. What news, Mr. Pilai?"

"You know I don't mean you no harm. I know you since you a child, and I call you that name so long now that it does be hard to remember. *Mala* does sound so strange. So, you mean you ent hear news? Well, I breaking news again!"

Mala liked Mr. Pilai well enough. She kept her eyes on the ground provisions as she picked through his tray of eddoes and cassava. He followed her closely.

"Ambrose . . ." Pilai was pleased to see the twitch in her body. His news would indeed be of certain import to her. He was all the more excited to be its bearer. "Ambrose, you remember Ambrose? Boyie, na. He coming home tonight."

Mala gasped and instantly regretted it. If he gossiped to her certainly he must do so to others, and she had no wish to be the subject of gossip. She had learned early the emotional bruising that came from whispered jeers and ice-cold stares. But still, the news that Ambrose, the closest friend she ever had, was returning to town was too thrilling to be elegantly contained.

"Ambrose Moha . . . ?"

"Yes, yes, yes, him self," said Pilai. "What other Ambrose I would tell you about? His mammy was in here not ten minutes before you come. You just miss she. She buy up all me good cassava. Look." He rummaged through the tray showing her that the ones left were a little bruised. "She take all me good provisions. She say to make big cook-up for him. Is like Christmas in Paradise Estate."

Mala allowed herself some curiosity. "His mammy must be real happy. Holidays? Holidays he come for, Mr. Pilai?"

"No, girl. He finish study. He get degree and thing. He back in truth. Coming home tonight, to sweet Lantanacamara by steamer. When we own fellas gone away to a place like the Shivering Northern Wetlands, they does hardly come back, you know. They does stay up there and marry foreign and forget about we. But Ambrose is a real Lantanacamara man. And Pohpoh-beti, how about you? You happy?" He asked the question with such real concern that Mala could not correct him again.

"I'm happy for his mammy. She must be cooking and cleaning all day for him."

Pilai gauged her response to his news not so much from anything Mala said, for she hardly spoke, but from the sudden shift in her purchasing manner. She got busier, buying flour, baking powder, eggs and dry chocolate. She even bought an ounce of the new colourful icing beads that he had got in only that week.

Even as she bought the baking ingredients, Mala wondered if Ambrose was returning alone or if he had found himself an exciting and educated foreign wife. Would he have children, would he even remember Mala? When they were in school together they had been inseparable, and he was the only one of the male species — besides Chandin Ramchandin, her father — who had ever touched her body, kissed her mouth. But they were children then and she had let him, not because she felt any love for him but because she wanted the ticklish feeling and moments of escape the act gave her. On her way home she thought only of Ambrose, of how he was before he left. Everyone in the town had been excited that he had won the one and only scholarship given out by the Bible Mission to go to the Shivering Northern Wetlands and study theology. He had been worried to be away for such a long time, afraid that anything could happen to his mother without his knowing. And now he was coming home to a healthy mother, older certainly, but well and happy. She wondered if in the Shivering Northern Wetlands he had ever seen her mother. Or Asha, who had run away from home when she was in her late teens, a deed Mala understood even though she cried for months when she realized Asha would be true to the penned word left for her on her bed. She would never return home again. She wondered daily what had become of her, if she had perhaps gone to the Wetlands in search of their mother. If, that is, the Shivering Northern Wetlands were where Mama and Aunt Lavinia had gone. She herself could hardly remember what any of them looked like, except in the photograph she had saved from a fire once. Asha was not in that photograph and sadly, there were none of her to be found. Mala wished that Ambrose would arrive on her doorstep with news of all three.

She went home and baked. Her father came late that evening. He had already been drinking and paid no attention to the smell of fresh roasted bread and angel cake. He was intoxicated enough not to notice the house was tidied up and cleaner than he'd ever seen it. With the kitchen floor and wood furniture all polished, the place looked and smelled like the early hours of Christmas morning. He was oblivious to it all.

That night Mala complied with Chandin Ramchandin's expectation that she lie down with him. She let him more easily than ordinarily lay his coarse hands on her belly, for she was in possession of a joy and hope that allowed her to block the whole thing out. She thought of Ambrose sitting with his mother in their house at the edge of the cane fields. She had heard that he sent money home regularly and that his mother had added two rooms with doors that could be locked. One for her and one for him. Mala wondered what Ambrose thought of the additions. She imagined him coming to say hello just as he had come to say good-bye years ago. She imagined herself in the kitchen when he knocked at the door. She changed the image and put herself in the garden. He would come around the back of the house to catch her tilling the soil around the rose bushes — or better yet, plucking wax-shiny yellow fruit from the passion fruit vine or collecting a basket of frangipani. Once, when they were in high school, he came to visit her. Realizing that her tyrannical father was home, he left a note of his visit in the form of a stolen stalk of frangipani shoved into the earth by the back fence, inside the yard. Her heart leapt with joy when she remembered the frangipani was in unusually full bloom these days. It must have been an omen.

When she was sure her father had succumbed completely to the sleep of his cheap alcohol, she removed his thick hand from her belly and slipped out of the bed. Mala ran to the window and looked out. Even in the dark night she could see the brightness of the frangipani blossoms by the fence. Her anxiousness to see Ambrose surprised her.

Next morning Mala was much less certain that the foreign-educated Ambrose would visit her. She busied herself around the kitchen, watching her father as he got ready to leave for the day.

Living had become a matter of habit for Chandin Ramchandin. He began his day as usual walking from house to house calling out, "Madam! Madam! Boss! You need help today?" He had learned to avoid some houses. Their inhabitants would come out wielding a broom, shouting to him to get away, that they did not want the likes of him around their children. While many shunned him there were those who took pity, for he was once the much respected teacher of the Gospel, and such a man would take to the bottle and to his own child, they reasoned, only if he suffered some madness. And, they further reasoned, what man would not suffer a rage akin to insanity if his own wife, with a devilish mind of her own, left her husband and children. Whether they disliked him or tolerated his existence, to everyone Chandin was Sir. He was often paid a goodwill shilling and pennies to weed a yard, sweep their drains, pick coconuts, kill a chicken or goat, or sharpen knives. When Chandin had enough coins he would quit work and head for the rum shop where he stayed until hunger gnawed at his belly.

Her father had hardly left the house for the day and Mala had only begun to straighten his smelly bed when she heard the soft voice, like cool, clear honey, cooing her name from the back porch. She straightened her hair, adjusted her dress and tried to calm her breathing.

"Pohpoh?"

She could find no voice to answer. She walked out to the back porch grinning.

"I hear you were coming back home, in truth, yes!" She could feel the blush on her face.

"Ah. How quickly news travels in a small town. I was hoping to surprise you."

"Well, I already knew. I was just wondering when I would see you. Yesterday I was in Pilai store, you remember Mr. Pilai? It was he who tell me that you was coming home. So Mammy must be too happy, eh? Pilai tell me your mammy was making big cook-up?"

He had put on a little weight but he never looked so fine. The fedora he removed with the fluency of a gentleman lent him an air of grandness. Ambrose E. Mohanty stood like a man, filling the porch with an elegant scent of cloves, cardamom and bay leaves. For the first time in her life Mala felt like a woman, a feeling both thrilling and frightening. She lifted her shoulders upright and her small breasts quietly announced themselves.

"Mammy is well, Pohpoh. And you? How are you? How have you been?"

"I good, yes," she said, suddenly afraid to know how he was, to know if he had married, if he were really back to stay. He had turned into an extraordinarily handsome man. Ambrose was more dapper than even the Wetlandish Reverends and white plantation owners who had not visited their home countries in many years. Except for his skin colour he looked like a man in a foreign magazine, and with a little twist of her imagination she could picture him fair skinned.

"Come in, na. Pappy isn't home. He left for the day already." Mala avoided his eyes.

"I know. I was outside for a good while, waiting for him to leave." Ambrose picked up a parcel he had set on the verandah floor and followed her into the kitchen.

"Pappy didn't changed much, na. You remember him?" How little could she tell him, she wondered, and still expect him to catch her meaning? She could never bring herself to graphically reveal her situation yet she desperately hoped that he, of all people, might understand the things she couldn't say. She wasn't really sure why she trusted he might understand. Several years had passed since she had last seen Ambrose, since he had last seen her. But in those years he had clearly outgrown the chubby, greasy Boyie she used to collect snails with in the schoolyard. Her father was still a menace and tyrant. Everyone knew that. She wondered if Ambrose had ever figured out that her father pretended she was the wife who had many years ago run out on him.

"So you come back to stay or you leaving again?" She busied herself getting out a plate and knife, the fresh bread and some butter and guava jelly. She couldn't bear to look at him. She wondered if the package he carried was for her.

"I have no plans to leave. I finished my studies and I am now back to stay." He lowered the parcel onto the kitchen table. "This is for you. Forgive my forwardness, Pohpoh, but I brought this novelty back home with me and I thought that it might be of some interest to you. May I offer it to you?"

"Well, that is kind of you. But I don't know what it is. You don't have to bring no gifts for me, you know. What is in the box, Mr. Mohanty?"

He had never heard her say his last name before and was amused by her formality. "Pohpoh, you must call me Ambrose. I am the same person you have known since we were children. Please accept my present."

He pushed the box toward her and encouraged her to look inside. She reluctantly opened the box. Inside was a portable gramophone with two seventy-eight r.p.m. disks stashed on the turntable. Mala covered her mouth in surprise and embarrassment.

"But I hardly know you. Is not right for a woman to take presents so expensive from a man. I am sorry but I can't accept this, Mr. Ambrose."

"Not *Mr.* Ambrose. Ambrose alone is fine. You do know me. And I only brought it back for you because I hold you in the highest esteem and wanted to pay my respects to you in the spirit that —" He broke off abruptly. It stunned Mala to realize he was about to cry.

"I expected you to be wearing a priest's collar," she quickly said.

His mood shifted. He dropped the topic of the gramophone and slid into an eloquence that he clearly delighted in displaying.

"After a year of schooling in theology," Ambrose began, "I found that certain concepts had the effect of turning me into a rather irascible fellow. Quite the antithesis of a theologian, don't you think?" He chuckled, looking to her for a response. Mala remained silent. "I left the seminary and went to a little-known university where I completed — quite successfully, might I add — a degree in entomology. I am an entomologist, a bloody entomologist, Pohpoh!" He laughed heartily. She stared at him blankly, not sure what he meant.

"Look. At the heart of theology there is a premise — they will try to tell you otherwise, but if one listens carefully there is a premise that we humans are the primary sun around which the entire universe revolves. Unstated but certainly implied is the assumption that humans are by far superior to the rest of all of nature, and that's why we are the inheritors of the earth. Arrogant, isn't it? What's more, not all humans are part of this sun. Some of us are considered to be much lesser than others — especially if we are not Wetlandish or European or full-blooded white."

She found his words and meanings too obscure for her to follow and Mala became interested in the musicality of his voice. His words were like cut-glass pendants tinkling on a string. He paused and waited for a response but she was far too lost.

"Ambrose, I never knew you to talk quite so much."

"Well, I feel as if I want to talk with you about everything and to talk and talk and talk forever and ever. With you, that is. Everything I learned while I was over there I wanted to discuss and share with you. How are you, Pohpoh? Tell me, how are you?"

"I am good, yes." Mala wasn't sure if she was hearing him correctly. "But I don't understand what you are talking about. What about the Reverend? What he say about you not finishing your studies? You must have to pay back the mission a lot of money, eh?"

"Ah, dear. Where should I begin?"

"You begin already. Just carry on. But go slow and explain so I can understand you."

"Look, it's not that I intended to turn my back on God. I just don't think that those instructors and eminent theologians are equal to their theories of theology. When I was asked about my special areas of interests I told them that I dearly wanted to map the importance of the insects and bugs mentioned in the Bible to the spiritual well-being of humankind and the earth on which we all, man and nature, co-exist. All of God's universe."

Mala began to giggle. He looked at her quizzically.

"I thought I wasn't understanding you but now it look like I am."

"Yes? Yes? Ah, Pohpoh. I knew you would! They thought I was loco but when they realized I was serious they let me begin a study of my own. Yet every step of the way they intervened, insisting that I posit the insects and the bugs and all creatures not of the human species as *lesser*, as *dumb*, and to relegate them to being God's *tools*, servants, or as doom that He would send down upon mankind as punishment, or that He would visit upon us as reward for our deeds. Well, I wrote a letter to the Reverend and he agreed that I could use the scholarship to study entomology as long as I promised to return and work as a good Christian in the ministry of agriculture."

"You goin to work in the cane fields, Ambrose?"

"I got him to agree that I would work in the area of tourism. Bringing people to God via the ministry of His marvellous nature. He told me that if I weren't so bright, and if Mammy weren't such a good and God-fearing woman he would take the scholarship away and give it to someone else. But he knew that ever since I was a child I had a heart for entomology. So I don't owe them any money. But I do owe you tremendous gratitude. It was you who introduced me to the world of insects, you know that, eh, Pohpoh?"

"So what kind of work it is you going to do?"

"Commerce. Some sort of enterprise of my own. Finding a position would be quite impossible, I tell you. It would be quickly discerned by any employer that I am incurably notional. I would be fired before the completion of my first day. The charges would fill a ledger: daydreaming, insolence, stubbornness, quixotism and so the list would go."

Mala couldn't quite follow him but somehow, to his delight, he made her chuckle. She glanced at the gramophone still sitting in the box. Its arm was brass coloured with ornate etchings. It was very pretty.

"So if I want to hold a job I must employ myself," Ambrose said happily. "I have so many ideas but I will bore you with only my most compelling."

"What is that?"

"I was thinking of harvesting spider silk. Do you remember how those imbeciles at school used to try to crush a strand of spider silk? They would smash at it with a rock but it never split apart.

There have been attempts already to harvest the silk but with little results. I think I might have stumbled upon a way, Pohpoh."

There was such affection in the way Ambrose said Pohpoh that Mala was unable to tell him that she could no longer bear the name. Pohpoh was what her father had lovingly called her since she was a baby, long before the crisis in the family. But when Chandin Ramchandin started touching her in ways that terrified and hurt her, she hated the way he whispered, "Pohpoh, my little Pohpoh, you must never leave me, eh?" She decided not to ask Ambrose to call her Mala just yet. The request might cause too many questions to hang like a curtain, separating them. She would wait for a time when she was sure nothing could wedge a distance between them.

"I am thinking also," he continued dreamily, "of purchasing a pirogue, a small boat, to take foreign visitors who come in search of nature's tropical wonders up the river and out to the vast swamp-lands on the eastern coast. The swamp is the home of magnificent birds, so colourful and varied in size, with fantastic appendages that make them appear to have escaped the pages of a fairy tale. The swamp is also home to countless species of fantastical crabs and lizards and crocodile. Those foreign naturalists would give their arm and a leg to see what lives in that swamp. I am certain, too, that there we could also find a copious supply of web-spinning spiders. What do you say?"

It was all too strange for Mala, especially his use of the word we.

"You like the bread?" was all that she could say.

"And you, Pohpoh, could serve them tea and hot bread at the end of the river trip. What do you say? I had no idea that you baked so competently. But of course I am not surprised. It is rather an excellent taste. I could eat such bread very happily for every meal for the rest of my life."

The surprise of such a revealing pronouncement quieted them both. They parted awkwardly, Ambrose pretending to forget the gramophone on the table and Mala pretending to not notice that it remained. He made his way out the back door.

Without removing the gift from the box she looked at it, touching the fat brass arm. She clutched the records to her chest, imagining that Ambrose knew these musical pieces well, had especially chosen them for her. She returned the disks and closed the box. With less difficulty than Ambrose, she lifted it and walked into her bedroom. She shoved the box under her bed, out of her father's sight.

IT WAS MARKET day. As he left the house that morning Chandin Ramchandin had, as usual, stated what he wanted for his evening meal. "Curry a brown fowl," he said but it was understood the meal must also include rice, split pea dhal, curried channa or aloo and one sadha roti. Chandin left six shillings on the kitchen table for Mala to go to market with. It was enough to buy the chicken but with all her baking for Ambrose she would also have to get flour for the roti. Before Ambrose left, Mala was distressed that she would have to shorten his visit so that she could make the trip to Pilai's Dry Goods and the market. She needed time to kill, gut and pluck the fowl before cooking it. There would be no lingering today.

Fortunately, Ambrose had left her just enough time to complete her work and cooking before Chandin returned. But so preoccupied was Mala with her intriguing beau, she entirely forgot what day it was. Before leaving for the market she fixed on her head a wide-brimmed hat with large red flowers and purple birds. She looked at herself in the mirror, pretending she was in the market and, unbeknownst to her, Ambrose too was in the market watching her. She turned and twisted her face, puckered her mouth and raised her eyebrows, mimicking the well-to-do women who sometimes made the market trip. She imitated them asking the vendors with benevolent arrogance for a fat young fowl, a bundle of cinnamon, a pineapple. She saw herself in the mirror as she imagined Ambrose might, the way he might watch and admire her.

Swinging her woven straw basket, humming and admiring the flowering shrubs and trees in neighbouring yards, Mala was ecstatic as she strolled down the five long blocks to the market. Cooking for her father was a chore she performed without much thought or caring. But now cooking had become a delightful production. She would cook more than enough food so that tomorrow she would be able to show off and offer her talents to Ambrose.

When she got to Pilai's store, to her horror, it was closed. Then she remembered the day was Wednesday. Her disbelief quickly turned to fear. On Wednesdays Pilai opened his shop for only two hours in the early morning. By nine o'clock he would close and make his once-a-week trip to the docks for provisions that came in by steamer from another island. Everyone in Paradise knew his schedule. She looked down at her feet and noted her shadow was short. It was well past ten o'clock. She was no longer very confident that she would get a chicken, let alone a brown one so late in the day.

The fowl, pork and beef vendors' tables had already been cleared. The fowl vendor was hosing off blood, feathers and snippets of entrails from the table and scales, and feathers and excrement from the stack of empty cages behind his stall. A couple of fish stalls were still running. Through a swarm of lazy flies she saw meagre piles of discoloured shrimp and some whole fish that had lost their gloss of freshness. All the king fish, red fish and cavalli were finished, the vendor said, but he had a shark and would give it to her cheap. Shark was always far cheaper than the other fish.

Mala knew it was said that only people whose souls were dark would eat the flesh of an animal that was known to eat the flesh of man.

Mala considered the shark. The vendor slit its belly with a flamboyant gesture and yanked out the guts. He stretched apart the slit intestine. She looked, and seeing nothing resembling human body parts or unusual colours, she agreed to take it. She sought solace in the fact that fish was cheaper than meat. She would spend her father's money carefully and take change home.

Spice and vegetable vendors were plentiful still. Mala bought tomatoes, onions, garlic, star anise seeds, sweet potatoes, eddoes, cassava, yam and scotch bonnet peppers. To compensate for her carelessness she bought a bundle of her father's favourite vegetable, string bean bodi. She still had a shilling and some pennies.

Chandin Ramchandin would not get his curry but Mala would cook up the tastiest stewed fish and provisions he had ever had. She would fry the bodi with onions and tomatoes, the way he liked best. He would not miss the curry. And the next day she would be able to give a plateful of the anise- and pepper-flavoured fish to Ambrose. It was indeed for Ambrose that she was cooking. It would be fine with him to be served shark. Ambrose was not one to be afraid to indulge in all kinds of pleasures. And Chandin Ramchandin would likely not ask what kind of fish he was eating. If he did she would simply say it was carite. He would never know the difference.

But when her father arrived home that afternoon, he expected the neighbourhood to be permeated with the bitter aromas of freshly roasted and ground curry paste. He was shocked to be greeted by the quieter aroma of fish tamed in burnt sugar and anise, the smells of a creole stew. Mala heard him drag open the front gate. She swiftly set the table for one. In a white enamel bowl she spooned out a large serving of the brilliant, tomato-coloured fish, decorated tastefully with the yellow scotch bonnet pepper floating in gravy. There was still enough left for herself and Ambrose. She put a portion of the bodi in a saucer and some rice in a sky-blue enamel bowl. She was finished by the time Chandin unlocked the front door.

She stood in the kitchen in full view, but he did not glance in her direction. He walked straight to his bedroom where he undressed, removed his shirt and changed from a pair of worn-out, stained khaki pants to worn-out, stained pajama pants. Mala anxiously brushed flies away from the plates of food. She expected a confrontation but trusted that after the first drop of her stew touched his tongue he would quietly finish his meal. In his pajama pants and a ragged merino vest, Chandin shuffled barefoot into the kitchen, still not looking at Mala.

He walked to the back verandah, looked around and came and stood in the doorway. His features were eclipsed by the evening glare.

"You wash clothes today?" he gruffly asked.

"No, Pappy. Today is Wednesday. I does wash clothes Tuesday and Friday."

"You sweep the yard? It didn't look to me like you sweep."

Becoming afraid, Mala whispered back, "No, I sweep yesterday. I will go and sweep now-now if you say so."

He looked at the plate of fish on the table. "I see you went and make market today," he said quietly. He shuffled into the drawing room and swiped a finger across a centre table.

"And I see you didn't dust today." His voice was low but Mala could tell that a hurricane was around the corner. Tears began to cloud her eyes.

"No, Pappy." The words were barely audible. His questioning was beginning to have its desired effect.

"So, if you didn't sweep, you didn't dust and you didn't wash, what make you late that you didn't get chicken?"

"Pappy, they didn't have chicken."

He walked over and stood by the table where the food waited. Mala watched flies settling on the dishes. She was trapped. Swatting the flies might provoke violence from her father, yet ignoring them was also perilous.

"So how is it that this morning I see Miss Barlo leaving the market with a fowl in her hand. And I see Miss Gomez with one and Mr. Samlal carrying two? Tell me?"

She opened her mouth to utter something that had not yet even formed itself into an idea, when he suddenly grabbed the bowl of fish and in one fluent motion rammed it into her face. In terror she gasped, inhaling stew in her mouth and nostrils. She kept her eyes on Chandin, even though the stew burned. She had learned to watch and anticipate his actions against her so she could control their impact.

Chandin Ramchandin's body shook with rage. Mala puffed her chest out against him like a bullfrog in full defiance. He growled, anger stripping him momentarily of his faculty to speak. Clutching a handful of hair at the back of her head, he shoved the bowl into her face again, twisting it back and forth. Her nose began to bleed. She concentrated on the sensation of enamel against her face, as though taking notes on an experiment. With every clockwise twist he slammed his pelvis into her, banging her against the counter of the sink. She felt no pain. She tapped her tongue against the roof of her mouth checking the stew for seasoning. She tasted blood. To stem the panic brought on by the recognition of blood, she focused her eyes on the half-moon-shaped, chicken pox scar on her father's forehead. He let the bowl drop and leaned against Mala, resting his forehead on hers. The smell of his alcoholic body and breath agitated her more than the injuries he had just then inflicted. She slipped her tongue out of her mouth and licked the stew on her face. The taste of garlic and anise erased his smell. The stew was indeed well seasoned, perhaps the best she had ever cooked. She was pleased she had saved some back for Ambrose.

Chandin straightened himself and moved away from her.

"Idleness is the workings of the devil, you lying bitch. You want to have your own way — just like your mother. You is a liar just like your mother. I will teach you. I will see to that. I tell you I want curry fowl. It don't matter to me where you get a fowl from but you will go and find one. Tonight self. You hear me? You ent sleeping until I eat curry fowl and this kitchen clean up good."

He ripped off his pajama shirt, which was spotted with bodi and tomato, bundled it up and flung it at her face. She caught it in time. Slyly pleased with herself, Mala hung her head low and stared at her bare feet. He shuffled out of the kitchen and into his room. He slammed the door so hard the dishes in the cupboard shook. She breathed a long sigh.

It was already dark outside except for the flashes of lightning that lit up the tropical night skies. Not that Mala needed light to find her way around the neighbourhood. In the first few months after her mother had left she had trekked through the streets many nights in despair, undetected. Ashamed that she had been forced out of her father's home to search for a chicken, Mala considered the possibilities. Her father clearly expected her to steal. How else would she find a chicken at night when no shop was open? Yet if she stole, her father would draw blood with his beating and berating — and would likely do the same if she returned empty handed. At the backyard gate Mala smelled a freshness. Something had recently died. It was not an offensive smell, perhaps a squirrel or cat. She followed her nose and waited for a flash of lightning to reveal what had met its death.

The garden was suddenly illuminated. On the bare earth lay a young pigeon. She knelt by it, sniffing. She poked it. Although the body had stiffened Mala could tell from its smell that the bird had died that day. She hid behind a thick majagua bush and began to cluck and clack. Her clucking heightened as though she were a bird being pursued and then, as though caught, she squawked and spat. Shaking the branches of the majagua she made a convincing imitation of a chicken struggling to free itself, and failing.

In the darkness of the yard she plucked the pigeon, slit the bird's belly and removed its entrails. She cut off its head with a machete. She snipped the soft breasts apart, separated the flesh and flung the bones over the fence. Then she cut up the rest of the small bird. By the time she was finished the mound of bird parts was not dissimilar to young chicken meat.

Chandin was more than halfway through a bottle of whiskey when he heard the sizzle and smelled the aroma of masala, garlic and onions frying in oil. He was too drunk to notice the foulness of a dish prepared with meat that was almost rotten. He tasted curry spices and that was enough to appease him, and besides, the spoonfuls of hot pepper sauce he doused the food with scorched his taste buds and eliminated the finer details of taste. He suffered nothing more than a slight stomach gripe and went to bed earlier than usual, believing the aches were the result of having eaten too much, too hot and too late: an entire chicken, two plates of rice floating in dhal and a quarter jar of pepper sauce. As she cleaned up the table and the kitchen, Mala heard him moaning in his bed. He called out to her twice but she pretended not to hear. By the time she was finished in the kitchen she heard snoring.

Mala turned out all the lights. While she had been washing all the cookware and cleaning up, the town had been sucked up into darkness. She leaned on the back porch banister and smelled the moistness of the earth. A million fireflies flickered on and off. Amidst the chirping of invisible crickets and frogs was her father's snoring. As long as the guttural sounds were audible she would be able to relax.

She thought of Ambrose, wondering if he too snored, of what he must look like while sleeping, of his lips. She tiptoed to her bedroom and quietly pulled the box from under her bed. The words *Cadence* and *The Shivering Northern Wetlands* and *Music Makers, Appointed by H.R.H. Rupert II* were stencilled on the side of the box. She whispered them to herself, savouring the sound of their exquisite foreignness. The box felt heavier than before. She toted it out to the verandah and lifted out the awkwardly balanced gramophone. She and Asha had once watched Aunt Lavinia crank up her gramophone. She tried to remember just how she made it work. She found the volume control knob and turned it down. She lifted the arm with the needle and placed it in the grooves of a disk. Even with the volume turned off Mala could hear the faint scratchiness, the suggestion of a Dixieland jazz band. She pressed her ear to the horn and smiled, filling once again with the feeling she had had watching her mother and Aunt Lavinia dance, her feet wanting to break out from under her and tap across the verandah, up and down the back stairs, from one end of the town to the next. She tapped a bare toe. She imagined herself in a flower-print dress, newly washed and pressed, twirling in the arms of her coattailed, top-hatted Ambrose, laughing and stepping from star to star all the way across the Lantanacamaran sky, and then back again before the first hint of dawn.

From then on, Mala schemed to get her father out of the house early. Usually still drunk from the night before, he barely noticed that she had washed and dressed herself before he had finished his cocoa and salt biscuits. One morning Ambrose had complimented her on her hair pinned back, and after that she fastened the long hair into a high bun especially for his pleasure.

Since Ambrose returned from the Shivering Northern Wetlands and started paying her frequent visits, she began washing and pressing her clothes the instant her father fell asleep. Looking forward to his visits gave her the strength to endure her father's night-time attacks. She wanted to look as elegant and as rich as she could for Ambrose, her gallant suitor, who dressed himself like a Wetlandish lord. She thought privately of him, indeed, as her black Wetlandish lord, and of herself as the lady who would one day be rescued by him and revealed to all the world as a princess stolen by commoners at birth.

And almost every single day — except for one day a fortnight when he was unable, and, to his credit, unwilling, to avoid his filial obligation of one kind or another to his mother — Ambrose rose with the sun to wait interminable minutes around the corner until he saw Chandin Ramchandin leave the house. Then he would visit Mala, his arms laden with some syrupy fruit he had picked especially for her or with bulbs and roots of wild plants, the pocket of his black slacks bulging with jars of the brilliantly coloured and weirdly shaped fungi he had found the day before in the forest or out on the banks of the swamp.

At the end of each visit they would cart the gramophone out from under the bed to the verandah, where they were afforded privacy by the backyard trees. He would put on one of the two records and the black lord and his poor brown princess would delicately hold the tips of each other's fingers and dance. Mala, at first cautious about moving her body freely, lost her shyness when her lord, with quiet, gentlemanly concern, acknowledged her fears and would neither touch nor gaze at her body in any way that made her uncomfortable. From the slightest touch of her fingertips he could feel her drawing the music into her soul and see it filling her from her feet to the dark hair gathered on her beautiful head. Quieting his desire, Ambrose would drop his eyes and stare at his own dancing feet and imagine the taste and texture and smell of her lips and tongue.

Ambrose quickly settled back into his homeland. He lived principally to visit Mala, the twinkling star of Lantanacamara as he had come to think of her. Dancing with her was the climax of his visits, which he simultaneously looked forward to and didn't want to arrive because it signalled the end. He plodded through evenings and at the first sign of darkness took to bed, long before the last rooster had settled itself down for the night. To induce sleep he lay with a fresh, young leaf of a black sage bush tucked under his tongue. And he waited.

How long these visits would remain hidden from Chandin worried them both, but did not deter them. Mala prayed for the day when Ambrose's dreams of his own enterprise would become a reality, yielding just enough money that they could elope to another town in Lantanacamara.

One morning Ambrose waited by the corner as usual, watching for Chandin to leave. Ambrose carried an empty aquarium in which he threw a branch of ripe, red gru-gru berries plucked from the palm tree under which he hid.

Even before Chandin had made it up the hill, Ambrose had entered the yard with his gifts. He placed the glass box under the house in a dark corner, an unlikely place for Chandin to come across. He grabbed the gru-gru branch and bolted up the back stairs. Mala was waiting for him on the porch.

Before entering the kitchen he invited her to take their old school days route and visit his mother, who had been asking to see the woman about whom her son could not stop talking. Mala found it curious that Ambrose would consider walking in public with the sullied daughter of Chandin Ramchandin. She could see he was not the same shy, easily led boy who had usually cringed in the face of disapproval. She would have loved to trek the old route with him but she feared being caught. Many people considered it an entertainment to watch Chandin become wildly angry, and they would vie to be the first to break such news to him.

"I have to be here when Pappy come home and I don't really know when he coming," Mala said halfheartedly. "He getting more and more crotchety, always have something he want me doing for him. I don't really think I could get to go away for too long a time." She wanted Ambrose to figure it out for himself. She had become so adept at not revealing her emotions that it was almost impossible for anyone else to detect her sadness and pleading. But Ambrose was learning.

"If your father might return soon shouldn't I leave right away?"

"Well, I don't know when he plan to come back but I shouldn't leave the house."

Ambrose felt as though he were being told a story in code. He entered the kitchen and put the berries on the table. They glowed between them as brilliantly as their still unspoken love for each other.

"You eat breakfast?" she asked.

"Mammy cooked me roti and salt fish which I ate, but I saved room in the hope that you would spoil me once more with your heavenly talents."

"Oh no, I make salt fish too."

"It is one of my favourites. I could eat it several times a day. And I am sure that yours will be different from Mammy's, and perhaps even better."

Mala set down a plate of fat bake and salted cod she had prepared for him the night before.

"Mmmm, this is unparallelled," he said, and so often that she stopped fretting that he had already had salted cod that morning.

Ambrose was in the presence of his most favourite and indulgent audience. (While his mother doted on his every move, she hardly understood a sentence he spoke.) Not long after he finished eating, words and phrases began to slide languorously from his lips. He was trying to express how he felt about her.

"A word is not the substance itself," Ambrose stated simply enough but soon slid into a morass. "A world freed of nomenclature, syntax and lexical form is experienced . . . named senses are enhanced . . . sensors in your joints open up like eager blossoms, their little receptors waving wildly, anxious to engage. Your entire being, the physical, and most of all the spiritual, is a vibrant network of synesthesia . . . throughout your body miles of blood, water, serums, toxins, effluvia and nutrients ebb and wane in tune to the moon . . . the tiniest random fraction of your being is connected to your sensorium, and your sensorium experienced as integral only when you recognize yourself as a conduit, a vibrant little cog in the functioning of the universe . . ."

Unable to directly tell Mala just then how aroused he became in her presence, Ambrose moved on to an intoxicating sermon on the potential uses of fine fabric spun by spiders. He asked Mala to imagine women's stockings and hair nets woven from the spiders' delicate threads. Hidden behind his words was his desire to know the delicacy of her skin, to sip from her lips. Yet he was also alerted to her need not to be smothered. The urgency of this need was so apparent that, without understanding its origins, he complied and hoped that with time she would come to trust him.

As he sat in the kitchen Mala too looked at him, at the shape of his lean chest underneath his shirt, his slender fingers, his velvet lips that were rendered much pronounced because of their stunning redness against skin as dark as the pods of the mudra tree. She fixated on his hair, which he no longer soaked in coconut oil, and wanted to bury her fingers in its tight coarseness. She scrutinized the stubby, sea-green area where he shaved. She imagined how the patch might feel and the scratchy noise the ball of her thumb rubbing up and down it might make. She gave his sweat an imagined odour and longed to feel the heat of his underarm against her face. The only man's sweat she knew was her father's, which made her nauseous, and so she was delighted that she could invent a smell for Ambrose that melted her with passion and momentarily overpowered her father's awful hold over her. Her desire for Ambrose made her body arch, reaching out, engulfing, drawing him deep inside her, yet she resisted converting these thoughts to actions.

Yet thorns of fear and treachery would prick her after Ambrose left the house. The fear that her father would discover that her head, heart and body were betraying him, if only because he could smell this new desire on her skin, rendered her inactive in Ambrose's presence. She would pace the upstairs of the house, tormented and confused by odd feelings of having betrayed her father. After all, she thought, her father had suffered immeasurably when her mother left them. Mala would chastise herself, pointing out that even she could not imagine the hurt he must have felt, or the embarrassment he endured. There were times when thoughts of Ambrose made her hate herself for being so cruel and thoughtless to her wounded father. But even at those times, her tenderness aroused, she wanted to be lifted up and taken away by Ambrose.

Ambrose took her outside and showed her the aquarium. They combed the underneath of her father's house for web-spinning spiders. Mala watched nervously when Ambrose gripped a strand of sticky fibre from a web attached to a mudra pole beneath the house. She followed as he walked slowly across the backyard, the unbroken fibre lengthening with each step he took. She admired his straight back and imitated his posture. Confident that the backyard was so overgrown that they were well hidden from view, she revelled in the magnificence of his attire. He walked as far as the back fence and still the filament remained unbroken.

"Imagine!" he whispered, "imagine a finely woven curtain miles high in the sky, hung between the Caribbean Sea and the Atlantic Ocean. A curtain that would not deny light, yet could contain and halt a hurricane!" She was so in awe of his inventiveness that she wanted him to whisper those words inside her mouth. She kept her eyes on the crook of his finger. He delighted in telling Mala the methods and principles of spider silk harvesting, and as he spoke he watched her, drinking in her beauty and suppressing his astonishing desire.

They stocked the aquarium with over forty spiders. Mala had little trouble catching the flies that clung lethargically to the nectar-stained petals of passion fruit flowers in her backyard. She put them in a bag, and then shook them into the aquarium.

Back upstairs, though thrilled with the first steps in their research adventure, Mala kept her distance, standing near the kitchen sink. Ambrose, red and puffed up with excitement, sat at the kitchen table. They sipped a cooling, good-luck tea that she had brewed from the leaves of the pigeonpea plant and ti marie, and snacked on the pale yellow meat of the gru-gru berry.

Ambrose produced a leather-bound notebook in which he entered the details of his fledgling business. Both agreed upon a name for the research business: STC–STS. *Softer Than Cotton–Stronger Than Steel.* On the inside front cover of the notebook he penned the name in letters with sprawling tails and elaborate feathers, and then in bold clean letters he set down his own name, *Ambrose E. Mohanty,* next to which he wrote *Principal.* And under this line he wrote *Pohpoh Ramchandin — Second Principal and Ultimate Inspiration.* He read it aloud and they laughed. Mala watched how he had scripted the word Pohpoh. His penmanship was crisp and artful. She could not bring herself to contradict him.

Ambrose leaned back in the caned chair and stretched his legs. Under the table she could see his sheer white stockings. With hands clasped behind his head, he related to Mala how he came to be fascinated by the properties and potentials of spider fibre. It happened as a result of the first winter he spent in the Shivering Northern Wetlands. He had never experienced such cold in his life.

"Don't even try to imagine it. You won't be able to. I had read about it. Even long before setting foot in the Shivering Northern Wetlands, I had seen photographs of the city dusted with this powder they call snow. But you know, Pohpoh, I was entirely unable to truly comprehend just exactly how cold such cold might be. Not until I experienced it for myself.

"This hellish, endless event takes over your entire existence and you can do nothing but think of artful connivances for remaining dry and warm. In the depth of this ruthless winter, while I nursed a demon of a cold, I sat indoors and mournfully contemplated the bleakness of snow-covered yards and walkways and streets from my window. I thought it would never end."

"Hmm," Mala responded simply.

"And then one spring day that same year, I chanced upon a thread of spider silk attached to the higher boughs of a naked tree. The glistening thread was stretched almost to the ground in a perfectly symmetrical V by the weight of an eight-inch-long icicle clinging to it. I stood there, under the warming spring sun and for hours watched as the icicle dripped itself thinner and shorter. Slowly unburdened, the thread itself rose elegantly, as if succumbing to spiritual levitation, higher and higher. When the icicle had succumbed to its watery demise, the spider-spun filament, now perfectly levitated, appeared not to have been stretched. It was, Pohpoh, glistening brilliantly and breathlessly, and as taut as any I had ever come across that had been freshly spun."

Mala grasped Ambrose's intent among the jumble of his words. "Ah! A bridge. You could make a bridge with the threads from this spider business, a bridge to cross the river and no matter how much people and animal and car they drive on it, it would never come falling down."

Mala laughed at her joke. Ambrose was still caught up in his reveries but when he noticed her enthusiasm, he leapt out of his chair, ran over to her, and in utter jubilation threw his arms around her, pulling her surprised and reluctant body into his. She instinctively crossed her arms in front of her chest yet when he looked at her she was smiling. In fact she was beginning to giggle. He knew the giggle from the long-ago days in the schoolyard. He also recognized the smile, yet instead of mirth he was overcome by concern.

"Ah, Pohpoh, my sweet, sweet Pohpoh."

Mala looked into his eyes. "Please don't call me by that name," she whispered. "Don't call me that. You remember my real name?"

Ambrose was taken aback.

"Which one? I am mortified. Tell me which name and it shall never be uttered again."

"*Pohpoh.* That is not my name."

After a quick joggle of his memory Ambrose smiled, pleased with himself. "Mala! You are right. Mala is indeed a name more fitting. The other one shall not be mentioned again." He continued, intending to make amends. "Come home with me. Come and see my dearest Mammy. She knows everything about you and she expects you soon. You will come, sweet Mala, won't you?" Her name, which he had not said aloud in many years, sounded foreign to him but he cottoned quickly to its adult sound. Mala relaxed her face into his chest. He pressed his lips against her thick hair. His chest smelled even more sweet than she had imagined.

There is no point trying to explain a phenomenon that took place in another part of Paradise, a good half mile away from the Ramchandin kitchen. Suffice it to say that these things do happen. Sitting in a rum shop Chandin Ramchandin felt a sudden tightness in his chest at the precise moment his daughter embraced her gentleman suitor. He winced and swallowed another mouthful of prickly babash. The pain in his chest did not lessen. On the contrary, he felt as though he were being stifled.

Mala was troubled. Was this the day when she would either put an end to their trysts or tell Ambrose about the heavy hand with which her father ruled her life? Ambrose breathed in the sugary aroma of her sweat. Her scalp had a faint scent of coconut oil. Even though he wore a concoction of clove oil, bay leaves and cardamom, the natural fragrance of his sweet-and-tangy skin rose from his shirt. She knew now the taste of his skin by its smell. She pressed her face against his chest. He didn't smell like her father, of rum and stale genitals, the shrill severity of soured secretions. Ambrose brought his lips down to her temples and she closed her eyes and lifted her head.

The pain gripping Chandin was like a thick metal chain being yanked around his torso. He finished his drink in one mouthful and, to his fellow drinkers' surprise, made his way out of the rum shop. He walked slowly at first. The pain eased and Chandin carried on as a seasoned drunk would: he swayed a little and mumbled to himself but because of the years and quantity of his consumption, he was in control of his faculties. The pain lessened further but Chandin continued to hold his chest, worried it might creep up on him again. For safety's sake he headed home.

Mala smelled Ambrose's lips close to hers and felt his breath. She pulled away, a little startled, feeling both the repulsion she knew when her father forced his tongue into her throat and also an unfathomable desire to take Ambrose's deep into her mouth and explore its taste and temperature and texture. Ambrose, startled by the sudden shift, responded to her shiver of discomfort.

He was, in truth, relieved at the interruption. Not since he was a child had he felt such a shimmering on the edges of his extremities.

He remembered Mala lying on his cattiya with nothing on but her underwear. He could feel her warm skin. There had been no shortage of women in the Shivering Northern Wetlands who offered to keep the handsome, unusual black man company through long winter evenings. Ambrose had no trouble resisting their temptations and he remained untouched, except in his thoughts of Mala. He had waited for the moment when he might do what he had dreamed of since he was a child: of putting that part of his anatomy that stiffened, making him dizzy with its trembling, so very close to . . . touching even . . . the place of mystery between Mala's legs, a place he imagined would exhale a hot mustiness with two very different scents — balsa wood from the silk cotton tree that he used to make spinners with, and the ripened fruit of the cannonball tree, a fearfully strong but very compelling odour. Lying in his bed in the Shivering Northern Wetlands he would close his eyes and lock onto an image of Mala. His blood would race around his body as he squeezed and rubbed himself, and he imagined placing his swollen self close enough to Mala to cause that mysterious mouth of hers to open in a wide yawn and pull him in.

Mala's abrupt withdrawal was welcome. It was as though, as time passed, Ambrose had fallen in love with desire itself and the act of desiring was its own fulfillment. Certainly, he craved the pleasures that would come from seeing Mala undressed, of delicately holding the nipple of her breast between his teeth and most of all, of his man's appendage moistened and caressed and drawn up into her body. But when Mala pushed him gently away, he was forced to acknowledge the companion that *desiring* had become for him over the years. He was, he realized, unwilling to jeopardize his relationship with desire. If he succumbed to Mala's treasures, *desire* could change, would disappear even.

Mala watched his face. She was so moved by his generous hesitation that she grabbed the front of his shirt and pulled his face toward hers. She closed her eyes and repeated to herself, Enjoy him, he is not my enemy, he loves me. She smelled his cheeks and felt the stubble on his face against her soft cheek. Little kisses from his voluptuous lips alighted on her cheek, skipping toward her mouth and then shyly away toward her ear again. She cupped his face tightly in both hands, opened her mouth and covered his with her strong, wet lips. Her lapping tongue slid across his lips. Ambrose felt completely weakened. He had never experienced a dizziness so pleasant. He opened his mouth to gasp for air and Mala reached in with her tongue and licked his. He pulled back from her and gasped for air. He had never seen her face so close before. His eyes roamed over her face, followed by the light touch of his fingers. His other hand hovered near her buttocks. Mala pressed her body against him, knowing he would be quite hard. The hovering hand found her buttocks, and the shape of her body — a woman's body — so disarmed him that he thought he would faint. Mala's movements were different from the day at his mother's house when they were children. This time she had no goal in mind. This time she let him touch her for his pleasure too. She met, mirrored and embraced his passion. She moved against his hardness. He began to pull her dress up in little increments.

It was his first time, and her first time with someone of her own choice. In the kitchen, on the wood floor that smelled of the onions and garlic ground over the years into its grooves, Ambrose experienced what it was like to empty his semen into a woman, into his childhood love, rather than onto the pages of a magazine. For the first time Mala felt no pain. It was the first time she felt what it was like to be touched and to have her nipples licked and tasted as though they were a delicacy. And though she had been forced to touch her father countless times, it was the first time she explored and felt on the tips of her fingers and the palm of her hand what a penis was really like.

They lay on the kitchen floor. Ambrose was propped on an elbow, his other hand caressing her pubic hair and delicately slipping a finger between her lips, amazed at her wetness. Suddenly Mala realized how late it had become. Her father would soon be home. She jumped up and started pulling her clothes on. It took Ambrose longer to dress, to tuck in his shirt, do up all the buttons and pull on his suspenders and socks. In less time than they liked, the day was coming to an end.

"We haven't danced today," Ambrose said. "But I must admit that loving you"— these words weakened her again —"quite rivals dancing. I do however promise you three extra sets to make up for today's missed one. It will be the pleasure of my life to hold you and to dance with you holding me."

"And I will practise and surprise you. Will you come tomorrow, Ambrose?"

How could he possibly stay away? He kissed her again and again to seal his response. It was the longest day Ambrose had spent with Mala since his return to Lantanacamara.

Chandin reached the gate at his front yard just as Ambrose took up his hat to leave the kitchen. Pressing the hat against his lower stomach he walked backwards out of the kitchen, not wanting to take his eyes off Mala as she lifted her hands to breathe in the traces of his body. He sniffed his own fingers and touched them to his lips. She closed her eyes. Ambrose slowly made his way down the back stairs.

Chandin grappled with the twisted front gate. It had been bent for years but he refused to fix it, convinced it contorted itself only to get the better of him after he had had a few drinks. He was determined not to be manipulated by its craftiness. He caught a glimpse of movement at the back of his house. Chandin stopped fiddling and focused his blurry eyes past the shrubs, past the underneath of the house with its high stilts, through to the back stairs. He saw a man slowly descending backwards, black coat, white shirt and hat in hand. He hid behind a shrub and peered out.

Looking around to make sure Mala's father was nowhere in sight, Ambrose made a quick detour under the house to check on the spiders in the aquarium. Chandin, anger rising, could not see what the man was up to under his house. He stayed hidden.

Ambrose was stunned to find that although all the flies remained alive only four spiders were moving. The others were headless, their torsos strewn on the floor of the glass cage. He quickly understood the evidence of natural selection. Overcrowded, the spiders had waged war. Only the fittest had survived and not a fragment of web had been spun.

The unfamiliarity of pessimism deflated him. Abrose turned his back on the spiders and pressing the hat against his chest again, reluctantly left the yard.

Chandin could hardly maintain his balance. He stumbled, holding on precariously to a handful of leaves from the shrub.

"What the ass. . . ?" he mumbled. "A man tiefing my baby? He brave to even try. I ent go let nobody tief my woman again. No man, no woman, no damn body go tief my property again. I go kill he. I go kill she too, if it come to that. I go kill meself too. I sharpenin' cutlass tonight."

Chandin crept up the front stairs and onto the verandah. He peered through the glass pane of the front door. His daughter still leaned against the kitchen sink, smiling to herself and smelling her hands. The plate and the cup that his wife once used for visitors were in full view on the table, and a chair was pulled out from the table.

Chandin's face was already flushed from alcohol, and anger caused the veins along his temples and neck to puff out a hard blue. He clutched his chest. His heart hurt with heaviness. He noisily pulled out a key ring from his pocket.

Hearing the keys and commotion on the front porch, Mala was shocked that her father had returned home so soon after Ambrose's departure. She whisked the cup and plate off the table and pushed the chair in. She shoved her mother's good dishes in the rubbish pan and pushed it out of sight. There was nothing unusual about her father's silence on entering. She glanced at his face for any sign that he might be suspicious but saw nothing. Mala took up a cloth and wiped the counter, pretending to be carrying on her regular chores. She watched him look at the table. He straightened the chair, then went over to her and spun her. He held her hands up to his face and pressed his lips to them. It was unmistakable that his intention was to smell her hands. She glanced over to the front porch to see from where he might have been watching. How much had he seen? Mala bent her neck in fear and began to sob.

Her father, silent since he entered the house, began to laugh. Then his face flared with anger, he jerked his body away from her and pulled out the chair. He held it by its back and lifted it high above his head and slammed it down on the kitchen floor. The chair shattered. Mala put her face in her hands and wailed, doubling over in fright. The memory of her father when he discovered her mother gone came flooding back. Chandin moved through the small kitchen like a hurricane. He stormed over to his cowering daughter and lifted his hand, splayed wide like a tennis paddle. When she cried out he slowly brought his hand back to his side, tears streaming down his face. Instead of hitting her he unbuckled his belt and unzipped his trousers. Mala ducked down and tried to slide past him. This infuriated him further. It was the first time she had ever tried to defy him. He caught her by her hair and pulled until she straightened up. He pressed his menacing face against hers and screamed.

"Mother ass! Don't try to make a fool out a me! I go kill you right here. I ent fraid."

"Please, Papa, please don't hurt me, don't hurt me. I beg forgiveness. Have mercy, Papa."

"I ever hurt you? I never before hurt you. You want to know what hurt is? Eh? Forgiveness? Mercy? I'll show you what hurt is."

He pushed her to the sink and shoved her face down into the basin, pressing his chin into her back as he used both hands to pull up her dress. He yanked out his penis, hardened weapon-like by anger. He used his knees to pry her legs open and his feet to kick and keep them apart. With his large fat fingers he parted her buttocks as she sobbed and whispered, "Have mercy, Lord, I beg, I beg." He rammed himself in and out of her. He reached around and squeezed her breasts, frantically pumping them to mimic the violent thrusting of his penis.

Then he pulled out of her and flung her around. Standing with his pants around his knees, his still erect penis pointing at her, Chandin slapped her back and forth with the palm and the back of his hand. Her lower lip split and the outer edge of her left eye tore. She tried to stop crying but her chest heaved. He slapped her so hard that she stumbled and fell onto the ground. He lowered his huge frame astride her, pulled her up by her hair and shoved his penis into her mouth. She choked and gagged as he rammed it down her throat. When she went limp, he took the weapon out of her mouth and spurted all over her face.

He began to throw the chairs around, to tear down the curtains. He flung ornaments at the walls and used a frying pan to smash glasses and plates and pictures hanging in the drawing room. Mala covered her ears and shut her eyes tight.

Chandin roared into her room and tore down the old, heavy cotton curtains her mother had sewn twenty years before. He ripped them to shreds. He turned around and saw himself in the full-length mirror on the armoire door. With the heel of his foot he attacked it with one lightning blow. The mirror shattered and fell in a hundred brilliant shards. Still unsatisfied, he wrenched the door from its top hinge, snatched a few dresses off their hangers and ripped them to pieces.

Chandin grabbed the edges of her bed and flipped it over. He saw the new box. Opening it and seeing the gramophone, he put his face in both hands and cried. For several minutes he contemplated the gramophone and what it seemed to signify. He lifted the needle arm and pulled it backwards. It snapped as easily as a crab's leg. Then he tried to do the same with the horn but it was more resistant. He stood up and thundered his bare foot onto the horn. His anger made him oblivious to the pain in his foot. He straightened himself up and marched back to the kitchen and kicked Mala where she lay sobbing on the ground. He pulled open a drawer and took up a cleaver. He dragged her into her bedroom.

"What is this, you whore? He give this to you? You taking presents from a man? What other presents you get? How long you doing this kind of thing? Everybody but Ramchandin know his daughter is the town whore?"

Mala turned her face to the ground and cried. He kicked her in the thighs.

"Answer me, you little whore. That man who was here give you this?" He flung the cleaver into the floor next to the gramophone. Mala looked up.

"Yes, Pappy. It was a gift for you and me."

"For me? What you think I is? don't give me that shit. And what you give him? Come give me what you give him."

Still carrying the cleaver, he pulled her up by the front of her dress and pushed her toward his bedroom. He threw her on the mattress of his sagging bed and ripped her dress off. She shut her eyes and cried out loudly. It was the first time since that very first time when she was a child that she felt so much pain.

Chandin locked the bedroom door. He set the cleaver down by the bed. He raped her three more times that night. He made her stay in his bed. Next morning he got up as usual. He left the bedroom door wide open, carried the cleaver into the kitchen, stepped over the broken furniture and glass and made his way out to the verandah.

Mala got up slowly. To her astonishment he did not hurry her. He did not utter a word. Every inch of her body pained. She licked her lip. She could tell it was swollen. She could feel that her eye was also swollen. Her pelvis and thighs hurt so much the slightest motion made her dizzy. As she made her way slowly to her room she noticed the cleaver was no longer by his bed.

The box was still on the floor, open. The gramophone lay inside, useless. It saddened her more than her bruises but she dared not touch it or be caught looking at it. She picked a dress off the floor and put it on.

Her father, to her embarrassment and fear, had boiled water and put the previous day's bread on the table. He was already eating. He did not look at her or say a word.

On the back porch, as she gently slapped water on her face, she heard the front door open and shut. She looked around the backyard hoping Ambrose would be nowhere in sight. She had no appetite to even think of him just then but she knew he would come as soon as her father had left. He would see her bruised face, he would see she was in pain. She would not tell him, she insisted to herself, what her father had done. After all, Mala berated herself, she should have known better than to cheat on her father. In the end she was to blame. She prayed that Ambrose had better things to do that morning.

She heard the front gate scrape shut. She hobbled in agony to the front door and looked out through the wooden jalousies that flanked the door. Her father was already out of sight yet she felt him in every nook of the house, in every corner of the yard, watching her every move. She hobbled back into the kitchen and looked around for the cleaver. It was nowhere to be seen. Mala latched the back door. She hoped Ambrose would assume she had gone to market or to run errands, and would leave.

Ambrose waited by the corner until he saw Chandin Ramchandin head up the road. He took off toward the backyard gate so eagerly that he did not see Chandin turn and duck behind a neighbour's cart. Chandin saw the ends of the tails of his daughter's suitor's black coat.

From the yard Ambrose noticed the bedroom curtains had been taken down. He thought nothing of it. When he got to the back door and found it latched he became curious. He knocked and called several times. He looked around to see if the curtains had been washed and were hanging on the clothesline. Seeing no signs of early morning activity and finding Mala's door shut on him only one day after the most glorious day of his life confused him. He juggled a fear of rejection with panic. Something ominous seemed to be hanging in the air.

Chandin crouched behind the cart until he felt sure Ambrose had entered the house, then he made his way back. He climbed the fence to avoid being given away by the creaky front gate. The cleaver was where he had concealed it: at the base of the oleander. Chandin wedged himself into the bush. Neither Ambrose nor Mala was in sight and the house appeared quiet. Chandin was about to come out, cleaver in hand, when he was startled by footsteps heading toward the front yard. He ducked back into the shrubbery.

Ambrose hurried around the house and to the front steps, bounding up two at a time. Chandin peered out and saw him staring through the front windows.

Ambrose's heart thundered. He became wide eyed when he saw the disarray inside, believing at first that the house had been burgled. Mala was nowhere to be seen. Fearing the worst, he urged himself to take control of his wits. He began a quiet, insistent knocking. He loudly whispered Mala's name, then called out more urgently. He knocked so many times that even Chandin wondered where his daughter had gone. Ambrose tried the door. It clicked and released, startling him.

Apprehensive, he pushed the front door open and stepped inside. A single glance took in the demolished drawing room and kitchen. His beloved was in neither. Ambrose broke out in a sweat. He tiptoed farther into the house. At Chandin's bedroom he took a slow breath and pushed the partly open door. He feared finding his sweetheart tied up and gagged or worse — but he would not allow himself to imagine what might be worse. He was both relieved and terrified to find no one there. He stood still and listened, wondering if the robber or murderer were still in the house. He tiptoed back to the drawing room. Hesitantly, he tried the door to the downstairs room. It was always locked and was still so.

Chandin, sneaking up the front stairs and crossing silently to the windows, saw the young man press his ear to the door. He watched him carry on toward Mala's room.

Ambrose felt nauseous. He placed his ear against her door and heard nothing. His eyes began to fill with tears of fright. He clenched his teeth, made a fist around the doorknob and very slowly turned it. The door gave way a hair and then shut again. He was so terrified he shoved the door with sudden and surprising force.

Mala had been hiding behind the door. She tumbled over. Keeping her face buried between her knees she sobbed so hard that her body shook violently. Ambrose saw everything except her face: the over-turned bed, the torn clothing, the broken gramophone and, worst of all, blue and violet bruises up and down Mala's arms and legs. He shrieked in alarm and threw himself over Mala like a protective blanket.

"Who did this? Who did this, Mala, tell me, tell me."

She sobbed louder, refusing to let him see her. "Please don't stay here. Go! Get away. Leave me, leave me."

Ambrose clutched her face by her chin. He forced her to face him. Damp hair clung to her face. Blood from her wounded eye had softened and smeared down her cheek. Mucus had run down and smeared her lips and chin.

Ambrose stared in disbelief. Mala stopped crying. She held her breath and looked defiantly straight ahead. Like a summer evening's first flash of lightning, Ambrose's face flared.

"Your father?" he whispered.

Mala closed her eyes. Suddenly Ambrose understood everything.

"So what you going to do about it?" Chandin said.

Mala's father stood in the doorway. Ambrose could not tell if the expression on Chandin Ramchandin's face was a grin or a snarl. Chandin grasped the handle of a cleaver firmly with his hands and lifted it high above his head, arching his body back for leverage. Ambrose scuttled backwards in disbelief. Mala, looking up and seeing her father about to swing the weapon, gave an icy shriek.

She lunged forward, grabbed Chandin by the knees and with a might that frightened even Ambrose, jerked his feet out from under him. Chandin fell on his back, still holding the cleaver. Mala dived across the floor, seized the handle and struggled to wrench it from her father's hand. He clenched her hair at the top of her head, tightened his fist and pulled and pulled.

Ambrose inched forward. He wanted to help but how? His mind felt fragile and timid. Chandin raised his foot and kicked in Ambrose's direction. Ambrose recoiled and the foot fell heavily on the gramophone.

Mala's fury was so uncontrollable she didn't notice her hair being ripped out. She forced her face toward the hand holding the cleaver and sunk her teeth deep into Chandin's wrist. Chandin released his grip on her hair and curled his body in sudden agony. Mala had drawn blood.

Ambrose saw the opportunity to go for help or perhaps find a tool with which to fight. He gathered the smashed-up gramophone, yanked open the door and dashed out of the room. The heavy door hit Chandin's head with enough force to stupefy him, and he slumped down, his eyes open. Mala tore the cleaver out of his suddenly limp hand. With the back of her other hand she wiped her father's blood from her face and spat at him. She charged out of the room.

When Ambrose entered the kitchen, he stood still, trying to make sense of what had been revealed to him. He assured himself that it was he whom Chandin wanted to kill and not his own daughter. He looked feebly around for a knife to protect himself, all the while feeling shame for her and for himself — as though he had been betrayed by Mala, and at the same time wrestling with the notion that she could not possibly, not conceivably have been agreeable to intimacies with her father. In that instant of hesitation he so distanced himself from Mala that, like an outside observer, he saw the world as he had known and dreamed it suddenly come undone. He rested the gramophone on the kitchen table and stumbled onto the verandah. At the bottom of the back stairs he hesitated again, wondering if and how to get help, and again shrank with the thought that a call for help would expose the shameful goings-on in the house, to which he had become connected.

Suddenly he heard a dreadful crashing. Mala was calling out his name. He ran back up the stairs as though jolted by a cord. In the kitchen he saw, instead of the woman he had made love to the day before, an unrecognizable wild creature with a blood-stained face, frothing at the mouth and hacking uncontrollably at the furniture in the drawing room. He watched her smash a side table with a single powerful blow. When she saw him she dropped the cleaver and moved heavily toward him, moaning lifelessly.

"Ambrose, don't go. Don't leave me, Ambrose. Please don't go." Ambrose couldn't make out her words. Thinking she had gone crazy and fearing once more for his life, he turned and bolted from the house.

Mala gasped in disbelief. She rushed to the verandah, screaming his name. He had already disappeared. She clutched the banister, choking as though there were no oxygen in the air. She fell to the ground. There was a bizarre familiarity in the moment. She remembered her father clutching at that same banister, and felt herself lying on the verandah in that same position. Long ago. Today.

Mala stopped crying and sat up slowly. She looked into the yard.

"Asha? Aunt Lavinia? You there? Mama? Boyie?" she whispered.

She looked and listened. Nothing. The house was quiet. She commanded herself to think. Shivering, she tiptoed back into the house, picking up the cleaver with a firm grip. Every few paces she stopped and listened for sounds of a buggy, her sister's voice, Ambrose returning, her father stirring. At the door of her room she listened. Unable to stand the tension, she nudged the door open and peeped in. Her father lay still on the floor, his eyes open and glazed, his legs limp, spread apart, his hands curled. The rage inside her ebbed. She stepped back, straightened her posture and pulled the door shut. She put down the cleaver. She walked to the door and lay both hands flat against it. She took a deep breath and pushed with all her power. The door hit Chandin's head and swung back shut. She took a deep breath and repeated the act until she was exhausted.

She opened the door that led to the sewing room downstairs and stared at the flight of steps. She walked back toward her own room and opened the door. Her father had not moved. She took up the cleaver and tiptoed around his body. She stooped down and waited. Still no movement. She lifted the gleaming cleaver to his face and rested the flat side under his nose. Did she only imagine the vapour of hot air that passed over the blade? She jumped up and, extremely vigilant, edged her way toward his feet. She grasped them and pulled. His body seemed oddly tensed. She hauled him with one sharp tug into the doorway. On the wood floor of the kitchen the body slid more easily. She dragged him to the open door. Positioning him on the top stair, she gave him a push and the body slid down two stairs and stopped. She kicked and pushed until she managed to get it all the way down to the bottom stair. Drenched in sweat, she stopped to catch her breath, not taking her eyes off the man. Then she dragged his unyielding weight into the sewing room. She ran out slamming the door shut behind her. Her mother used to keep a key on the ledge. She reached up and found it. She locked the door. She leaned against it with relief and then mounted the stairs. At the top she shut and locked the door.

She looked, not for Ambrose but for Boyie, for Asha, for her mother and for Aunt Lavinia. She picked up the broken gramophone and went down into the garden searching for them. She peered under the house. She left the gramophone there and went to the fence. She walked the length of the fence looking up and down the road. There was no one to be seen.

She tore up the boards that had lain on the soil so that the yard would still be passable in the rainy season. She dragged the boards to the sewing room and hammered them over the window. She ran back upstairs. The door to the sewing room was still shut. She tried it and was relieved to find it was indeed locked. She sat down in the kitchen facing the door to the sewing room, waiting and wondering.

As evening approached Mala sat there still. She thought about the night and how she dared not sleep in her room. She dreaded the idea of sleep and refused to do so inside the house. She jumped up and ran into her room and dragged a dresser, an arm chair and a stool into the centre of the drawing room. She went into her father's room and did the same with his furniture. She spent the evening intricately arranging these and every piece from the drawing room and kitchen, including pieces she smashed apart, into a tight barricade from floor to ceiling. She worked until she had created an admirable wall that was almost impenetrable. It would be dangerous to anyone who attempted to dismantle it. Realizing she would need to know her father's condition and how much care would be needed to be safe from him, she made a small, well-camouflaged doorway.

When she finished she went out on the verandah. In the frothy wind that wildly stirred the trees in the yard she sat and waited.

She never lit a lantern in that house again. Nor did she, since that day, pass a night inside its walls.

IV

THERE WAS NO dawn on the morning after the fire on Hill Side. The town, exhausted by the previous day's excitement, lay under a low umbrella of soot that had the fragrance of mudra-scented charcoal. Across Paradise could be heard a constant, scratchy coughing and sneezing as the town awakened. Most townspeople did not realize that morning had already come. They arose from their beds in darkness.

Ambrose E. Mohanty had stayed on his verandah all night. Otoh was utterly worn out and could have slept had he chosen to. He opted to stay with his father. In recent hours time seemed to have caught up with Ambrose. Otoh watched his father, amazed at how shrunken his posture had become since the afternoon, how stooped his shoulders, how pale and drooped his skin and eyes, as though they could no longer fight gravity. It occurred to Otoh that being awake really did not agree with his father. His father tapped delicately on the banister during the silences between them, as though with a jeweller's hammer. He often paused, sometimes for so long that Otoh resumed his own thoughts and quite forgot what had been said before.

"I appreciate your company, son." Otoh had heard this once already.

"You're so quiet though," Ambrose ventured. Silence.

"It's disconcerting, your quiet I mean," he tried again. Otoh nodded sadly.

"Each time I glance over at you, I feel obliged to respond to the questions that you have every right to ask but are polite enough not to voice." His father tapped.

"Is it my imagination or are there a thousand unspoken whys streaming out, swimming from your temples? I look at your silent face, and in my throat the feeble word *because* forms itself only to become stuck. *Because, because, because,* a menacing little word whose mere utterance tastes like an admission of culpability." Ambrose drummed a little on the wood railing.

"Save me my shame, son, and ask me, I beg you, those things that line your face and discolour your eyes. What say you, my son? What a terrible thing to be disgusted, or even disappointed with one's father."

And so the night passed. Otoh had questions but they were not foremost in his mind. Even as his father's verbosity irritated him he wanted to embrace him protectively.

"Have you ever wondered why I slept so much?" his father continued. "Have you? You know there was a time when I thought there was so much to do and life was so wonderful that I would sleep only when I was dead and buried.

"I slept not because I was avoiding you or your mother, as you both had every right to assume. I slept because I couldn't face myself. Whenever I caught sight of my own reflection what I saw was my own face watching me, mocking me, and shaking its head in disgust with my performance in the entire Ramchandin affair. I slept to avoid the nausea that seemed to sour my insides and the weight of defeat crushing my heart whenever I thought of my inaction . . . of my indecisiveness that day Mr. Ramchandin brandished his cleaver at me. In a way I didn't merely lose Mala Ramchandin. I lost myself also. Did I lose you too, son? Hmmm? At the end of each month of sleeping, I awoke to find that the beast caged in my sternum had grown, making me even more fatigued and ill. So I hurried to smother the monster with sleep. Goodness. Sleep is an inactivity too, is it not? An act of indecision? Hmmm."

During this nonsensical ramble Otoh began to feel like his mother, to at last understand her fury at Ambrose's dance with words.

"Phew! Dear, dear, dear," said Ambrose, reading the look on his son's face.

"Otoh, I want you to know that I did go back the following day. In fact I returned three times. The first time I reached only as far as the bottom of the back stairs and she came flying at me with a stick, brandishing it and growling like an animal. My love charged at me with a long guava stick. She chased me out of the yard. She had no idea who I was. She had no idea who I was, Otoh.

"She just screamed sounds that had no meaning, and she beat the air in front of her with that stick, and it occurred to me then, and the thought broke my heart, that my sweet one's mind had flown out of her head.

"I managed on the second occasion to retrieve the gramophone, with the ambition to have it repaired and to present it to her again, god willing. God willing. That gramophone brought us such enjoyment.

"I went again and again, three times I tell you, I returned only to be met with the same fate. Mala, my sweet Mala, had aged overnight and was keeping her hair as wild as a worn-down, coconut-fibre broom. I decided it was unsafe for me to go back. On all three occasions her father was nowhere to be seen. So I thought she was safe from him, at least. I assumed he had gotten the hell out of there.

"But it was clear. I couldn't go back up there. All I could do to make up for my confusion and, call it neglect if you will, was to make sure that she had provisions and the essentials. Leaving those food supplies for her, you know the salted cod, butter, sugar and such, was all I could really do to try and loosen the knot that was growing in my heart."

The sounds of the townspeople finally rousing found them still on the verandah. (Elsie Mohanty, however, continued to sleep well into the day.) Otoh was weary. He resigned himself to the way things had turned out and the futility of dredging it all out and laying blame.

"Pappy, I would very much like to go and see her as soon as it is possible. Do you want to go with me?"

Ambrose clasped his hands at his chest as though in prayer and nodded, half grinning, half crying.

"Well, I will find out where she will be and when she can be visited. We will both go. I've got something up my sleeve."

"I'm sure you have. I'm sure you have!" An embarrassed chuckle came from Ambrose. Otoh remained serious.

"Also, I want to take a clipping of this plant for her. I wonder what it's called. Pappy, do you know?"

BEFORE ELSIE MOHANTY left Paradise she searched for an appropriate moment to have a talk with her son. She found such an opportunity in his restlessness one morning.

"Otoh, you walking in circles around me," Elsie said. "You making me dizzy. You couldn't be hungry — unless you have worms — you just eat lunch, child. If you have something on your mind why you don't just settle down and tell me?"

Otoh continued circling his mother, unsure how to ask her what she knew about Miss Ramchandin's life. Unskillfully broached, such a topic was bound to explode in every direction but the one he wanted. His mother could not have guessed that it was The Bird that he wanted to discuss, so she assumed that what made him uneasy was exactly what was on her own mind.

"All right. What about if I guess what it is that is on your mind? Hmmm?"

"No, Ma, you can't guess . . ." he mumbled. He turned on his heels and circled her in the opposite direction.

"Yes, I am a mother. I must know my child. You are behaving like somebody who is ready to settle down. You have marriage on your mind, not so?" Otoh's circling came to an abrupt halt but he didn't answer. He did not, that is, have time to answer. Pleased that she had caught his attention, Elsie rushed ahead.

"Is time, you right about that. Is definitely time for you to be married. Now I know for a fact that Mavis interested in you. Mavis is a nice girl. I get on good with she and with she family. She like you too bad, long time now. If you want Mavis I will go and speak with her mother today self." She could not have been more to the point, nor more wrong, Otoh thought. Although she had never contradicted him, this talk about marriage showed that his mother had more fully accepted him as a man than he had ever realized. Otoh was both thrilled and too shocked for words. He stared at her.

"Now I have to admit, I am just a little confused. She knows about you?" Elsie asked.

Again she caught him by surprise. This time she waited for his reply. "Knows what?" Otoh asked.

"What you mean, 'knows what?' You know *what* I am talking about!"

He remained silent and she barged on. "She know you don't have anything between those two stick legs of yours? Don't watch me so. You think because I never say anything that I forget what you are? You are my child, child. I just want to know if she know. She know?"

"Ma!" was all Otoh, thoroughly embarrassed, could utter.

"What you ma-ing me for? You think I am stupid or what? Now the fact of the matter is that you are not the first or the only one of your kind in this place. You grow up here and you don't realize almost everybody in this place wish they could be somebody or something else? That is the story of life here in Lantanacamara. Look at you father. Why you think The Bird end up in that situation? Look at her own father. And the mother . . ."

So his mother knew something about The Bird. "Well, actually that is what I wanted to . . ." Otoh interjected.

"Yes but we not concerned with that now. I want to talk with you about your situation. Now as I was saying, every village in this place have a handful of people like you. And is not easy to tell who is who. How many people here know about you, eh? I does watch out over the banister and wonder if *who* I see is really *what* I see. Look here, what I want to ask you is, you sure Mavis is a woman? I not asking you to tell me your business, but I just want as a mother to advise you to make sure she is what you want. Is a woman you want? I don't want to go and talk to her mother and then have to go back and retract. What you want? In a case like yours you just have to know, careful-careful, what you really want."

Otoh was reeling with the astonishing discovery that his mother had thought about his situation in even greater depth than he had ever done before. He quickly assured her that he would take her advice and think carefully. He implored her, in the meantime, not to approach Mavis' mother until he had time to decide.

THE DAY AMBROSE E. Mohanty rose from his wheelchair and became a regular man was the most upsetting day of Elsie Mohanty's life. She had not realized the peace and quiet that his month-long sleeps had afforded her. Now he was always in her midst, messing up her house, leaving his clothes for her to fold and put away. She found herself tripping over his shoes, bumping into him, having to cook three meals a day and wash three sets of dishes and pots and pans, and, most tedious of all, having to listen when he talked to her. He cluttered the space she had come to regard unconsciously as her very own. And, besides, he was almost indistinguishable from the person she had married so many years ago — whereas she had changed and aged with the passing of time. Other than his body Ambrose had not changed at all. She wished he would go back to sleep. When it was clear that he wouldn't she packed her things, hugged and kissed her son and made him promise he would visit her in the north of the island where she had friends. She wrote one line on a piece of paper, left the sheet on the kitchen table and, without discussing the matter with Ambrose, departed.

"You was simpler when you was sleeping." When Ambrose found the note he shed a few tears, after which he took a red pen, made corrections to her grammar and saved the paper, just in case she were to return some day and he could explain the errors to her.

V

MISS RAMCHANDIN HAS had a most unexpected visitor. Judge Walter Bissey.

Unknown to Otoh and me, Mr. Mohanty had contacted his high school tormentor, requesting him to use his good office to locate Asha Ramchandin. It was difficult to weigh which was more wonderful: that Ambrose Mohanty had finally taken action or that some news of Asha Ramchandin had been uncovered.

Judge Bissey, no doubt tending to skeletons of his own, set his staff on a trail that ended on a dusty top shelf in a back room at the local post office. He came to the alms house bearing a shoe box with Mala Ramchandin's name pencilled on top.

Over the course of eight years Asha had written Mala enough letters to fill the box. The majority were sent from Upnorth in the far end of Lantanacamara. Several were mailed from the Shivering Northern Wetlands and one card was sent from Canada. After the first six years the frequency of correspondence had diminished. None of Asha's letters were ever delivered because the righteous postman, deeming the Ramchandin house to be a place of sin and moral corruption, refused to go up there.

Judge Bissey inquired after her health yet seemed unable to look directly at Miss Ramchandin's face. He didn't stay long, quietly promising as he left to look into the matter of the undelivered mail.

My dearest sister Pohpoh,
I didn't get ten minutes away from the house before I wanted to run back and make you come with me. I am not sorry that I left, only that you didn't come with me. That is my biggest worry now. Pohpoh, I hope we will see each other very soon. We must. I don't understand why you worry so much about Papa. He hurt us so much and still you think of him. The day after I got up here I got a job helping out a nice woman, and going to do market for her, and a little cooking. She said I can't cook so she will teach me how. You can write me at the above address. That is not where I am staying but I go there to collect my letters, because I don't want Papa to come looking for me. I am going to send money for you to come and meet me. I am not coming back . . .

My one and only dearest sister,
Did you get my letter? Please write me back. Don't be angry with me. I think of you every day and night. I love you and miss you. I send you enough money in the same envelope as this letter (I hope and pray you get it) so that you could take the train and come and meet me. It simple. When Papa go out in the morning, put a dress and some underwear in a brown bag. Don't forget the picture of Mammy and Aunt Lavinia. You don't need anything more. We will manage. Then go to the train station. A train leaves Paradise for Upnorth Junction every day at

ten o'clock in the morning. That is a good one to take. I can get time off any day to come and meet you. I told the lady I work for about you. She is a nice woman, she said you could come and stay here until you get work. She might even get you a job. She knows a lot of people. I am waiting to hear from you, so write and tell me when you coming. Give the letter about ten days to arrive. Just don't tell anybody your plan. Pohpoh, I can't wait to see you. I really want to go and look for Mammy. I have a feeling like I can do anything I want now. I can even make my way to the Shivering Northern Wetlands to look for her. Let us go together. I am waiting . . .

Dear Pohpoh,
It is a month now and I still didn't get a letter from you. Please don't be angry with me. I think of you all the time . . . I am saving all my money so that we could go abroad and find Mammy. Please write me. I am so sad that I didn't hear from you . . .

From the Shivering Northern Wetlands Asha first wrote:

Darling Sister,
I found work here. I will send money for you every month. It is cold here. I never imagined that cold could be so cold. I thought it would be easy to find Mammy here. But the city here is bigger than even Lantanacamara.

How are you? I am too stubborn to ask how Papa is, but I do wonder about him. I hope you are all right. I don't understand why you don't write me . . . You always protected me, Pohpoh, and I was hoping I could do that for you now, but since you don't even write me I feel as

> if instead of protecting you I left you. I am beginning to understand why Mammy left. I hope that one day you will understand why I left . . .

Other letters reported on Asha's work, which I am happy to say was nursing, in the Shivering Northern Wetlands. None of them suggested she had made any inroads in contacting her mother or her mother's lover. Some letters contained Wetlandish currency. The last one from the Wetlands said:

> *Pohpoh, my dearest sister,*
> Long ago I left one country and now am leaving this one too. I am crossing the ocean and going to Canada. I don't even know if my letters are reaching you. I fear the worst. I will write you again when I get over there and settle down. What are you doing with your life? I still think all the time of you and love you. I am sure that is how Mammy must feel about us, wherever she is. I won't give up hope of seeing you. Just tell me that you want to come, even for holidays, and I will send you the passage . . .

Finally, there was a card from Canada:

> *Dearest Pohpoh,*
> Think of you every day. If you get this card please write me back.
>
> I want to see you. I miss you. I am well and happy—except that I wish I knew how you were.
> *All my love, Asha.*

Miss Ramchandin sat in her rocker, stroking the cat on her lap, while I read the letters out loud, one by one. By the time I finished, she appeared to be asleep. Her cheeks were stained with tears.

Lately restraint and I have been hostile strangers to one another. I find myself defying caution. To hell with Toby. I have powdered my nose on days that were not visiting days. To gentler hell with Sister and the nurses. I must, as a matter of life and death, wear scent in the crock of my elbows. I am readier than ever to present myself like a peacock in heat.

Otty — things have progressed so that he calls me Ty, I call him Otty — Otty's deportment has changed too. I recognize and appreciate the studied swagger of the lone bushwhacker he has cultivated since we met. In light of his manly inability to bare his heart, I consider these eloquent declarations.

Otty and his charming father still visit the Paradise Alms House often. Mr. Mohanty treats the occasion as an opportunity to wear his swallow-tail jacket — regardless of the weather — a bow tie far too oversized for his small body, and a bowler that Otty recently purchased for him.

On visiting days Miss Ramchandin and I practically hover above the ground with excitement. She puts aside her mutterings and I put away my book and pencil. Before our visitors arrive I wash her, mildly rubbing her skin with frangipani petals from Mr. Hector's hedge and pay special attention in dressing her. She sits on a stool while I pin her hair up into a waterfall, or braid and set it off with a little ribbon or flowers. She giggles and twitches her feet. On visiting days she wears a garland of snail shells about her neck or a crown of wreaths that we wove with feathers and the wings of expired insects. Hours before the visitors arrive she and I, I more discreetly than she, are decked out and waiting.

The time inevitably arrived. I decided to unabashedly declare myself, as it were.

And so, last visit, I wore lip colour more thickly than usual, shades brighter than my dark lips. With powder I blotted the shine that tends to develop on my nose and cheeks on hot days. I tied a flower-patterned scarf around my neck, and on my temples I daubed enough scent to make a Puritan cross his legs and swoon. Miss Mala grinned and clapped her hands when I entered her room. She squealed when I pulled the nurse's uniform from behind her dresser and put it on.

They arrived. I could hardly look him in the eyes, suddenly thinking I was about to cross his line. I held Miss Mala by an elbow and Mr. Ambrose took the other arm. Otty, subtly attired in loose, off-white trousers and a shirt of such delicate white cotton that he might as well have been bare-chested, supported his father's free arm.

We walked slowly to a bench. I could see the nurses had come to a halt and were watching us. I held my head high. The gossip mill began to rumble but I listened instead to the leaves in the trees. Otty took my arm and we walked off, leaving our companions to a private visit. We headed for the residents' garden. Mr. Hector was working and seeing us, he dropped his tools and stared.

"Well, I never! If I didn't know better . . . I wish my brother could meet you two. Christ where he is, I wonder? Where my brother? By any chance, you know my brother?"

From the cereus hung pink buds on the ends of long stems. Otty kneeled down in the garden with no regard for his white trousers and proceeded to pack the soil around its base. He patted it with his bare, slender hands not because it needed work but rather to show it some attention and, I imagine, to honour its place in Miss Ramchandin's life. When he stood up I reached over to brush the soil off the knees of his pants. I felt the form of his shapely leg and when he braced himself, I heard him catch his breath. He too was stirring. I got up, my legs unstable, and walked as best I could throughout the garden, picking a bouquet of shrimp bush, lilac, rose bay and flame ixora. I presented the arrangement to Otty. He deliberately cupped my hands and held them to his chest. With practised elegance I moistened my lips and continued to stare at him.

"The cereus will bloom in just another few nights. Can you wait?" I whispered to him.

"Yes, yes. Just barely, but I will wait."

Mr. Mohanty and Miss Ramchandin were still seated next to each other when we arrived back at the bench. He was staring at his surroundings, shaking his head in a gesture of approval and saying, "No time to waste, not a moment to be wasted."

Miss Ramchandin bounced on the bench. She pointed up into the sky and traced a distant flight pattern that she alone could see. She laughed as her eyes followed what her finger described, and waved to whatever it was she saw. She trembled with joy. In a tiny whispering voice, she uttered her first public words: "Poh, Pohpohpoh, Poh, Poh, Poh."

The cereus will surely bloom within days — an excitement diminished only by the fact that there is still no word from Asha Ramchandin. Judge Walter Bissey has contacted a colleague in Canada, who promises to use all legal means to determine if an Asha Ramchandin still resides in that cold country.

Asha, if these words have already found your eyes, for the sake of your sister who worships your memory please return and pay her a visit: Paradise Alms House, Paradise, Lantanacamara. If for some reason you are physically unable to come here, please write, send a message, a photograph. I will respond immediately with the same. And if you were indeed reunited with your mother, Sarah, and with

Lavinia Thoroughly, in the Wetlands or in Canada, please tell us how they fared. Not a day passes that you are not foremost in our minds. We await a letter, and better yet, your arrival. She expects you any day soon. You are, to her, the promise of a cereus-scented breeze on a Paradise night.

Acknowledgements

It is often assumed that writing is a solitary occupation, a one-person show. Yet if it weren't for a number of people who encouraged and supported — and even distracted — me, *Cereus* would still be inside me, wrestling to be released.

From as far away as England and Trinidad I could feel my parents and four siblings awaiting this book, almost drawing it out of me with their ardent curiosity. My friends — and I am happy to say they still permit me to refer to them as friends — generously listened each time I excitedly changed or added sometimes no more than a word or a sentence. Their unflagging interest spurred me on, and often I felt as though I were writing for each of them. When my grant money was depleted before I had wrapped up the manuscript they brought me bags of groceries, took me out to eat — at great restaurants, no less — and bought my paintings so that I could continue to write without worrying too much. When they could see I was buried too deeply in the story and beginning to disappear under reams of paper, or on the verge of becoming obnoxiously boring, they dragged me away and took me for great coffee, or went hiking, bicycling, canoeing and kayaking with me. I eventually found that it was while "playing" that snags and cobwebs in my story and my mind got unravelled.

My parents, siblings and good friends Persimmon Blackbridge, Lorna Boschman, Cyndia Cole, Monika Kin Gagnon, Angie Joyce, Larissa Lai, Shannon McFarlane, Zaphura Mohamed, Hidemi Nishibata, Shelina Velji and Zara Velji are my true fortune.

It was a real gift and honour to have Larissa Lai share with me, through reading and discussing my manuscript, her experiences writing and editing her novel *When Fox Is a Thousand.*

I greatly appreciate the active support of Cynthia Flood who, by twice inviting me to read from the work-in-progress to her class at Langara College, helped to fuel my confidence and desire to continue.

Inventing the story, chasing and being chased by the characters has been one of the most enjoyable creative journeys I have undertaken. It was not, however, until Jennifer Glossop and Nancy Pollak started editing the manuscript that the true, mesmerizing magic of this kind of writing began to be revealed to me. I want now to shower them with a piñata of compliments and gratitude but I hesitate because I imagine them editing out and whittling away all but one or two of the adjectives I might use. In a nutshell, by making the editing process a vital and significant experience, Jennifer and Nancy have stoked my desire to write.

As an admirer of Val Speidel's design work it is a privilege to have my book designed by her.

Della McCreary and Barbara Kuhne of Press Gang Publishers maintained a warm, caring closeness, even when in private they might well have been tearing their hair out wondering if I would ever finish the manuscript.

The last person to be mentioned in a thank-you list tends, more often than not, to be the one you wanted to mention from the very first. Kathy High was there in my dark moments of doubting, ready to shine her light of enthusiasm and belief in my abilities. She indulged me by discussing and celebrating each of my changes without expressing any tedium. I am happily indebted to her.

*